WHAT HELL MAY COME

REX HURST

Let the world know:
#IGotMyCLPBook!

Crystal Lake Publishing
www.CrystalLakePub.com

WELCOME
TO ANOTHER

CRYSTAL LAKE PUBLISHING
CREATION

Welcome to another Crystal Lake Publishing creation.

Thank you for supporting independent publishing and small presses. You rock, and hopefully you'll quickly realize why we've become one of the world's leading publishers of Dark and Speculative Fiction. We have some of the world's best fans for a reason, and hopefully we'll be able to add you to that list really soon. Be sure to sign up for our newsletter to receive some free eBooks, as well as info on new releases, special offers, and so much more.

**Welcome to Crystal Lake Publishing—
Tales from the Darkest Depths.**

OTHER NOVELS BY CRYSTAL LAKE PUBLISHING

Lilitu: The Memoirs of a Succubus by Jonathan Fortin
Doll Crimes by Karen Runge
House of Sighs (with sequel novella) by Aaron Dries
Beyond Night by Eric S. Brown and Steven L. Shrewsbury
The Third Twin: A Dark Psychological Thriller by Darren Speegle
Aletheia: A Supernatural Thriller by J.S. Breukelaar
Where the Dead Go to Die by Mark Allan Gunnells and Aaron Dries
Sarah Killian: Serial Killer (For Hire!) by Mark Sheldon
The Final Cut by Jasper Bark
Blackwater Val by William Gorman
Nameless: The Darkness Comes by Mercedes M. Yardley

Or check out other Crystal Lake Publishing books for more Tales from the Darkest Depths.

AUTHOR'S NOTE

The Satanic Panic was a moral panic which swept through the United States during the 1980s. Concerned political and religious groups jumped all over the new imagined trend of "Satanism" found in popular youth culture at the time. Preachers, pundits, and politicos all spun the yarn that a vast underground network of Satanists were in control of secular society and corrupting the youth away from moral righteousness.

It began in 1972 with the laughably bad book *The Satan Seller* by Michael Warnke. The author claimed to have been a satanic high priest who recruited over 50,000 members to the Dark Lord before finding Jesus. All of his claims have been subsequently debunked. It continued on with a series of short illustrated tracks produced at cost by the infamous Jack Chick. The tracks became crazier and crazier until they eventually claimed that every other religion, including non-fundamentalist denominations of Christianity, are under the control of a Satanic illuminati. You can still order his tracks online, if you want a good laugh. They cost about 10 cents per, plus shipping. In the 1980s, the popular memoir *Michelle*

Remembers was published. It is a supposedly autobiographical account of a mentally ill woman whose psychiatrist hypnotically helped her recall repressed memories of Satanic ritual abuse at the hands of her family. The technique used to "recover" memories has also been thoroughly debunked. Then in 1987 came *Turmoil in the Toybox*, my favorite accidently hysterical book, which claims, among other things, that He-Man was designed by "occultists" to recruit boys into homosexuality and that Yoda is a demonic figure.

Eventually these ideas stuck around long enough to filter into everyday life. Halloween was banned in many communities for years. Geraldo Rivera got massive attention with an hour and a half long exploitative special on ABC about supposed Satanic influences. The panic culminated in a witch hunt among childcare workers in California that were claimed to be part of an organized system of Satanic ritual abuse on children. Thirty low paid workers were sent to prison. All but one of the convictions were eventually overturned.

Why did it happen? Well, a good moral crusade, especially against an imaginary foe, is an easy target. One that guarantees to generate money and power. Many certainly profited from it. Televangelists in their '80s heyday raked in a combined billion dollars a year. Politicians could prove their virtue by attacking a boogeyman they would never have to answer to. Corrupt district attorneys could gain name recognition with bogus prosecutions.

In hindsight, these are all ridiculous claims and are easily disproved in the internet age. However, I want you to imagine a world where all of these allegations are true. Satanism secretly rules popular culture. Playing an elf in *Dungeons and Dragons* can lead to learning true witchcraft. Heavy metal music has secret brainwashing messages encoded backwards in each song encouraging fans to rape and kill. What would such a world actually look like? Turn the page and find out.

PROLOGUE

THE RITUAL HAD taken eighty-one days.

They were at it for more than a quarter of a year.

Eighty-one days of smoke, and animal shrieks, and groans of pleasure, and spilled blood. Months of heady incense burning. The occasional hallucinogen was tossed into the mixture, turning the world into a fever dream. Weeks of chanting. The constant intonation fell behind the ears and awoke powers in the subconscious. Robed heroes of all races and classes came and went, adding to the celebration, until they collapsed and were dragged off to recuperate.

Crixen Runeburner, elf mage, had been there for all of it. The chanting, the killing, the sex. He had cast down enemies, seen proud heroes fall, and evaded all magical traps to come here at this time. Many adventures across bleak and alien landscapes had led him to this ancient crypt. He had faced dagger fanged monsters, green skinned humans with cruel blades, and pale shadows of the formerly alive. All of these he had struck down to reach his goal. Now, he just had to hang on.

He was on the verge of physical ruin. His eyes were raw around the rims, skin deathly pale for lack of sunlight, hair wild and shaggy, gums juicy red, and teeth yellowed from neglect. The elf had lost too much weight and seemed to have shrunk in height as well. Crixen Runeburner knew he was in danger, but he had volunteered for this, begged for it, and he would not fail!

The underground chamber had once been a family tomb from an unnamed religion. The bones of the occupants rested no longer in saintly contemplation but were added to the altar decorations. Each of the eight walls, the ceiling, and the floors, had been painted with eldritch symbols and phrases in angelic script. Each rune was designed to beckon, focus, and bind. All the signs and symbols were directed at one bare patch in the center of a pentagram, located behind the altar of stone and bone.

It was The Feast of the Beast, an ancient rite established—if you believe the musty grimoires—in the year of their lord, six hundred and sixty-six. On the surface, its purpose was general hedonism and over-indulgence, but in reality, the room became a meeting point where the upper echelons of the infernal family made contact with the beyond.

Here it was. The final day. Crixen Runeburner pushed forth the last of his physical reserves, burning whatever proteins were still circling his stomach. He couldn't remember the last time food had passed his lips. All the hunger pains had died off after the third day. The elf had only managed to choke down a few cups of sugar water every few hours.

Heavy gongs rang. Six naked bearers, three of each sex, their heads swathed in black hoods, carried in a cushioned litter. On it lounged The Scarlet Woman.

Round and succulent, her face lolled to the left and right, barely taking in the environment. Her legs were tied with silken rope to the poles, forcing them open to reveal her sex between. She didn't complain. Long had she been prepared for this event.

Behind her entered the High Priest, decorated in a shining purple robe, wearing a mask knitted from the flesh of unbaptized children. Other heroes of old campaigns shuffled in behind him, garbed in the same gruesome fare. They wrestled in a figure that was tied up in a burlap tarp.

"Glory. Glory. Glory," he roared. "Let us commence the communion of our race."

The Scarlet Woman was positioned at the northern point of the pentacle, legs spread open to embrace the blank spot. The unseen figure was dumped onto the altar and strapped down on the stone. It was a woman. Her shrieks of fear could do nothing but add to the discordant harmony rolling about the room.

"By the power of earth. By the power of air. By the power of water. By the power of fire. Let forth the spirit. Descend to the lantern of sorrows of the South, to the trumpets of doom of the West, to the praise of harlots to the East, to the horns of death to the North. Descend!"

The heroes cheered, repeating the ends of his sentences. They howled and gibbered in triumph. Everyone was focused on the blank spot. Everyone waiting for the end. Everyone except Crixen. He had spotted one odd thing in the eyes of the High Priest. Terror. Why was that? What had he missed?

"Descend and clothe thyself in one of the sacred shrouds, one of the mystic mantles. Asmodeus, creature of judgement. Abaddon, who destroys both body and soul. Af, the sower of hatred. Belial, angel of hostility. Samael, who poisons the world. Lucifer, lord of proud spirits. Satan, the great adversary."

Crixen Runeburner was lead forward and placed before the altar. A golden knife slapped into his hand. The victim before him, a mask of blank terror, screamed his name. He saw her then. It was the girl who had taken his virginity

He raised the blade.

CHAPTER 1

DO UNTO OTHERS FIRST

EVIL HAD ALWAYS been in Jon St. Fond's life. Lurking behind the wallpaper. Breathing down vents. He would turn quickly and in the span of an eye blink, the beast would be there. A horned shadow on the wall, a cold dusk of air, a tail slap on the door, a fallen picture frame, a deformed insect scuttling over the ceiling. It was there.

Right now, he couldn't care about any of that. Right now, Jon was kicking open the screen door at the back of his parents' suburban home and bringing something cupped in his hands over to the sink. He placed it gently into the basin and wrapped a hand towel around it.

It was the end of Indian summer in 1986. School had just started up and all of the anxieties that went with being a teen in the '80s plagued Jon. Lack of social graces, teenage awkwardness, no money—all these bothered him, but none of his problems loomed as large as his family.

Jon heard a sharp intake of breath. The warning "Oooooo," of his snitchy little sister rose behind him. Jon knew it by instinct. How many times had he suffered after that preamble? He swung around and snarled at her.

"What, Catherine? What do you want?"

"You not 'spousta use your feet to kick open the door like tha'," she stuttered out. "And those towels are for hands, Mom says."

She stood at the kitchen door, her mouth a flat frowning line of defiance at Jon's heinous breach of protocol. Six-years-old and ready to rat on the world, Catherine was wearing her ugly tan Brownie uniform and clutching an empty plastic soda bottle in each arm. Behind her, he heard the murmur of his mother lecturing the other girls in Catherine's scout troop, as she did every other week.

"Don't say anything Catherine," Jon pleaded. He heard the whine in his voice and hated himself for it. But she held the power and only an earnest plea might stop her smiting tongue.

No dice. She stared at him blank-eyed for a moment, and then ran back to the living room calling for mother. "Jon's doing . . . " whatever. He knew the drill but wanted to delay it as long as possible. He scooped up his cargo and ran for the cellar door.

Inside the living room, his mother's high-pitched squawk rang out, "I'll deal with Jon in a minute, sit down. Now remember girls, any man who makes you feel uncomfortable should be immediately reported to the police. If he touches you, talks to you, looks at you, is near you, and you don't like it then he should be locked up. It can be a stranger, a teacher, your father, your uncle, your brother, your grandfather, your cousin. Report them and keep talking until they are locked up. What's the number again?"

"911!" the gaggle of girls shouted.

Jon groaned. He had actually been victim to one such call by his younger sister wherein she made some pretty evil accusations. His parents convinced the police to leave the matter alone, but how close he came to being locked up stuck with him. He paused at the cellar door and sucked in a deep breath. The package in his arms squirmed and eeked.

"I'm not scared. I'm not scared. I'm not scared," he intoned three times, then spun around and spat behind.

Jon flung open the door and jumped down the stairs, hoping to avoid— No, it gripped him as it always did. A wave of nausea ran through him. Some hidden scent, some forgotten childhood nightmare, some trick of the light always triggered unease in his soul. His gorge would rise and his bottom would drop. Every time his appetite dried up upon walking down the steps. He never actually did vomit but felt constantly on the verge of it. The ritual followed was to ward off the evil which lurked there. Childish, yes, but it was the only thing that gave him confidence.

He didn't know why this happened. It was just a normal-looking cellar filled with standard cellar junk. Old holiday decorations, the water heater, a warped workbench with rusty tools, and the washer and dryer. It smelled dank and musty, but that wasn't different from any of his friends' cellars and he never had the gripping nausea when at their homes.

That was a mystery for another time, though. He needed to take care of his charge. Jon laid the towel down in a slightly grimy sink next to the washer and unwrapped the creature inside. It was a squirrel he had accidently run over with his Huffy on the way home from school. Its back legs were crushed and bent in weird angles. Its eyes fluttered open and shut, and the animal's breathing came in rapid short breaths.

Guilt washed over him. He didn't know what to do. It was an accident, yet he was responsible. The creature's feeble eeking made the whole thing even worse. Jon paced back and forth, anxiety sending tremors of panic down his spine. He had to help, but how?

Maybe some splints for its legs? What could he make them out of? Twigs? Popsicle sticks? Oh, hell, its back was probably broken. Maybe something to eat, or some water, or some whiskey to ease the pain. Could squirrels drink alcohol?

He went back upstairs and ransacked the kitchen, finally coming across a can of Spanish peanuts favored by Father. Taking that was a mortal sin, but he recklessly did it anyway. Jon filled a saucer with water and hurried back down to the animal.

Inside the living room, his mother was wrapping things up. "Okay girls. Remember, you deserve to be given the best of everything. If someone can't provide what you need, then take what you can and move on."

The squirrel had gone silent. He slid a peanut between the squirrel's weird thumb and fingers. It fell out, so he tried again. The creature's eyes flitted a bit then dropped the food. All right, it was too far gone for that. Jon edged the saucer to the animal's snout. Surely it could use some liquid. That was the one thing you always needed when you were sick or run over by a vehicle.

"Jon, Jon, where are you?" His mother was

stomping around above. "What's this about you kicking the screen door again?"

He froze. This would not end well. He knew it. His mother took a sadistic glee in ranting about petty crapola. It was only Jon who received these assaults. She left her other two daughters alone. He was her favorite stress ball.

Though he couldn't end it, Jon hoped to delay the attack for a while. He remained still by the sink, watching and waiting. His focus was on the door exclusively and didn't notice that his hand had strayed a little too close to the squirrel's mouth. The animal roused a bit and, whether he recognized Jon or just lashed out because of the pain, the squirrel bit deep into the webbing between Jon's thumb and forefinger.

Pain. Scream. Crying.

"Ah ha!"

The cellar door kicked open. His mother, all five-foot-two-inches of her, stood silhouetted against the dying afternoon light. As she stomped down the stairs, a hideous joy was revealed on her face. She loved having the high ground. She loved having an excuse, no matter how petty, to rip into someone. It filled her with a cold warmth that neither children, nor marriage, nor church could supply. These moments were what she truly lived for.

"How many times do I have to tell you to use your hands to open the fucking door, you idiot. Your feet will bend the metal if you kick it enough times," Slim figured and large breasted, her visage was the living definition of a 'bitch face.' Her shrill words spat out rapid fire. "Why are you such a fucking retard? This house is going to be yours one day, stupid. You might want to fucking take care of it a little."

Catherine peeked around the cellar door, barely stifling a giggle. Her face mimicked her mother's as she absorbed the scene, excited by the chaos she'd caused.

"Is Jon in a lot of trouble?" she asked.

"No, dear." Mother's tone twisted to doting parent mid-syllable. "Why don't you get a popsicle for being a good girl and watch cartoons."

"Okay." But she didn't leave. No cartoon could beat the show in the basement.

"Why can't you ever follow simple directions? It's not much. It's not fucking rocket science. I ask you not the kick the door open, but that's too difficult for you. I send you to get some Hellman's mayonnaise, you get some other goddamn brand. I tell you to cut the lawn a quarter of an inch, you cut it half. You're so incompetent. When are you gonna pull your head out of your dumb ass and stop being the biggest fuck-up in the world?"

Anger. Hurt. Depression.

It would be *so* satisfying to break her face. He could almost feel the crunch of her teeth across his knuckles. The rules of society held back his blow. One just didn't hit their mother, did they? No matter what she did, she was still a mother and that meant something. So he took the emotional wounds, withstood the verbal battering, without complaint. He became the proverbial whipped dog since society left him no other options.

Despite his resolution, Jon was not the type to do absolutely *nothing*. Robbed of using violence, the only thing he could manage was tears. That made him hate himself more. He wanted to be a man, be strong, but . . .

"Holy shit. Are you crying, you little wimp?"

Eyes downcast, a sniffle wiped away. "No."

"Yes, you are!"

Why was his life like this? Why couldn't she be a normal mother who cared for her children? Cared about them as people, not just about their basic needs. Father supplied him with clothes and food, but not much else.

"Time to step up and start being a man. No one loves a pussy," she continued on without missing a beat. "That means doing what you're told. And why the hell are you bleeding?"

A little pool of blood had developed in the webbing of his hand. It spread over the lines of his knuckles. He had forgotten it under the abuse. Only after it was pointed out to him did he feel pain. That and the nausea.

"Well?" she demanded.

He mutely pointed to the sink. She stomped over and screeched. "Why is there a half-dead animal stinking up my good basement?"

"I . . . I . . ."

"*What*?"

"I kind of hit it with my bike."

"Jesus fuck, so you bring it home?"

"It's not dead."

"We'll see about that." She grabbed the squirrel and dashed its head open against the bottom of the sink. This time the nausea overwhelmed him, and he vomited on the slate floor.

Jon retreated into his inner thoughts. In his room, he

scribbled furiously away in a spiral notebook. He had labeled it "geometry notes" to prevent any curious snooping, but it really contained his secret diary—or journal. Yes, journal was more masculine—where he raged against his parents, his insecurity, his lingering virginity, and whatever was left in the world.

It had taken him an hour to clean up the puke and dispose of the squirrel carcass, All the while he endured vicious barbs and nasty giggling from the two females who had decided to "supervise" rather than help. The dead animal was all but forgotten now, only hate rattled around his brain.

If that stupid bitch wants me dead then she should just shoot me, but that would mean she would have to get off her lazy ass and do something besides whining out of her cunt. She can't do anything but complain that's why she never gets anything done. She just complains and waits for someone else to fix it because she's such a lazy whore.

This was one of his escapes. Not the big one, but a minor oasis to deal with the garbage of life. A place to expel the venom from his soul. With each word he tossed out, he felt a cathartic warmth, a rush of pleasure, which stabilized his mood. Pressure slowly decreased.

And it's only ME! She doesn't treat Michelle or Catherine bad. And it's not just because I'm a boy. She has some special hate in her heart for my presence. She won't talk like that to Father. Or anyone else! Bitch is always looking for some excuse to attack, like I'm ruining the house that'll be mine.

He paused. Technically, Mother was right. The place probably would go to him as the only male heir.

Michelle was older, but considering her toxic waste lifestyle, it would be turned into a crack den five minutes after her claws snatched up the deed. Father would never let that happen. The house's legacy was very important to him.

Their home had been in the St. Fond family ever since Jon's great-great-grandfather ordered the two-story house out of the Sears Roebuck catalogue in 1922—The Puritan, model no. 3190—paying the princely sum of $1,947 for the whole thing. Once the thirty thousand pieces had been shipped down the Erie Canal, the old patriarch had the dwelling installed over a pre-existing cellar. He must have been a cheap bastard because he refused to shell out for frills like plumbing, electricity, or a boiler. The old time ways were the best to him apparently, including having to wipe your asshole with your own hand. All of the staples of modern life had been added later by less sturdy descendants.

While being forced to write some stupid essay about his family, Jon had stumbled on a whole box of old papers detailing his great-great-grandfather's legal troubles over the construction. The old man would hire a crew for a day, fire them without paying, and then hire a different crew for the next day. He kept this up until the house was finished. Eventually, the various crews banded together and sued for their wages. The old man refused to settle and strung the proceedings out for six years before finally settling on a quarter of what they were owed. The land appeared to have belonged to the family for longer than the house stood, though most of the records had been destroyed by some flash flood in 1959.

And even if I will inherit it, there's some horrible thing just waiting underneath. I know it. They always half-ass it with me. Like there's a lot of taxes owed on the house or it's on a sinkhole or something like that. That's how they work. Catherine gets all the latest Barbie crap, but when I ask for that new VHS copy of Star Wars, they get me some knock-off episodes of Jason of Star Command, the shittiest of shitty sci-fi shows.

The phone rang. Someone else answered, then his mother squawked up the stairs that the call was for him and he needed to hurry the hell up. Jon stashed the book in its hiding place under a small black and white TV on his desk. That was another way his parents screwed him. Michelle had a massive twenty-five-inch Zenith television with cable hookup—the little snot got thirteen whole channels right to her room—while he had been given this crappy ten-inch Mexican knock-off with rabbit ear antenna that he had to wrap half a yard of tinfoil around to get even the lousy PBS channel.

He snatched up the receiver and waited for the other extension to click off. It didn't. Jon breathed heavy and waited, and waited, and waited some more. God damn it . . .

"Mom, can you hang up?"

"I don't think so. If you need to talk, go ahead. There's no reason why I shouldn't listen in. I mean, are you talking about drugs or robbing a bank? No? Well then it doesn't matter if I hear."

"It's okay, dude," the caller chimed in.

Michael Dutch was on the other end. Jon's oldest friend. His non-biological brother. Michael also had the distinction of being one of the few people with a worse home life than Jon. His parents were self-absorbed assholes just like Jon's, but they also had the added handicap of being poor. A hand-to-mouth existence had been Michael's entire life. He needed an escape as much as Jon did.

"Are we still on?"

"Definitely."

"All right, I'll meet you in a bit."

"Remember, you have to do all your chores first," butted in Mother. "I'll be double-checking and reporting to Father. Anything not done well and you're not going anywhere, mister."

Jon slammed down the phone and panted a while in near-rabid frenzy. Fuck her! This was one of her little games. No matter how much he scrubbed the floor or how long he vacuumed the rug, there would always be a problem, real or imagined. It didn't matter.

He was going out and she could shove the chores. If she did tell Father . . . a cold dread seized him . . . it was a problem to deal with later. Right now, Jon needed to get away.

He gathered up a number of hardbound books with bits of loose-leaf paper sticking haphazardly between the pages and put them carefully into a backpack. These were precious objects, holier than any ancient script. They were the tools and keys with which Jon escaped the world. They were how he kept his sanity and maintained stability in his soul. They let him be . . . something else.

He donned a baseball cap and sauntered down the stairs. The Girl Scout gear stowed away, Catherine was now decked-out in a brightly colored leotard. She pranced around the living room with the best ballerina flats money could buy adorning her feet. As she spun, an infectious grin of true joy broke out over her face. Mother clapped, pure maternal love leaking from her smile.

"Beautiful. Just beautiful," she muttered.

And it was. For a split second, he forgot all about the horrible snitching and lies Catherine had made up about him and took in her happiness. There wasn't much grace, but her laughter made up for all that. It was a side of his sister that only occasionally snuck out. Then she saw him and evil reclaimed her face.

Mother joined her in the stare. "Are you going to make a stand or something?" she mocked Jon.

"Nope, I'm just going." He strode past them.

"Fine," Mother said, shaking her head, "you're the one who'll deal with Father, not me."

He slammed the screen door behind him and yanked his Huffy from the garage. There was still a smear of blood down the center of his front wheel. The guilt stabbed him again. *Just an accident,* he reminded himself. Jon gave a brief salute to the trash can which was the animal's final resting place. Then hesitated, thinking there should be more that he could do.

Inside, Mother heaped praise on Catherine. "When we go, you're gonna be number one. Oh, I know it! You'll be the prettiest girl there. Everyone will be jealous."

Mother and daughter spent a lot of time touring the child pageant circuit. The pair primped and preened, teased up hair, rubbed Vaseline on teeth, danced, and sang. Many times Jon had come home to see Catherine standing on the kitchen table practicing cute quips to say to the judges or reciting rote speeches on how much she loved herself some Jesus. Catherine did fairly well, too. A shelf on the upper walkway was loaded with ribbons and trophies. Rather than be jealous, Jon was all for it. It got them out of his hair.

His mother went on and on in her praise of her youngest child.

Jon spat. Nothing like that had ever been thrown his way. The squirrel's soul would have to migrate on without any more salutations. He stomped on the pedals and rode off into the night.

CHAPTER 2

THE TRAGEDY OF MAN

BUFFALO WAS THE faded queen of old New York, the leftovers of an industrial era ground to shit. It had once been a showpiece of culture and success, industry and shipping, where the working slobs could pull down beer money and the educated snobs could twitter their noses at a host of artistic feasts. It wasn't *fully* gone, but the city was quickly fading into a new Detroit or Baltimore—hubs of corruption and squalor. As opportunity slowly leaked away, so did Buffalo's best and brightest. More and more vanished each year, leaving behind only those who were too lazy or stupid to get the hell out. Nowadays, all the city had to boast about was a chronically losing football team and the invention of Buffalo wings.

If the city proper was that bad, Jon's home of Black Rock, the area he now pedaled through, was its retarded cousin. Once the berg had been a commercial rival for its dominant sister and had nearly been the chosen terminus of the Erie Canal. The War of 1812 changed everything. While it was raging on, Buffalo got the nod for the canal exit, as it was further away from the enemy's forts. This turned out to be good planning as the township of Black Rock was razed and raped twice by blood hungry Canuck marauders.

The township took its name from an outcropping of black limestone along a nearby river that was blown up by engineers in the building of said Erie Canal, adding insult to injury in the minds of its low-wage residents. Nowadays the typical Black Rockian barely sported a high school diploma and lived paycheck-to-paycheck from an ever-shifting menagerie of minimum-wage jobs. Their dreams of bettering themselves revolved solely around hitting it big on the lottery, rather than actually working toward a goal.

Their dwellings reflected their poor life planning. Cardboard squares duct-taped in place of broken windows. Screen doors with the mesh half hanging out. Red brick stoops that were missing a few bricks. Old paint jobs with flaked-out gray splotches like leper spots. These were common sights. Last decade's broken down Chevys and germ-ridden public transportation were the rides of choice. Dented corner bars. Cheap wing shacks. Gas stations with rusted nozzles. All of this was Jon's world.

Which begged the question as to why his parents insisted on staying in the area, despite the fact that they could easily afford something ten times as luxurious. Well, it was the land, the family land that anchored them all to this dead spot. Father had an uncharacteristic soft spot for his heredity, so everyone else had to suffer because of it.

Jon pulled up at Michael Dutch's house. It was a crumbling brick affair, a thrown together cheap structure, shoved at the very back of a dead end street.

The cement stairs to the front door were bare. The iron railings, embedded in the stone, had been twisted off years ago. A barebones carport, just a roof and poles to hold it up, lay to the right, with a beat up truck missing the front tires underneath. The truck's forward plate dangled by a single stripped-out bolt.

Jon tapped on the front door. Mrs. Dutch answered and, without acknowledging Jon's presence, yelled for Michael. He came to the door quickly, a backpack slung over his shoulder. Jon was glad of that. He didn't want to linger inside. It seemed like the Dutch family never cleaned their carpets and the house constantly stunk of cheap cigars and fried bologna. That night was no exception.

He peeked inside as Michael laced up his sneakers. A three legged dog gnawed a rawhide bone. The youngest child rattled the bars of his playpen with savage determination. Mrs. Dutch went back to singing unharmoniously along with the radio. Michael's dad sat in his boxer shorts and hole-ridden undershirt, swearing at the game on TV. A slab of greasy pizza oozed over his leg.

"God damn losers. Get the ball!"

Michael slapped on a ball cap similar to Jon's and said, "Let's go."

You didn't have to tell Jon twice. He had plenty of bad memories of the place, and he didn't even live there. Who knew what barnacles Michael had sticking to the bottom of his soul. They got Michael's bike out of the back, negotiating through a clump of dropouts sniffing gasoline from an aluminum container. Shaggy hair and shaggy brains, they were friends of Michael's older brother, an eternal doper who was finally kicked out of the ninth grade at the age of twenty. Michael shouted into the house that he was leaving and didn't even receive a grunt in reply.

It was a miracle he still even bothered. Michael was shooting for the moon if he thought his parents were going to change. Neither of them had progressed beyond the idiot high schooler's need to appear tough. They took every new idea as a challenge against them personally, as an attack on their ego, and the easiest way for them to deal with something and still "look cool" was to shit all over it. As if anyone was paying attention.

Jon remembered in the fifth grade they had to do a diorama for their science class. The projects had been all laid out in the school atrium and parents, teachers, and the principal sauntered by and judged them. Michael had worked for days on his, adding all sorts of glitter and streamers, the accoutrements that make an elementary school project pop. He won first place and got a little ribbon to go along with the honor. He was so proud and raced home to show off his achievement. Jon followed him along.

"Look, Daddy," he had said, heart pounding with pride, "I won this."

The elder Dutch had half-glanced at the award and snorted, "What the fuck you want me to do?"

The light had switched off in Michael's eyes. Downtrodden, he slumped out of the house, the project dragging on the ground behind. He had lugged it with a limp hand, glitter sparked up over every bump, like the dying gasps of a fairy. Michael had tossed the whole thing into the trashcan and sat down by it, staring at ants making their rounds.

Jon had tried to cheer him up by buying him an ice cream, the one true cure all for an eight year old's ills, but nothing could shake him from this slump.

This was just one of many soul-crushing incidents. Michael never spoke about his parents after that, just focused on his studies, hoping that school was his ticket away. To deal with stress, he composed limericks. No, really. Actual limericks. The dirtier the better. It was a side of him that you might not have otherwise known existed.

"There was a young fellow named Simon,
Who tried to discover a hymen,
But he found every girl,
Had given up her pearl,
In exchange for a single fake diamond."

"Sounds about right for Black Rock," Jon sneered. "Heard they're adding a maternity ward to the middle school."

"Yeah," Michael laughed. "The girls around here are all dumb sluts. They spread for anyone."

Except me! They both lamented silently.

Dusk was rapidly running at them. A crisp autumn wind shot down the street. They pedaled through old roads designed for horses and buggies, half the streetlights were out. The pair stopped at an unassuming house surrounded by a tired chain link fence. A figure detached from a porch swing and leapt onto the small patch of lawn.

"Thought y'all might not be comin'," the figure drawled.

"Well, we're here."

"Yep, ya'll here," the boy said and picked up a bike. It was his granddaddy's Schwinn from the 1950s.

Not something he was proud of. Even with the basket ripped off, it was an embarrassment. Old and clunky. A "hand-me down" his parents had called it, but it was more of a castaway. Mostly it was their way of avoiding having to admit they couldn't afford a new one.

"Everything alright at yer home?" the boy asked Jon.

"Why?"

"Yer daddy called up here lookin' fer you."

"He did?"

"Yep. Didn't think he knew who I was."

"Me neither."

The boy, Louis Norton, had a muscular frame and straddled the bike like a pro. He was a transplant from North Carolina. The family had drifted northwards to take advantage of the very generous welfare system New York State had to offer. Like all who migrated to the city from the Bible Belt, Louis was mocked constantly due to his thick corn whiskey accent. Nothing would stop that. No matter how many teeth he knocked out, it never ended. The fact that he had a starting position on the school football team, something that would've stilled tongues in the small towns of the Carolinas, meant nothing. The collective Irish, Italian, Polish, and Black communities still ganged up to poke fun at the hick, which was why the jock preferred to hang out with the fringe elements of the school.

Not that they didn't give him some friendly ribbing.

"There was a girl out of Carolina,
Who had an erratic vagina,
To the surprise of the fucker,
It would suddenly pucker,

And whistle a song made in China.”
“Yeah, y’all are real fucking funny.”
“Just kidding.”
“Uh huh, let’s get out of here.”
They zipped out into the night. How did Father know about Louis? He never seemed to pay attention to Jon’s coming and goings, or never commented on it, except to dole out punishment. What else did he know? Had he been reading Jon’s journal? After a moment’s thought, he rejected the idea. There was nothing in there about the guys. It was all filled with the fallout of his venting against the family. Still . . .

They came up canal-side by that great trench of Victorian-Era engineering, the Erie Canal, then followed it up near to the end where the great grain elevators, a marvel of Edwardian era engineering, punched the sky. One-hundred-and-twenty-feet tall, made from steel and cement, this once magnificent structure was designed to hold, weigh, and dispense grain being shipped all across the country.

The place had seen better days. The main building—called the head house—rose five-stories and was about as gutted a wreck as you can imagine. Next to the head house were eight storage silos with “Agway” written down the side in three-foot long letters. Various spindly support towers arched up next to the silos, none of which had any floors left in them. The entire structure half slumped over the water. An old marine leg, which used to scoop grain out of passing ships, had long rotted away, leaving only a damaged hump over the tops of the buildings.

In past days, two-thousand men would have been working this area. Pulling up, weighing, and dropping off grain sacks. Now, the only ones who used it were teenagers having illicit rendezvous. Waiting for them just outside was a portly girl in a jean jacket also slinging a backpack. She waved when they rode up.

"You guys are late," she chided.

"But we're here now," Michael said flatly and walked past her.

"Hi, Jon," she said, a touch of mousiness creeping around the edges of her voice. He smiled in reply, and she blushed.

"Hey, Kathy. Any trouble sneaking out?"

"No. The parents are at some exhibit opening at the museum."

They pulled their bikes into the head house and hid them behind a half-collapsed wall. It was unlikely anyone would want them, but better safe than sorry. More sinister people than they lurked there sometimes. All the old machinery had long been removed, leaving giant holes descending through the floors, and the left-behind parts always felt shaky. No glass remained in the windows, and most of the staircases were missing stairs, but somehow they traversed all the obstacles until they reached a small claustrophobic room with a low ceiling on the fifth floor. They called it the midget room. It was their broken playroom.

Once in and the door safely sealed with a beam, Kathy took out a pack of red candles and laid them all about the room, while Louis lit them. Michael took several old tomes from his pack and settled in cross-legged. The others soon followed suit, each presenting their own books. Michael then opened a trapper keeper and took out several sheets of loose leaf paper tucked away in a folder. Jon took out his own paper. All looked at Michael with intense concentration.

"When last we met," Michael began in an ominous tone, "you had recovered the Sunsword from the disused chapel and fought off some ghouls. You are currently back in the grand foyer."

"After we just knock'd off that wax dummy that look'd like the vampire Strahd, hiding behind the mirror," Louis added. "Which ah still call bullshit on. My guy woulda taken his head off. Bait and switch."

"It's in the module," Michael yelled, holding up a thin blue book. "The guy there was a fake out. A dummy to trick you."

"But ah rolled a natural twenty!"

"It doesn't matter. Now, focus," Michael commanded, producing a handful of glittering dice from his pack. "You're being attacked by a gang of zombies. Your move, Louis."

"I hit one, ah reckon," Louis stared down at his own blue-colored dice, confused by their complex shapes. "Christ, which one do I roll again?"

"The twenty sided," Kathy offered. "You just said it."

"I can't keep track of all these gawd-damned rules."

As Louis fumbled with his dice, Jon consulted his character. Crixen Runeburner, elf mage, tall and proud. He was from a noble line of adventurers and princes. Magical rings glistened on his fingers. Multi-colored robes flowed about his willowy frame. They mystically staved off attacks and turned back spells. Around his feet flowed silken boots that allowed him to run with the speed of a pony. His right hand held a mighty heft of oak, an enchanted quarterstaff of kicking-your-fucking-ass.

Jon looked at this character sheet, thin in some places due to erasures, with pride. He had worked and sweated and rolled long and hard to raise this character with sub-standard statistics up into the powerhouse he was now. He had become a mighty hero who had conquered many a fearsome foe.

He had to admit, it wasn't just him. The group had all built great characters with Michael running the game. They had campaigned against the giants, discovered the sinister secret of Saltmarsh, survived the Isle of Dread, unraveled the Assassin's Knot, nearly died in the depths of Dungeonland, and now they were storming Castle Ravenloft to destroy an ancient evil that had been fouling the land for centuries.

The group had been meeting three times a week for over a year now and Jon wished they could play more. When the game was on and the die rolled, he could completely lose himself. He could see the mystic world where Crixen Runeburner strode, hear his character's breath, and feel the power that crackled in his veins. Better than a book. Better than a movie. It was a tale they all told together. One where *they* were the heroes, great deeds were accomplished, and even death itself was negotiable. Quite frankly, it was better than life itself.

They played on into the night. Fighting, making discoveries, gathering treasure, uncovering secrets. All in all, having a blast. Each successful roll of the dice was a badge of honor. Every failure, a slap of shame. For Jon, this was all about the triumph, about his character becoming the best. When his guy was doing well, it made him feel good, as if he was doing good in life as well. Perhaps it was a poor substitute for actual achievement, but Jon didn't care.

With the others, things were slightly different. Michael enjoyed controlling the world, being the man in charge. Louis . . . well he just liked to hit things. The idea of his over-muscled warrior decapitating some monster thrilled him. And Kathy— he didn't know exactly why she played, but considering how violent her character, Black Leaf, acted, she must be burning off some sort of frustration.

"Why the hell is there an Iron Golem down here?"

"Two of them," Michael corrected.

"Two, Christ. And we got this here gas comin' out of the treasure chest . . . "

"Maybe we should run?" offered Kathy.

Louis lifted his character sheet and said with utter seriousness, "Big Jim Umbrage, he don't run from nobody, no how." He nudged Jon, "You ready to rock?"

"Fuck yeah!"

"Cast giant form on me."

They played up in the midget room for the atmosphere mostly. The place had a sense of complete isolation, a leftover box of a dead generation. The walls and ceiling were well over a hundred years old and in that ruined building it seemed easier for them to slip into their mythological fantasy realm.

Michael had found it after the group was run out of Louis's place by his strict and loud Anabaptist parents. They had listened to some half-baked tele-preacher rattle on about the evils of D&D and were convinced it was a tool of the devil. Of course, they also believed that about most music, TV, films, toys—He-Man in particular for some reason—and popular video games, like Pac Man and Donkey Kong. Hell, even Root Beer Tapper gave them pause.

For obvious reasons, Jon and Michael's homes were out. Kathy gave only vague reasons, but they got the impression she was ashamed of her parents. So they used the midget room, which turned out to be an ideal place. There they didn't need to be polite or watch their language.

"Goddamn son of a bitch, hit that fucker with a fucking lightnin' bolt before he knocks the shit out of us."

Or clean up after themselves. The room was littered with crushed cola cans and candy bar wrappers. Or respect the property. The building was practically a ghost in any case.

They gamed on and on, well past the witching hour, until their first yawns indicated that they might have to stop. It was easy to lose track of time while in the game.

"Alright, I guess we better pack it in," Michael concluded. "We all got school tomorrow."

"You mean today."

He laughed, "Yeah."

"And ah got practice."

"Have fun with that."

"Whatever. Just 'cause you all couldn't make the cut—"

They carefully exited the head house. Michael almost slipped on some rickety stairs, but he grabbed the holes in the wall and steadied himself. Jon felt joy slip away. Back to the grind of life. Back to the family bullshit. Every time the group started up, he wished they would keep going until they all passed out, then wake up and start over.

Once out, Kathy tugged Jon's sleeve. "Can you ride with me home? It's later than usual."

"Sure."

"Oooh-la-la," joked Michael and rode off. Louis followed, pulling huge yawns that stretched out his face.

"Oh, whatever," she called after Michael. "It's not even like that."

Of course not. Not even the rotund girls with pizza faces, like Kathy, wanted Jon. And forget about the ones he actually lusted after, the Playboy bunnies and Sears underwear models. They haunted his dreams and stoked his loins, leading to many a sticky night. Jon had spent too much time watching the idiot box and believing that the big lie would come true. That just around the corner the magical supermodel would beckon towards him, lusting for his body. All he wanted was one incredibly hot woman to have sex with all the time. Him and the rest of the male population. He despaired of ever getting sexual pleasure from anything other than his right hand.

Jon had run across some abstinence literature once that described his virginity as a "noble choice" and one of the "greatest gifts he had to give." What a load of horseshit. It was a millstone. A giant obstacle he needed to knock over if he was really going to start living his life. At that moment, he would happily let some toothless crack-whore gum his cock into an explosion just to get it all over with. So he could finally feel like a man and stop lying about being a virgin.

They rode on through the chilly streets. An occasional neighborhood bar would flash by, the local drunks all clustered together yelling about the game or whatever, but otherwise the roads were dead.

Everyone was tucked away somewhere warm, away from the night air, where Jon should have been.

It took a while to get to her house and Jon was near exhausted when they finally zipped up to a two-story townhouse done in a neo-colonial style. It was on the cusp of a much more affluent neighborhood, where the houses were wider, the bars almost nonexistent, and the corner groceries didn't universally proclaim, "We Accept Food Stamps." It was the sort of neighborhood Jon felt he belonged in.

"What do your parents do again?"

"My dad's the director of the Museum of History and mom teaches archeology at Buff State."

"Nice place."

"Yeah, it's okay," she replied and walked over to him, eyes nervously looking at her fingers. "Thanks for the escort."

"Oh, no problem."

She gave him a quick peck on the cheek and walked away. That caught him off guard, even though it shouldn't have. The signs had been there. He had just missed them. There was his opportunity for sexual exploration, but Jon shrugged it off. He was getting too tired to care about anything. Jon watched her walk down the path to her house and enter. Then he cycled away into the night, yawning all the while.

CHAPTER 3

What Rough Beast

FATHER FOUND HIM on the way back from Kathy's house.

A town car, freshly minted and fully loaded, pulled up to Jon on an empty street. It sparkled under the streetlights and the yellow eyes of its driver sparkled along with it. Jon's father stepped out. Well-muscled and trim, he was always perfectly dressed with neat crisp lines. He never seemed to sweat or get dirty. He always knew what to say and how to act, to get what he wanted. Perfection clung naturally to him. From that perfection came a confidence Jon could never hope for.

Punishment was looming. Mother found the problems. Father corrected them. He towered over Jon like a giant. The teen shrank under his shadow. The elder fixed him with his eyes, seeming to drink in Jon's every weakness before saying, "So you didn't do as you were ordered."

He let that dangle like a viper between them.

"What do you have to say for yourself?"

Jon's head hung down, his ball cap shading all but the lower jut of his chin. He felt anger at having to be in this spot. *What the hell does it matter if I went off with some friends?* Then shame at having failed in other's eyes. *It* was *my job. I was told to do it.* Then acceptance that he needed to be punished. *Better take it then. Sooner it begins, sooner it's over.*

"I'm sorry," he said in his patented whipped dog tone.

Father stared for a moment. His implacable gaze burned into Jon's body. Once again, the boy was a failure. Once again, he needed to be punished. Father sighed.

"You're sorry. Here's what sorry gets you."

He pulled a large monkey wrench from the trunk and walked over to the bicycle. He paused, waiting for an objection from Jon, then shoved his son aside and began pounding away. He smashed through the handlebars, bent the axle, broke the tire rims, ripped out the spokes, and snapped the chain.

Father backed away still perfectly dressed, not a hair out of place. "Bring this junk heap back home," he ordered and drove off in his car, leaving Jon to eat his dust.

Jon hefted the bike and stumbled over the uneven cement blocks of the sidewalk. It was a long, savage haul at that time of night, with the temperature rapidly falling. The cold numbed his legs, while the weight of the bike bit into his hand and strained his muscles to their limit. Little weeds and sticky plants grew up between them. Jon cursed each one, then cursed his family, their house, and kept cursing until he had reached back to his great-great-grandfather. With every curse, he forgot some of his burden. Each spark of hate warmed him a little.

By the time he made it back home, the birds were chirping. He dumped the bike at the end of the driveway, right behind Father's car. Hopefully the old man wouldn't notice, would back over it and ruin some of that car's perfection. Probably not, though. Father just didn't make those kinds of mistakes. The best revenge Jon could hope for was to make the old man move the wreckage himself. He'd take whatever he could get. He went inside.

The jokes he and Michael had made earlier about the whorishness of the average Black Rock teenage girl had a germ of truth embedded at its heart. The most average example of that type lay sprawled before him on the living room divan. His older sister, Michelle, snored away. Blobs of puke were smeared down her pinhole-burn-ridden shirt and collected into a grimy pool on the antique oriental carpet. A half-empty Beefeaters bottle lay curled under her arm like an adored child.

She was the greatest whore Jon had ever heard of, except she never got paid. She sucked a new cock every other day. Alcohol was her mother's milk. There wasn't a drug that she hadn't smoked or snorted. Track marks ran up and down her arms. Every one of her teeth had rotted out of her head and had been replaced with dentures.

All this decadence was abetted by their parents. They had let Michelle effectively drop out of school at twelve. Technically, she was enrolled under the Home-School Act in New York State, but no actual educating, except how to apply makeup, went on. All assignments and tests that the state required be submitted had been forged. Jon knew this because he had been forced to write a few papers for her. On her sixteenth birthday, they officially let her withdraw from her education requirements. Father had a party to celebrate the event where Michelle was presented with her first bong, a blue glass affair with her name emblazoned along the stem in rhinestones.

She was rail thin from the substance abuse and her parents had invested in a portable IV rack, so they could inject her with nutrients whenever she passed out. At nineteen, she still looked good. The amount of slavering hormonal boys tramping through the house was testament enough to this, but that would soon pass. No one could abuse their body so much without it eventually collapsing into a wreck, or at least Jon hoped that was the case.

He felt a twinge of guilt at the schadenfreude of the idea of his sister turning into a bar hag. In a very real sense, she was as much a victim of her parents, as he was. This dead-end street her life was on had been foisted onto her by the pair. She may never really have had a choice. When a world of pleasure is tossed at you, it's difficult to say no. Especially when you're too young to know better. Still it *was* pleasure and not a similar pain that was constantly pounded onto him, and for that he was jealous. For that, he would have a little nasty fun at her expense. He needed a pick-me-up after witnessing his bike's destruction.

Jon pulled a frozen hotdog from the freezer and thawed it a little by swirling it around in the toilet after he'd pissed in the bowl. He picked up an iron poker from the fireplace—the thing had been bricked up years ago, but they kept the paraphernalia lying around for some reason—and jabbed her with the poker. She stirred and blurted an incomprehensible phrase in a dreamy accent. He poked her again.

"All right, Ian," she burbled, still three quarters unconscious. "Just gimme the shit, man. I'll get you the money later. My daddy will give it to me."

"No," Jon said, barely suppressing an evil laugh. "You pay me now."

"I'll suck your dick. I'll suck your dick. Just gimme!"

He shoved the soiled hot dog into her mouth and laughed as her filthy gums worked around it expertly. Eyes crusted over, she grunted in appreciation as she fellated the dead meat. Every time she shifted, a new foul smell wafted towards Jon. One way, vomit and stale beer. Another, a yeasty fish. Third, diseased semen. Fourth, spoiled mayonnaise.

"You've gotten bigger, baby," she burped onto the hot dog.

Suddenly thirsty, he went back to the kitchen and poured himself some green apple Kool Aid from a glass pitcher.

"I forgot you weren't cut. Sexy," she burbled in a bad seductress voice.

It was disgusting and fascinating at the same time, like a horrific accident, impossible to tear your eyes away from. He slurped heavily from the glass as her tongue expertly worked along the meat stick's edges. It was rhythmic, hypnotic in a way. The weird taste of the off-brand Kool Aid hung thick on his tongue.

"Are you gonna cum soon baby? I need. *Need . . .*"

Reality became shiny along the edges. Some underpaid editor had over-saturated the colors. Things behind him? A door creek? Cold air? The world began to . . . No, not the world. His mind! His mind began drip-drip-dripping

plop
drip
drip
collecting
into a puddle of
nonsense at his feet
lights and boxers and monsters
in a pool of liquid rock, shaking sticks
waved and played and talked the stock market
then drank a bubbling milky scum from a big skull
Aya. They yelled. Hua. They barked. Ska. Ska
monoamine oxidase inhibitor their god
there was a man from Nantucket
who showed a left hand
until until
Plop!

Where the hell was he? His room? Yes, his room. It had to be . . . but. Oh Christ, he was tired. If he had slept, it couldn't have been for long. He was naked in his bed on top of the covers . . . and his mother stood over him, frowning as usual. He covered up with his hands quickly.

"Oh, please, there's nothing worth looking at on you."

She threw a piece of paper on his skinny chest. A note written in Father's hand.

"It's for yesterday," she said. "An excuse for school."

"Yesterday?" he said weakly. "I went there yesterday."

She stuck her face close to his, snarling contempt.

"You got home late two nights ago and literally slept all of yesterday. Lazy asshole. I would've woken you up, but Father said to let you lie around. Not today, though. Get up and get out."

A day? A whole day gone? He flipped his feet over the bed and tried to stand, but his legs were spaghetti. Jon's face hit the hardwood floor. His arms barely had the strength to push himself into a sitting position.

"Hurry, I don't have time to mess around with you," his mother yelled and stormed out. "I have to take your sister to her school and check up on Michelle at the hospital. She almost choked to death after she fell asleep eating a hot dog."

That woke him. "What? Is she alright?"

"What do *you* care?" she stepped into his doorway and considered him intently.

Long ago, Jon had mastered the art of the unintelligent blank stare. A man under as much enemy scrutiny as himself needed a defensive mechanism, a fallback face to deflect any suspicion. It was a masterful expression. Blank unintelligent surprise with a touch of sadness at the corners. The eyes mutely crying *how can you suspect me?* It had gotten him out of more than one jam. This time, Mother bought it.

"Father is down there now threatening a lawsuit. They're trying to put her in rehab or some Narcotics Anonymous bullshit. We'll have to slam the sue hammer down on them."

His younger sister appeared briefly behind her mother's legs and stuck her tongue out at him, then ran down the stairs giggling with evil intent. His mother burrowed into his blank face, mentally trying to tear it away and expose some dark guilt. Her brow furrowed and lips pinched in concentration, but the eternal enemy, time, got in the way. She glanced at her watch and stomped off. The front door slammed. Now that the source of tension had evaporated, blackness claimed Jon.

He snorted awake sometime later, still sitting propped up against the bed. The alarm clock was blaring, must have been for hours. He wiped the crud from his eyes. 11:30. Christ, half the day gone. Well, no point in going now. The way punishment worked at the school, missing part of the day was as bad as the whole of it, so he might as well take full advantage. The malaise affecting him earlier had washed away. A few minutes of stretching later, he felt absolutely great. Ready to take on the world.

The clothes he had been wearing were thrown in a pile by his closet. Like everything else, he had no memory of taking them off. Jon did an inventory. Jeans, T-shirt, underwear, socks. Sneaker- singular. Sneaker? Where was the other one? Damn it. He franticly began digging through the mess that was his room. In the closet, under the bed, by the dresser, around the desk. Nothing. He had to find it.

Not that he even liked them. They were just another reminder how his parents cheapened his life. All his pals, even broke-ass Louis, had Nikes. And what did Jon's affluent parents bequeath him? KangaROOS, a knock-off Australian brand in ugly grey with pink trim. Their only distinguishing feature was a little pocket and zipper on the side. The pocket might sound pretty cool, but it was too small to hold anything thicker than a dime. Essentially it was just a useless zipper to spice up the look of a poorly stitched shoe.

Still, there would be hell to pay if it was lost. He could feel his mother's tongue lashing against his back already, yelling at him for hours. Maybe buying him an even worse pair if that was possible. He scoured the living room, the last place he remembered being, but there was nothing. All of the puke had been expertly scrubbed out of the carpet and couch. Maybe they'd found the sneaker and tossed it somewhere.

The rest of the downstairs also yielded nothing, so he hit the upper floors. Perhaps Catherine had taken it. That would explain her laughter earlier. He kicked open her door. Decorated in the style of a fantasy princess, her room was full of pink and white, silk and lace. The bed was the most comfortable around. The TV was prominently displayed with a horde of plush animals surrounding it. Every Barbie accessory a little girl could want was crammed in there. Every top-of-the-line ballerina accouterment, batons for twirling, and makeup as well as jewelry for when they hit the child pageant circuit. Everything was beautiful and spotless. He hated it. And as far his rooting could tell, there was no sneaker.

Michelle's room, actually a converted attic space, was locked up tight. The only way in was a ladder that extended from a pull-down rope. Jon had never seen up there. He'd only smelled dubious odors wafting down.

That left his parents' room. A place he feared to tread. He creaked the door open, half-afraid some booby trap would swing out and decapitate him. It was pleasantly arranged. Nothing audacious. The decor was almost muted. Catherine's room was far more extravagant. It wasn't until he opened drawers and closets that the decadence shined. Designer clothes, racks of fashionable shoes, expensive scents, tasteful jewelry, a drawer full of Rolexes. The St. Fonds did not practice self-denial.

He was digging through Father's shoe trees, filled with Testoni Italian leather shoes, when he heard a click. His elbow had hit a concealed button along the line of the wall, invisible to the naked eye. The back of the closet dislodged from its base and retracted a quarter of an inch. He pushed and the back slid to the left. There was a small alcove with an electric hum.

Inside was filled with monitors, each displaying a different room. There must have been a hidden camera hook-up riddling the house. As he looked closer, there were multiple views of every room, each from a different angle. No stone was left unturned. No blind spots were obvious. His room was there. Catherine's as well. The attic, the *bathrooms* (ugh), the master bedroom, the kitchen, the basement. Two even displayed the back and front yards. These all connected up to a high shelf, full of VCRs recording every movement. Jon had never suspected anything like this.

A padded fold-out chair was in the corner, next to a Waterford glass and bottle of—he picked it up— Glenlivet Nadurra. The label identified it as an eighteen-year-old single malt. Jon didn't know much about liquor, the smell nauseated him, but made the educated guess it was expensive.

He flipped the chair open and plopped down, holding the bottle by the neck, taking in the enormity of the find. This room wasn't supposed to be here. He knew the architectural specs, the original ones from the 1920s he had come across in his research, and every square inch was accounted for. All of the rooms were roughly of the same dimension as originally designed. Or were they?

He moved his hands across the walls. Solid yellow pine on both sides. The nails and studs seemed to be aged the same as well, but the shelves holding the VCRs and monitors were made of plywood, and were screwed in, not nailed. The screw heads were shinier, obviously having been added at a later date. Logic dictated that this little room had been a detail added to the original blueprints at the orders of his great-great-grandfather, who went through workmen like toilet paper. How many other little rooms were there?

He unscrewed the whiskey and took a snort, then suppressed a blob of vomit. How could people drink that shit? He'd take a slug of Mountain Dew over that piss any day of the week. He had an emergency stash of the soda in the back of his own closet, which of course his parents knew.

So they had been watching him his whole life. Every cry, every panic attack, every imaginary conversation, every masturbatory incident, everything. It must be how they knew about Louis. They wouldn't have had to read his journal. They probably knew about Kathy too. Course he didn't remember ever dialing Louis from his house, but his memory wasn't perfect. Maybe he should rewind the tape. How far back did they go? He popped one out. It was a specialty job, very expensive, and contained enough tape to last twenty-four hours. He returned it to the machine and pressed record.

He looked closer at the screen, was the definition

good enough to pick up phone calls? Each of the monitors had a joystick that allowed the camera angle to be adjusted, a little button on top zoomed the image in. He pushed it in on the rotary phone at his little desk—another way they screwed him, everyone else had a touchpad phone extension. Yeah, the picture was clear enough.

Movement caught his eye. The front door swung open. In sauntered his mother and a stranger. He was tall and bald of pate with a black goatee, dressed in a cream-colored turtleneck and black slacks. The stranger had the same bearing Father did, command and obedience. Jon zoomed in on his mother's face. There was something odd about it, she was almost giddy?

"Make yourself at home," she said, surprising Jon. He didn't realize the cameras included sound.

"I will," the man replied. His tone was dusky and thick. A heavy smoker's voice, with a faint trace of a French accent. "And I'll have a drink as well."

"Of course!" his mother tittered and scurried off like a schoolgirl. "I think we have some Privilège Cognac left."

The man seated himself at the dining room table and threw a manila folder, thick with papers, on it. Mother returned with a glass and a bottle and stood over him, pouring. As she served, the stranger's hand crept up her leg, feeling the muscles in his hard grip, then slipped it up under her skirt. Her teeth gnashed together and lips fluttered. In pleasure? In pain? Impossible to tell at this angle.

"You've been keeping yourself fit," he said.

"Oh yes."

"Absolom?" came the dark voice of Father.

They turned, Jon jumped. So intent was he on the scene, he didn't notice the patriarch's entrance. This would be interesting. A fight? A murder? An orgy? But it was none of the above.

Father sat across from the stranger, unperturbed by where the newcomer had lodged his right hand. The bald Frenchman, named Absolom, squeezed harder. Mother was paralyzed. Her fingers ground into the table varnish.

"What brings you here," Father asked in his calm commanding manner, "besides a cheap distraction."

Absolom chuckled to himself and pushed the folder over. "We think we may have found the perfect place. The Osbourne Canning Company has a few acres that they need to get rid of. It's close, isolated, but not too isolated. Has that special tint we require. They bought it originally as equity to borrow against for a further business venture. On paper it looks like prime land, until you realize what's actually there."

Father glanced at the papers then laughed long and loud. "That's a novel way to handle a loan. Very admirable in fact. Sneaky and bold, simultaneously."

"It was all financed through a bank in Wisconsin. They must have sent an inspector, but he was either bribed off or was an idiot."

"Or something else."

"Quite," came the grinning reply, his hand clutching deeper under the skirt, pulling out a groan from Jon's mother. Father was absorbed by the paperwork. "Still the loan went through. Now, fifty years later, the business is about to go under, so they need to raise some capital. It's perfect for what we want. Now that the great—"

"Enough proselytizing. Let's focus on details. The asking price is still pretty high considering the area. What about the structures? How are they holding up?"

"Left to decay. The company just needed the deed to the land. They didn't maintain it, couldn't build on it, now they can't get rid of it. Wear and tear, lot of vandalism, but that's not important."

"No, it isn't," Father agreed. "Still, there's no reason we should get raped here."

"Be as unfair as you want. The thing's a millstone to them. I'm almost certain we'll be the only bid. May I?" The Frenchman nodded to Jon's near-drooling mother.

"Hmmm? Oh," Father said absentmindedly. "Help yourself." Then leafed over the next page.

Absolom manhandled her back into the kitchen. She screeched hysterically with joy, as her skirt was roughly ripped away and he ravaged her over the sink.

She submissively took the pounding, gasping in pleasure over the dirty dishes. Eventually he loosed his sperm and fell back, red face and swearing. Absolom had cum so hard that he lost control of his legs and fell, bare ass streaking across the linoleum. Jon's mother just stood there quivering.

Father leaned against the doorframe, the snifter of cognac swirling between two fingers, dark amusement smeared on his face. "Having fun there?" he asked his fallen comrade. The other just laughed, still completely spent.

"You two's fuckplay has fired me up," Father growled, and grabbed his wife by the throat, forcing her to bend backwards over the counter, "though I prefer the front hole." And he plunged in, rough and bestial.

Jon couldn't tear himself away. It was an erotic car wreck. There was a dark hilarity in watching a parent you despise get hate-fucked. Still, there was something fundamentally wrong about watching family members having sex. Okay, it was a natural biological urge everyone indulged in, but his instincts revolted at the sight of his parents below.

"No, no. The ass, the ass, mon ami," Absolom chided, still lying on the floor. "Never was a passage created that could give such pleasure as that noble channel. No slimy cunt ever fulfilled me as much as a beautifully tight anus."

Father finished with a roaring bellow and several short hard pelvic thrusts. His wife's face had gone purple from his grip on her throat. He threw her aside and staggered, a few stray specks of semen spat into the sink. Onto his younger sister's favorite dish, Jon noted. His mother fell to the floor as well, gasping for air, hand massaging her neck, staring up at Father in fear, excitement, and adoration.

No one could blame Jon from taking that second slug of whiskey. This time he barely flinched at its bouquet. His parents' kinks were something he didn't want to know about. It actually wasn't *that* much of a surprise. He had caught some clues in the past. Discarded sex toys in the trash and the like. However, that didn't mean he wanted to be slapped in the face with a bird's eye view. It also blew up a popular theory of Jon's that his mother acted like she did towards him out of sexual frustration. Clearly not the case. That bummed him. The thought of her misery darkly lightened his own.

He turned off the kitchen monitors. Enough of

that. Their voices still drifted in from other cameras, but it was lower, babbling. He was probably stuck there for the duration. Out of boredom he chugged a third shot and began playing with the joysticks. Nothing, nothing, nothing. Wait! What was that?

In the basement monitor, near a far corner was a sneaker. No, not *a* sneaker. *His* sneaker. He zoomed in. The little zipper on the side confirmed it. How the fuck did it get down there? He knew that, no matter what state he was in, there was no way he would've entered that dank hole.

The rewind button was pushed. The image of the basement spooled backwards. Nothing, nothing, nothing. It was like a slug negotiating a staircase. Was that . . . ? Nope, just his mother taking out a load of laundry, his younger sister dancing behind her in ballet shoes, then walking backwards up the stairs. Time zipped on. She came back down and put the laundry in. Then nothing. Nothing stirred, not even a mouse. It wasn't until the very end, the last minute of tape that he saw—

Four figures in black hooded robes carrying his naked body. Weird marks were painted in red up and down his frame, circling the genitals and nipples. His face had been coated with a white paste. One figure held his clothes and accidently dropped the sneaker. Then they went upstairs.

He leapt to the other cameras and rewound those tapes. After frantic pushing and waiting, he pieced together a few more scenes. One was him being hauled through the living room. No one's face was visible. His older sister still lay there, hotdog dangling from her mouth. Another scene had him being propped up in the shower. The red and white body paint trickled down the drain. Finally, he was tossed onto the bed and his clothes thrown in a corner.

Okay . . . okay . . . calm down. Wipe away the cold sweat. Another shot? Hell, make it two. Regrettably, the terror of what he'd uncovered chased away any effects of the alcohol. Was it some perverted sex thing? What were those symbols? Assuming two were his parents, who were the others? Absolom seemed to be a new arrival, so that, at least, left two others. His parents didn't have any friends that he knew of. A statement that spoke volumes about them.

Then he heard his name from a live camera. Clear as a bell, his mother had said, "Jon." The rest was garbled by distance from the camera. He flipped the monitors back on. The three of them were standing, pants pulled back up. His mother wearing a different skirt. Absolom was examining an earthenware bowl while the others drank cognac.

" . . . will happen like we wanted to," Father was saying.

"I'm worried," his mother said. "The way he's been acting is troubling."

Troubling? Troubling how? In what manner? Hadn't he gone along with whatever they told him? And if they were troubled, what would they do to him—beyond, apparently, what they were doing while he was unconscious. No sleep tonight.

"I know better than you do. No woman could understand what a boy goes through. You've never had to do it yourself."

"But . . . "

"That's enough," Father ordered and she immediately shut her mouth.

Absolom gave up the bowl with a wink. "It is good," he proclaimed. "Just what the physician ordered. Now, when can it be delivered?"

"Later," Father said, handing his wife the item. "Put it in the safe."

Safe? What safe? Jon's mother nodded and ascended the stairs. To his horror Jon realized she must be coming into the master bedroom. He fumbled over the chair and, as quietly as he could, replaced the concealed door. Retaking his seat, he peered at the bedroom monitors. His blood froze.

Mother was already in the room. She stood at the end of the bed and was staring at the closet. Long minutes dragged by and she just stood there. Motionless, looking, listening. He held his breath and clutched the bottle close like it was a comfort animal. Finally, eyes still on the closet, she began to move to the head of the bed. She flipped up the ugly picture over the headboard. It was some Blake print of a nearly naked guy doodling with an old-fashioned compass. Underneath it was a safe embedded in the wall. It was rather modern with a computerized keypad, Jon had no idea when they could have had it installed. As she jabbed in a key code, Jon pushed the picture in as close as he could, mentally repeating the numbers over and over. The bowl was deposited and the room restored.

Downstairs there was laughing. When Mother joined them, it was suggested that they all go out for steaks, drinking, and dancing. The proposal was roundly applauded and the trio left. After emerging from the hidden hole, the first thing Jon did was flip the picture and yank the safe open. Inside, there was about ten-thousand dollars, two .45 automatic pistols, various deeds to properties around the city, a very detailed genealogical chart of the St. Fond family, and the bowl.

The outside of the bowl was fired red earthenware with a thick glaze. Crude symbols were etched all through it, then painted in white. Intersecting lines and circles mainly, with pluses and Os darting inside and along the closed sections of the lines. One fat wave ran all along the bowl, connecting every symbol. The inside was something else entirely. The bottom half was inlaid with a convex shaped bone, possibly a skull cap. Scrimshawed on it was a complex circular pattern, much more skillful than the outside.

The pattern was a series of concentric circles, each with runes or glyphs or just decoration that Jon couldn't decipher. The center was an ugly face, grimacing up at the world with a pleated knife for its tongue. Two clawed hands clutched a human heart. Four squares surrounded the center, each depicting a monstrous face. Two animal skulls snarled out at the rest of the circles that were all filled with bizarre symbols. They became smaller and smaller, until you needed a microscope to see the images.

Jon couldn't see much point to the item, but he assumed it wasn't for anything good. He quickly became much more interested in the charts. Once unfolded, it spread across the whole of king-sized bed like an extra comforter. Hundreds of names and dates were recorded on the yellowed paper, right up into modern times, with the addition of a 5th cousin born only two weeks ago from a family branch in

Louisiana. Many of his relatives were still in France, it seemed.

Jon knew his family's origin was French. He had some famous ancestor who wrote various important books on geology and ballooning—well "important" to people who cared about any of that stuff. Benjamin Franklin had had a brief correspondence with the man, and their letters were warehoused at the National Archives. The extent shown on the chart, however, surprised him. Obviously, his parents still kept in touch with the extended family, but Jon had never been exposed to them. He did remember one trip his mother had made to France, about three years ago, along with his younger sister. He'd been told the trip was something to do with her feminist business, but that may have been a lie.

Mildly curious, he looked for his own name and found it listed with his two sisters. Above it, he saw his parents' names and something odd. It seemed his mother's maiden name was St. Fond as well. A further line connected her to a branch of the family residing in Key West. His parents were cousins . . . distant cousins, but still blood related. Was he the product of incest? The thought nauseated him. He saw many other such pairings all across the chart. Yuck.

So, what to do? There was money. He could run. But where? The only place that might be a refuge was Michael's house. Well, Michael's room. The rest of that family was disinterested in him. Louis and Kathy might be able to help him out as well. Then he remembered that Kathy's parents had something to do with archeology and historical junk. Perhaps they could shed light on this weird thing.

He grabbed a Polaroid camera from his parents' closet and shot twelve photos of the bowl. As for the cash, he grabbed about a hundred dollars, a little back payment for the abuse he had suffered. He thought about taking more but decided to leave the rest. If he needed to run, *then* he'd grab it. Maybe there was some possible non-sinister explanation for all this. He laughed at himself. Highly unlikely.

The bowl was shut back up in the safe and the painting restored. The problem was how to erase himself from the tapes. He couldn't just leave them off, that would attract suspicion, but now they were un-synced. Several of them would stop before the rest. Maybe they would automatically rewind and start over, some of these machines did that. Or perhaps no one would look at the tapes. After all, his parents couldn't go through them every day, could they? Then if he stayed away from the house, that would give them the incentive to look at the tapes and see what he had discovered.

Screw it. He could go round and round like this forever. Jon stopped all of the tapes, retrieved the sneaker from the basement—doing his ritual, running as fast as he could in and out of there, the sick feeling gripped him harder now—then rewound all of the tapes back two hours and hit record. If they checked, he would still be seen leaving the master bedroom. A risk he had to take.

After grabbing a few juice packs and granola bars from the pantry, he zipped off down the road to meet his gaming buddies. But somehow the adventures of Crixen Runeburner were dim and lifeless that night.

CHAPTER 4

THE JUDAS GOAT

JON WOKE WITH a start on Michael's bedroom floor. The grungy shag carpeting had scored a number of macaroni-sized ruts in his face. The usual disorders of not knowing where he was claimed him for a second, but his senses took in reality quick enough. The stink of yesterday's clothes, hard particles of crud from a carpet that had never been vacuumed, stale air from an unventilated room.

A typical teenage boy's room. Iron Maiden posters on the wall. A pile of dirty laundry in the closet. A tottering stack of well-read comics next to the bed. Porno mags hidden under the bed. Trashcan filled to the brim. Loose leaf paper, pens, spiral notebooks, backpack. Textbooks with a brown paper bag cover to minimize damage. Not much different from his own, except the furniture was more ragged.

He shook the sleep from his face. Michael was elsewhere, which was just as well, Jon needed to scratch his balls and didn't want anyone around for that. After the game last night, when they had extricated themselves from the grain elevator ruins, Jon called in a favor and asked to flop at Michael's place. There was no question of refusing, the two were close enough that he almost didn't have to ask. However, the latter kept pushing for details as to why Jon needed a new place and Jon clammed up. What was he going to say? That he didn't want to be sexually manhandled in some occult ritual? If that's even what his parents were doing.

Through a crack in the bedroom door, he heard Michael down below, talking on the phone. Others shuffled about, getting ready to commence the daily grind.

"I can pick that up later," he was saying. "No, no. It's great . . . Everything's fine . . . Well that might be a little tricky, he uh . . . "

"Are you gonna be on the phone all goddamn day?" Michael's dad yelled at him. "Some of us got to go ta work."

"How is me taking a call stopping that?"

"Well, uh, maybe *I* gotta make a call. You think of that? *No.*"

"Besides you need to eat," his mom chimed in.

"Did you make me something?" Michael asked hopefully.

"What? Your arm's broken?"

The rest of the family laughed with bovine idiocy. The joke had probably been made a hundred times before and they still found it just as funny. Michael hung up.

"You're always talking to people and stuff. All ritzy," his dad commented, as if it were some great crime.

"I'm planning for my future," Michael whined. "I've got to meet people who know other people if I'm gonna get ahead. That will be very useful once I graduate college.”

“Gct ahead. Please,” his dad snorted.

“You’re not even out of high school yet,” his mom scolded,” and you’re wasting your time talking about going to college. It’s a long ways off.”

“Only a year.”

“This is giving me a headache,” Michael’s father declared. Scraping sounds of a chair pushing across linoleum. “I’m out of here. Oh, tell your brother to get off his lazy butt and go find a job today.”

The dad walked into view, slipping on a plaid work shirt over his stained wife-beater T, a lunchbox stuffed in his armpit. Dishes clanked on the table.

“Is that kid, what’s his name, still here?” his mom asked.

“Jon? Yes.”

“I want him out when you leave.”

Jon retreated to the bed and wiped a greasy hand over his face. The pair had been friends for over nine years, a good chunk of their lives, and Michael’s parents still didn’t know Jon’s name. Oh well, that lack of interest could work in his favor. He might be able to sneak back in another night. If not, there weren’t many places for him to go. Maybe Kathy . . .

“Kathy is such a sad sack of shit,
That no one will tickle her tit,
It would make her so glad,
To be banged by a lad,
Her jeans cream at the mere thought of it.”

The words floated back from yesterday when Michael spat out this limerick as they headed to the game. Sexual jealousy? Sour grapes? Maybe he just wanted attention. Maybe he just hated the idea of anyone else having sex besides himself. Whatever was bothering him about the girl, Michael wasn't coughing up, but suddenly he was very down on her. Not to her face, of course. The Black Rock way was to always talk trash just out of earshot.

Kathy had agreed readily enough when Jon asked her to pass on the photos of the bowl to her parents. Then she repeated the kiss of the other night, much to Michael's amusement. He didn't spend a thought on whether he should go out with her. Things were way too weird to waste time on it. Besides, the fantasy of the horny supermodel who was into underage boys always lingered just around the corner of his mind.

Michael appeared, scratching his head shamefacedly. "Um, we—"

"Yeah, I heard."

"You heard?"

"Your mom wants me out."

"Yeah. Were you listening in?"

"She was kind of loud."

"That's true. Alright. We missed the bus, so we gotta bike. You can use my brother's since he's usually too stoned to stay on it anymore."

School was the same chore it had been for the last eleven years. Droning classes. Homework, given and received. Notes taken, but never read again. Lessons learned, then forgotten with the first footfall out the door. Yawns stifled. Clock ticking. Bored teachers. Bored students. Bored janitors.

At a break between classes, a laughing mick by the name of Coughlin told him that a group of Italians was smacking Michael around by the bathroom.

Apparently, they had pulled down his pants to impress some girls, then things took a dark turn. Jon went to see.

A large crowd had gathered around, looking and mocking. Vinnie Gabbaducci had the half-naked boy on the ground and was straddled across his chest, battering him about the head and neck. His hook-nosed butt-buddies, Carlo Abandanzo and Gino Giordino, were right behind the bully, egging him on, taking mock shots in the air. The sight of blood excited them to frenzy.

Behind the boys were the tittering girls. Their lips all warbled about what disgusting brutes the boys were, but their eyes sang high praise. A restless gleam shone in them, and their thighs rubbed together at the bravado. Jon's heart skipped a beat. Among the girls, wearing a tight sweater and short skirt, was his dream girl, Maria Maleventum. Large breasts, thin waist, pearl skin, bountiful auburn curls. She was perfect.

Whenever she hovered into view, his mind melted, the blood drained southwards, and all he could do was babble stupidly.

It took a few minutes before a few brave teachers ventured in and pulled the boys apart. The blood lust was deep on Gabbaducci now and it took three full grown men to wrestle him down the hall and toss him into the detention room.

Michael, red-faced with shame and choking back tears, was sympathetically led to the nurse's station to be looked over by the geriatric employed there. His pants, tossed into the girl's bathroom, were retrieved and slung over his shoulder.

The poor guy could never catch a break. The Dutch

family was—well, probably Dutch in origin, even though it could easily been some other WASP delineation. The main ethnic groups in the school were the Irish, Italians, and blacks, and they did not get along. It was almost taboo for a member of one pack to speak to someone of a different lineage. On a good day, they would only hurl insults at each other. On the worst, mini race riots would break out. Michael, not related to any group even by marriage, was alone.

Jon was, too. Not many St. Fonds in the area, the genealogical chart pointed that out, but something about Michael attracted these groups to bully him. He had the smell of an easy mark. His stooped shoulders and downward glance, gave away his beta gene. Whatever it was, the vermin would flock to feed on his corpse.

After that scene, he decided not to risk going to Michael's house a second night, and instead approached Louis. The jock agreed readily enough, saying that his family always had a couch open in case a stray member of their extended family should amble on up. Jon then sought out Kathy and caught up to her as she was about to enter a class.

"Hi," she said, eyes dancing eagerly over his face.

Some females nearby whispered softly and giggled at them. Suddenly self-conscious, Jon stared at the floor as they talked.

"So what did they say?"

"Say?"

"About the photos. Your parents."

"Oh, I'm sorry. I didn't get a chance to show them."

"Jesus Christ, it's important you know." He stalked away, shaking in head in irritation.

"I'm sorry," she called after him.

The night at Louis's place was odd. Well, not really odd, they were just more like a typical TV family than Jon was used to. They seemed actually *happy* to be around one another. Spending time together was something they wanted to do, rather than it being an obligation. Instead of watching TV and gulping down food, they sat around at a table for their evening meal and talked happily. They even said a prayer while holding hands, something Jon had never done. Afterwards, they spent time playing games, doing homework, reading, and generally enjoying each other's company without one of them verbally attacking the other.

What foreign land was this? Louis lived only six block away, but it might as well have been on Mars. These people were a unit, a team. Seeing them together made his own home seem like a farce. He slept well that night, better than he had in ages.

"My mother wants to talk to you," Kathy told him the next day. "I showed her the photos and she took them into her study, then came out and asked me all sorts of questions I couldn't answer. She was real agitated."

"Agitated?"

"Excited and nervous. She gets like that when she thinks she found something new. Like when she thought some jewelry she found in a dig in Yaxuna came from a lost civilization because they were made from a type of amber that is only found in New Zealand. Turns out it wasn't, but she believed that it might be from the Empire of Heva."

"And that's what the bowl is?"

"No, but she said it was weird and connected to

something old and hidden. Where did you get those photos?"

"Never mind. I've got to talk to your mom."

"Okay," she brightened up. "We can go to my place after school and then go to the game afterwards."

It was a game night. He had forgotten. All of his books and dice, and, most importantly, his character sheet were back at the house. Without that, Crixen Runeburner couldn't come alive. Should he risk returning for a sheet of paper? The class bell disrupted his thoughts. He had to hurry up to be bored.

Time stretched on to an infinitesimal crawl, but all bad things eventually come to an end and he was hit with an explosion of energy when the last bell finally rang. He flew out the door and found Kathy unchaining her bike. They took off, dodging cars and buses filled with joyful teens. On the road away, Jon looked back at the school and, wasn't sure, but thought he saw Michael on a street corner staring after him.

Thirty minutes later, they pulled up to Kathy's house. Inside, it was spare but tasteful. Bits of pottery from long dead Mesoamerican cultures decorated the rooms. Beakers, jars, a few knives and so on. As Kathy ran off to find her mother, Jon picked up a pipe shaped like a fornicating couple. It was designed so that the tobacco was stuffed into his anus and the smoke emerged from her mouth. Ingenious and obscene.

"She's in her office," Kathy said.

In traditional academic fashion, the room was a paper nightmare. Book, charts, pictures, journals, folders, and files were piled up on every conceivable space. The shelves were double-stacked with books. A couch near the window was flooded with loose leaf items. Jon looked about in dismay. And he used to think *his* room was messy.

"It looks a mess, but I know where everything is," Kathy's mother said, rising from a leather chair. A boxy computer hummed beside her. "I have my own system of organization."

Early forties, short iron-gray hair, the mother had the look of a deep thinker and the distracted mannerisms of one as well. She was barefoot and had donned riding jodhpurs topped with a red flannel shirt. The smile given to Jon was genuine and warm.

She looked around. "I'm afraid there isn't anywhere to sit . . . " Her voice trailed off as she stared at an empty spot on the carpet. There were in fact several chairs but, like the couch, they too were full.

"Kathy go to the garage and get one of those canvas chairs we use at the beach—"

"That's not necessary," Jon interjected. "I can stand."

"Are you sure? Uh . . . "

"Jon. Yes. Yes."

"Okay then," she clapped her hands, mind blanking, distracted by lofty thoughts.

"Photos."

"Right!" She extricated them from the middle of a large stack of folders, then regarded them. "Where did you find these, because this is right, but wrong at the same time. If you understand."

"No."

"Have you ever heard of something called Palo or Palo Mayombe?"

"No."

"Or Las Reglas de Congo?"

"Again, no."

"It was, or is, an underground religion that developed in Cuba and a few other Caribbean Islands. When the French first brought over African slaves from the Congo, they didn't bother to Christianize them. As long as they could cut sugarcane, the overseers weren't too interested in what else they got up to. That's why you have many more religious oddities, like Voodoo, floating about in former French colonies than where the Spanish held dominion."

"So the bowl . . . ?"

"Of course in the Spanish places, they just hid their old religions in the Catholic one. Adapting the old into the new. It's how La Dia De Los Muertes became a church event. In some regions you'll find curse cards, where they use an invocation to St. Peter to damn their enemies' souls or give them leprosy. Not exactly a traditional Christian sentiment."

"And what do they do in this religion?"

"Most of them are the same, just the cast of celestial characters change. Palo believes in the veneration of ancestors and in harnessing natural earth powers. Sticks, bones, wax, and the like, have power and are infused with spirits called Kimpungulu. Tell me, were there any candles?"

"Candles?"

"Near the bowl where you took the photos. Orange, white, red, yellow, black, shaped like a woman, like a crucifix, a skull? Anything?"

"I didn't see any."

"So you *did* take the photos," she said.

Jon was about to swear, but shrugged. What did it matter if she knew?

"The candles are often used in rituals. A different type, or collection of types, for each invocation. The lack of candles might mean whoever has possession of this item isn't a practitioner or a priest."

"Are they called priests?"

"Sort of. Palo is the Hispanic derivation of an unnamed religion. The word *palo* means stick in Spanish. The practitioner takes these earthbound spiritual objects, called *nkisni*, and collects them in his *nganga*. The more he has, the more spiritual power he gathers. Specific types, such as bones of animals, gives powers associated with that animal. Spiritual stones add toughness and so on. The *nganga* is the center of the priest's power. They then mark them with sacred symbols like we see on this bowl."

"So the bowl is a *nganga*?"

"No, that's the problem! The *nganga* is always a cauldron or cast iron pot. The working of metal in ancient times was one of the greatest mysteries, next to masonry, so it contained quite a bit of spiritual power. Man taking what the gods wrought and shaping it to his own desires. Very powerful stuff. A pottery bowl marked with Palo symbols is unique."

She walked to another stack of folders and, almost at random, whipped out a photograph. Jon looked. In it was an old-fashioned black cauldron. On it, a large 'S' was painted in white and adorned with crosses. The cauldron was filled with a large collection of junk. Rusted knives, Mardi Gras beads, a crude face chiseled in obsidian, some steel chains, a host of black feathers, and various other unidentified lumps. Jon would never have guessed it was a religious altar. The whole thing looked like a bucket of trash.

"That's a proper *nganga* uncovered six months ago in Nicaragua. The Sandinista government has been . . . let's say forcibly discouraging practitioners from selling their wares to the peasants. It's all part of their 're-education' of the oppressed class. Of course, they do it with bullets instead of books."

Jon still couldn't put together what his parents and their weird associate would want with this thing. Before the other night, he wouldn't have believed his parents were part of any religion. He couldn't see them indulging in one that dealt with collecting sticks and chicken bones. Not unless there was some money involved.

"What kind of wares," he asked, "does a Palo priest provide?"

"They offer curses, wards against evil, protection fetishes, good luck charms, cleansing rites, and so on. Primitive superstition some call it, maybe with reason, but there is an overriding belief in it throughout Central America. There are plenty who grew up in the region that might scoff in public, but secretly still fear its practitioners and their powers."

That didn't sound like much money. He couldn't see his successful parents wasting their time collecting pesos from Hispanic peons. So the bowl had to be for something else. He thought about the markings that had been painted on his unconscious body. Were they similar to those on the bowl? He couldn't remember and the tape would have been recorded over by now.

"Do they sacrifice animals or people?"

"Animals, definitely," she nodded. "As I said

before, the bones of various creatures hold significant spiritual value and they must be consecrated in a specific rite to trap the spirit. Human sacrifice, not really. There have been some practitioners linked to grave robbing, but uh . . . " She blanked for a moment, ideas cascading into her from all sides. Then, bingo! "Oh! Human sacrifice. That's the other part."

She rifled through the photos and pulled out the one showing the pattern inside the bowl.

"Now this is interesting and as unique as the pottery itself. The decoration inside is identical to the Aztec calendar stone. Whoever etched this in whatever that is in the bowl—"

"It's bone."

"I see . . . Well they must have used the actual one as a reference. It's just that the symbolism here is out of place. These are two incongruent religions. Ones that couldn't have had any contact with each other."

"Aren't they from the same region?"

"Yes. However, the Aztecs died out at least two hundred years before the rise of Palo and its cousins. That's why they hid Palo in the Christian religion instead of the Aztec one. All the old medicine men had been swept away. In fact, the stone had been buried in the wall of the Mexico City Cathedral when Palo was developing."

"What do these etchings mean? They're like hieroglyphics, correct?"

"A lot of this is up to speculation, but the center seems to represent the face of their sun god with the glyph of movement inside his mouth. These four squares with the skulls represent the death of the previous suns. These other symbols represent various important dates such as—"

"Death of the four suns?"

"Possibly a symbolic death. The end of the usefulness of the previous calendar certainly. Symbolically, it means the destruction of the world and humanity, only to be reborn again with the next sun. This could be represented by a solar eclipse, or be just more apocalyptic mythology, like the Norse Ragnarok or the Christian Day of Judgement."

"Or be true."

She laughed, taken by surprise at the suggestion. She tried to grope for the appropriate words, before blurting, "No!"

"Did they make another calendar with a new sun?"

"Their civilization was extinguished by the Spanish conquistadors in the 16th Century. This one doesn't run out until 2012, twenty six years from now. They had no need to make a new one. The Spanish replaced the Aztec calendar with the Christian one."

"Yet it *could* mean something more, like the end of the world.

"You're looking for the fantastical in the mundane, which I must admit is much more exciting. Think of it this way, if we stopped making calendars at the end of this year, would time end? Would the world explode? Even if we wrote on the last day of the final calendar, 'after this everyone dies', that wouldn't make it true. The Aztecs had four previous calendars, why not a sixth. They just never had a chance to make one."

That made sense. With the odd occurrences happening in his house, this bowl being the only physical manifestation of it, his mind had begun to race in all sorts of weird directions. All this old pottery and leftover religion didn't fit in with his parents and their lifestyle. Maybe they were going to sell it? Was there some sinister figure in the shadows eager for such an item?

Kathy's mother licked her lips, eyes gleaming with greed. Greed for knowledge that is.

"Can I meet them?"

"Who?"

"Whoever has the bowl. Is it your parents?"

Alarm bells! What would this disorganized woman do if he admitted who had possession of the bowl. Probably contact them, demanding answers. Then his parents would know he knew, and then . . . His imagination flared with ideas, each more hideous than the last.

"No. It's not them."

"Whoever it is. I just want to know about the bowl. What's it for and its connection to Palo Mayombe? What spiritual forces is it supposed to represent?"

"I'll ask them, but they don't know I took the photos."

She looked concerned. "Would you be in any danger if they found out?"

"Maybe."

"And it's definitely not your parents."

"No. It's not."

The conversation wandered from there. Kathy's mother flipped into a long diatribe about Aztec history and their religion, or what was presumed of their religion. Little of it had been recorded by their conquerors as they destroyed the Aztec civilization. Jon only really took in the most grisly parts, particularly about human sacrifice.

At Kathy's insistence, a dinner invitation was extended and Jon accepted. He wanted to see how the other half lived. Once again, it was an odd affair. The only child, Kathy, and her parents sat around a tasteful table making small talk about the minutiae of their day and minor vagaries of the weather. A rotund maid waddled around dishing up soup and boiled carrots, completely ignored by those seated.

The room had a stifled air. No one was relaxed. Each acted as if the others were strangers and held their true selves back to avoid offending anyone. This was not a happy affair. It was simply something that must be done in a civilized household. A required ritual. A few questions were tossed at Jon. How was school going? Where did he plan to attend college? What was going to be his major? Blah, blah, blah. Meaningless drivel which the adults barely took in. It was just noise to fill the emptiness. Kathy spent most of the dinner sending mooneyes Jon's way.

After the meal, the parents departed to their separate corners, while the teens left to join the others at the grain elevator. The question of whether to retrieve his gaming material popped up on the way. Even though he was sorely tempted, Jon nixed it. He couldn't take the risk right then.

The bikes were hidden in the usual place and they took the treacherous route to the midget room. New broken beer bottles and empty potato chip wrappers indicated someone else had been partying there recently. Louis and Michael were already present, arguing.

"Man, I don't know. We've been dewn' this a long ass time. Why change now?"

"What's the matter?" Jon asked.

Michael seemed triumphant, smirking at some hidden knowledge, "I've got a new game for us." He held up a black box. Embossed in white letters on it was the name *Dark Dungeons*. A wicked gleam rolled through his eyes. "This is something else."

A new game? Forget it. Jon didn't want to abandon Crixen Runeburner. Right now, it was the only escape he had in life. He needed to slip into the elf mage's skin and get away from the cryptic garbage cluttering up his life. Jon St. Fond could take a backseat in his own body for a bit.

"I spent a lot of time buildin' up Big Jim Umbrage and his sword arm," Louis yelled. His harsh voice thudded heavily against the small room's walls. "I ain't throwin' that away."

"We're not going to throw anything away," Michael consoled him. "The game comes with conversion rules, so you can bring in your character. There's something else about this game that's really great. Take a look."

He opened the box, which was full of beige plastic pieces. Torsos, arms, legs, heads. Hundreds of the dismembered things. Plucking out a few, Michael quickly snapped together a warrior. A silent scream of bloodlust was molded onto the figure's face as it raised a battle axe to destroy an enemy.

"You can customize your character, then paint it. It'll make the whole thing come alive."

"Well, that's kinda cool. But these look real small for paintin'."

"I'll do it for you. All of you," Michael offered. "Let's build our guys, while I run you through the rules."

Sounded good. Jon was intrigued. The players pawed through the box, shifting from limb to limb. The work on the miniatures was high quality. Each piece was from a unique mold, there was no repetition in style among the various disembodied heads and torsos. It was fascinating to play with the near endless variety of combinations available to build a character.

Michael went on and on about the rules. Jon only half-listened. Trying to take it all in now was futile, he'd forget half of it in twenty minutes. Repetition and actual use was how he learned best.

No numbers were used for statistics in the game. A series of descriptive words replaced them, so the player could focus more on the story. A series of action cards were produced and thrown out by the players at appropriate moments when designated by the Game Master, which would succeed or fail based upon the precision of the players and the descriptive text on their character sheet. The more precisely the players played the cards in unison, the greater the chance for success. A cassette of various dungeon noises and other things was provided to set the mood, along with some sticks of incense to be lit at certain times. They smelled weird, not a soothing remedy, but could actually heighten nervousness and add tension to a scenario. Jon thought that was a neat touch.

A pentagon shaped battle board was set up. Each of the character miniatures were placed on a corner. Combat occurred when the players, after being prompted by the Game Master, indicated they should throw down their combat cards and intone their desired action.

"And then what kinda dice do we throw to hit?" Louis asked.

"None."

"None?"

Outrage at the suggestion.

"It's diceless. Nothing is randomized here. The flick of your wrist and how fast you can all recite together determine things in your favor."

Jon let them hammer it out. His mind was elsewhere. The image of Crixen Runeburner was ready. It was perfect. Noble face with sharp elven ears, flowing robes, a mighty quarterstaff in hand. Somehow the artists had managed to create everything Jon envisioned his character to be. And for a moment, the fear that had been building a web in his brain for the last few days was gone.

As they went through a few practice rounds and got the rhythm of the game, Jon found himself drawn further into the life of his character than ever before. His hair rippled under fictional air. The tips of his fingers tingled when a spell was cast. It was exhilarating.

This might be a good game after all.

CHAPTER 5

SIGN OF THE BEAST

HE STAYED WITH Michael the next two nights, at the latter's insistence. Jon didn't need much of an arm twisting. Where else did he have to go? Michael's parents didn't want him there, but they paid so little attention it was easy to sneak by. The dad got up early to go to his job repairing conveyor belts, while the mom ran out soon after for her job as a crossing guard at the elementary school. Most nights, they went out bowling after a fast-food meal. Meanwhile, Michael's brother was always high or in the process of getting high, so he didn't care. He just stayed in the room reading comics when the parents were home, then scavenged for food afterwards.

It couldn't last, though. What was he to do? Become some kind of homeless derelict, eating garbage and collecting aluminum cans? There was no job he could get above minimum wage. Even if he could work full-time, he would be living out of an abandoned car or with ten other guys in a fly-trap college flop. Even with Michael's assurances that he could stay hidden in his room forever, it was bleak.

The vague plan he concocted was to graduate next May, somehow avoiding total homelessness, and then enlist in the armed forces. Recruiters constantly prowled the school's corridors offering a life of low-paid adventure to the dregs of the senior class. Right then, it seemed his best bet.

The alternative was to go home, which freaked Jon out. The emotional impact of what he had seen had worn off some, but the unknown—what his parents would do to him—kept him away. His mother's words: *"The way he's been acting is troubling,"* haunted him.

Things were made even clearer when Michael started collecting college brochures and applications. They spent a few hours poring over each one, then filling it out, along with a host of student loan applications, tuition grants, and any scholarship he came across. Jon didn't bother. All the applications had non-refundable fees attached to them. The Ivory Tower demanded a little tribute for the honor of being rejected by them. Jon had more lint than pennies in his pockets. Not that Michael's parents helped their son either. The teen dipped into his own savings account to pay off the college's bribes.

"I think I've got a good chance for Stanford," Michael said, not bragging. "They've got a great department for chemical engineering."

Michael had maintained his grades well enough and had joined the science club like a good nerd. Stanford was not out of the question, except economically. At that point, anything seemed better than Jon's imagined fate. He kept grasping at straws. Only out of desperation did he decide to keep an assigned meeting with the school guidance counselor to discuss college prospects.

All new seniors had to go through the process. An entire week was given over to it. A month earlier, each senior had been given an appointment time. Jon wasn't sure why he bothered. Mr. Demorray, the counselor, a rapidly balding and bitter man, upset that his words had forked no lightning, inevitably told ninety percent of the student body that they weren't college material and wouldn't amount to much in life.

When he opened the door, the world fell into an ice age and he trembled. Not at the broken-down administrator, desperately trying to make a comb over work with significantly less material than required, but at the sleek, perfectly groomed, confident man seated in front of him. Father tilted his head and motioned for Jon to be seated.

"I'm glad you could make it, Mr. St. Fond. So many of the parents don't turn up for these meetings, no matter how often we remind them. It's a sign of the times, I'm afraid."

Sign of a shithole neighborhood more like. The meeting commenced. Both adults talked as if Jon wasn't there. Demorray went on and on about how Jon's somewhat mediocre grades debarred him from the Ivy Leagues. The man was obsessed with those colleges, as if a student he had counseled going to them would somehow justify his own lackluster life.

"We want to keep him close to home in any case," Father said smoothly.

"Well, then I suggest Buffalo State College or SUNY at Buffalo. Either of them is economical and won't mind building up a student with less than stellar grades who would be rejected by Harvard."

They continued. Jon being the subject of much discussion but not a participant of said discussion. Eventually the meeting ended with an exhausted sigh by the counselor and Jon being led out of the office by Father's firm hand. The bell had rung and the halls filled with students.

"Time to come home, boy," Father whispered in Jon's ear. "You've had some fun, but where does it go? Does running away make anything better?"

Jon had to admit defeat. He wasn't prepared to become a bum on the street. A return was in the cards. That didn't mean he would put up with any more nonsense, or stop looking into whatever the hell his parents did to him in the basement, or what they were up to with the bowl. No, they hadn't beaten him. Just the opposite. He felt stronger than he ever had before.

"I borrowed a bike from Michael. I have to see if he'll let me keep on using it."

Father only nodded. Jon was about to add on to that statement, something about needing more respect at home, when his attention was hijacked by the lithe form of Maria Maleventum walking by with a cohort of Italians. They were smacking gum on their lips while discussing which of the absent girls from their clique was the biggest skank.

His pants tightened. Mouth watered. Gabbaducci was with her. He grabbed her ass and sneered when he caught Jon looking, then whispered something to his buddies. Maria giggled under the assault, playfully smacking him. Father leaned behind his son.

"You want that girl?" he asked. "Why don't you have her?"

"She only goes for jerks. You know nice guys finish last."

"Well, you're not that nice. I know what you did to your sister with the hot dog. Don't deny it."

Jon didn't. No point. He knew how Father collected information.

"Her death would've caused quite a few problems."

Jon bit his tongue, the reflexive *I'm sorry* was on the tip of it, but every time it came out in Father's presence things got worse. He choked it back down. Besides, he *wasn't* sorry. His older sister was a disgusting mass of putrefied desires and she made him sick. She was an idol of self-indulgence that his parents enabled for some reason.

He had never considered it before, but maybe there was a sinister reason for their actions. Jon had blamed all of his woes on bad parenting. Could there be a method to the madness? The rituals in the basement. The impossible bowl. How were they connected? His mind reeled. Too much he didn't know. Too many gaps in the narrative that he could fill with fears. That sealed it. He had to go home, if only to discover more about what was happening.

"And it isn't 'nice guys' that finish last," Father continued. "It's weak men who do so. Men who hang in the back and wait for the woman to slink to them. Who are too scared to go for what they want. Who are too lazy to figure out how to get it. You've all been brainwashed to assume that being a submissive to a woman's ever-shifting wants is somehow being a 'good guy.' No, it's being weak."

Jon stared at him. Father had never been so frank and open before, even if it was somewhat sexist. Looking back over the chunks he could remember from his childhood, Jon had almost never gotten any direction from his elder. Mostly it had been one perpetual emasculation by Mother. Otherwise, the young Jon had been left to develop on his own.

"Then," Jon began, bracing for a verbal smack down from Father, "what do you do?"

"If they want something, don't just give it to them. Make them work for it, plead for it. Humans value something that they've sweated for over something just handed to them. If a woman has to struggle for your attention or your favor, they'll automatically put you in a higher bracket than those who run behind trying to sniff her ass."

First bit of fatherly advice, how to pick up chicks. What a life. The late bell rang and the halls quickly became a ghost town. Father lit a cigar, completely indifferent to the school's no-smoking policy.

"Better get to class," he said. "I expect you at dinner tonight."

He walked down the hall, somehow larger than the room. A mousy secretary tried to scold him for smoking, but he ignored her completely and disappeared around a corner. Jon ran to class, puzzled and nervous.

The rest of the school day passed in a blur.

Michael accompanied him home, talking a mile a minute about how Jon could keep the bike, about going to Stanford, about how great the game was going, about a big surprise he had for next week. Jon barely took it in. With each pedal towards home, his anxiety hiked just a bit. He was sure something horrible was waiting for him.

The only thing at home was his younger sister sticking out her tongue, though. Decked out in her frilly ballerina costume, she was a pink snarling nightmare when Jon walked in the door, then went back to stuffing a huge mound of sherbet into her maw off her favorite plate. Mother was talking to someone over the phone, growing increasingly agitated.

"How do you know you're not a homosexual if you don't try it?"

A pause. She rolled her eyes at the excuses. "Well *I* think it's a good idea. There's a guy I want to match you up with."

Another pause. Another excuse. An offended huff from Mother.

"What does it matter what he looks like? We're trying to get past this sexist corporate imagery of beauty and here you are diving right back into it. If you really believe looks don't matter, then you'd go out with whomever I say."

Objection from the phone. A shriek of outrage.

"You're just not gay? It's not you? Well then maybe who *you* are doesn't work for us anymore and *you* can't be part of any of our activist groups!"

She slammed the phone. She glanced at Jon briefly, noting him as one would a stray fly, and rummaged through her purse.

"I've got to take Catherine to dance class," she said without looking up. Keys jingled under her fingers. "Michelle's upstairs with a friend. Don't disturb her. There's some food and stuff in the fridge."

Brushing past Jon, she led the young ballerina out

the door, cooing sweetly about how pretty the little girl was. The door slammed. Silence, except for the faint hum of a bass line from the attic, where his whore sister held court.

The first thing Jon did was check out his room to make sure none of his second-hand stuff was missing. Nothing had been taken, or cleaned, the smell attested to that, but under the portable TV set he found something had been slipped into his journal.

A tarot card. An old one. Incredibly brittle, it felt like it would crumble under his touch. The tarot wasn't printed on card stock and waxed, as modern cards were. It seemed to be a hand painted woodblock imprint. Back when they were twelve, Michael had been briefly fascinated with the tarot and had gone on about it for weeks.

It was the fifteenth trump of the major arcana, The Devil. Though this one was marked as Le Diable. It was a much cruder drawing from ones he had seen before. While still sporting the goatish mane and horns, the devil also had prodigious breasts and a massive phallus. There was a blue face in the devil's midsection sticking its tongue out. Two chained demons, one male, one female, lay at a round pedestal at his feet.

From what he remembered, the image represented mankind seduced by the material world and physical pleasures. A lust for power and money. Its opposition meaning—represented when the card was dealt upside down—meant a person chained in fear. One who lived in bondage to a more powerful image. The card had been slid into the notebook sideways, as if its symbolism was still up in the air. One that Jon was meant to choose.

What was this? A little wave from his parents that they were on to him? Or maybe it was some sort of magic thing, some devil worship. Kathy's mother had mentioned curse cards being used by those weird religions. All of those had used catholic saints, but did it matter? Had his parents cursed him? Mother had certainly cursed *at* him plenty. He slipped the card into his pocket.

The hatch to Michelle's room was open a tad. Oily smoke from the illegal herb she was inhaling billowed out. Its thick fragrance penetrated the entire upper floor. Some ancient The Door's song rumbled out, punctuated by inane giggling.

"This isn't Thai stick. I've had Thai stick and this shit ain't it," Michelle's voice warbled.

"Hey, baby," a deep masculine voice replied. "There's a pot drought on. I take what kind I can get. Should be happy I give you any at all."

"Well, don't call it Thai stick. It's terrible . . . Don't hog it!"

"You want it, huh? You know what that costs."

"Okay," Michelle said. "But you gotta use the back door, the front's all raw and puffy."

Ugh. Jon retreated to the first floor, where the godawful noises they started to make were reduced to low droning. He snagged half a cheese sandwich lying on a plate for him and some red flavored Kool Aid, just to line his gut.

Once again, he squashed down the fears regarding the cellar and forced himself to descend into the musky gray room.

He repeated his protective ritual in his mind. *I'm not scared.* One might expect the terror to dwindle with repeated exposure, but it never did. *I'm not scared.* He took one step, then another. *I'm not . . .*

The stairs extended and dropped a

Long way, then it

       sna

        ked

         sna

          ked

         sna

        ked

       sna

       ked

        sna

         ked

          sna

           ked

          sna

          ked

         sna

       ked

      snake

      snaked

      snake

       sn

        a

        k

         e

      d   d

He made snow angels on the gray slate floor. Burning fumed from his pocket. What was there? Was it the Devil? Yes, it was.

The ancient tarot card was burning a hole in his pants.

His fingers sizzled behind a lavender scent as he yanked it forth.

The Devil roared its rage. The mouth in its stomach vomited up red ink that stained his hands. The floor cracked open and fiery stairs led the way down.

"What is this?" Jon yelled.

"Communion," The Devil answered. "One step beyond."

"Always just one step beyond."

The demons chained at the Devil's feet simpered and cried. From their mouths came a stream of unending babble.

The Male Demon thundered:

The invention of the left-hand-path as the direction where "evil" treads is based purely on the idea that polar opposites in moral deliberations exist as a force outside of the human mind. Whereas in reality, the "good" and the "evil" are cultural constructs designed to corral the local populace into accepted mental boxes, so the ruling elite may then dispose of them as per their fiat. Such ideas exist solely to fellate the individual's ego. When one applies the adjective "good" to oneself, then those who have a viewpoint not in alignment, must out of necessity, be "evil." Yet if each person views themselves as the "good" or the "hero", then what actually constitutes evil? Is then each man a beacon of evil? Or does it mean that evil does not actually exist beyond our own warped vanity? Will you let yourself be defined by others? Or will you . . .

The Female Demon screeched:

Crixen Runeburner held the globe of brilliance in his hand. For hours, he stood there pondering its icy depths. All about him, his comrades in arms, his fellow adventurers, lay crumpled like bits of paper. The rabid orc horde they had cut through was broken, the bleeding survivors running back into the hills. Only their master, the Ogre Mage, with one foul horn between its yellow beady eyes, remained. They clashed. The Ogre's spells and raw strength had battered down the heroes. The fighter, the cleric, the thief. They all fell beneath the monster's might. Crixen channeled power from hidden depths of will and sent a blast of destruction that enveloped the monster's head, leaving only charred bone and melted flesh in its wake. "You can do this too, Jon," the elf whispered into the gem. "All the power of the world lies at your feet. All you must do is . . .

TAKE ONE STEP BEYOND

Jon woke up, dehydrated as before. At least his clothes were still on this time. A post-it note had been slapped on his forehead. "You have to stop sleeping in strange places," it read in Father's handwriting.

Goddamn it. What was happening? He had been drugged, not a doubt about it. But how? The food? The drink? Wonderful, to protect himself it'd have to be nothing but tap water and stolen saltine packets from now on.

The bathroom mirror revealed a wretch of a face.

Despite being unconscious for however long he had been, he was exhausted. The sallow pull of his flesh, combined with the black rings around his eyes, attested to that. He peeled a milky scum off his tongue that had congealed there.

He consulted the note again. Its tone was almost playful. Not a threat, more a smirk. Father knew Jon knew something, but how much? And how much did Father care? Not much, judging by their lack of reaction. That just might be their downfall, the underestimating of their son.

After slapping himself awake, Jon plunged back into the hidden room behind his parents' closet. The bottle of whiskey was still in the hiding place. He helped himself to a slug while he pulled up the chair. Jon snapped off the VCRs and rewound the basement feed as far back as it could go. There he was on the basement floor. A robed figure descends, glances at him, then plugs something into the wall. He paused the image and leaned in, squinting to get as much detail as he could squeeze from the small sight. It looked like a crockpot with some kind of white liquid—very white, like alfredo sauce—cooking away in it.

Others in robes came down, five of them. They carried the semi-conscious, naked, carcass of his sister, Michelle. She kept rolling around the floor and they had to re-flip her onto her back. Two of them grabbed Jon's body—his eyes were wide open, barely blinking—and stuffed him into a corner. One of them put a boot into Jon's stomach to make sure he was as out of the way as possible. Each drank a tablespoon of the white liquid.

The five stood equidistant from each other, with his sister in the middle. They linked hands and began to chant in an unknown tongue. Obscene intonations swirled around his ears. The language had twisting syllables and an odd high-pitched lilt, sometimes it seemed to disappear out of human range altogether.

Then a flash, or the lens flared up, or something. Something extraordinary had occurred. He rewound and inspected it closer. Yes. There it was, for a brief few seconds before the flash on the floor, a blue outline of a pentagram had appeared, and each of the robed ones stood at its cardinal points. After the flash, they were all on different points. He could tell due to their height. Plus, his sister was now lying on her front instead of her back. All of them dropped to the floor, exhausted. One vomited up green slime.

After several minutes of rest, they rose and took away his sister as well as the crockpot. Then one came back for Jon and dragged him away as well. That called for another shot of whiskey. A victory one. There really *was* something off about his basement. It wasn't just some weird childhood phobia. But what caused it? A communion spot the Devil had said in his hallucination. A place to meet with the realm infernal. That scared him enough to take another drink.

That scene filled in a puzzle piece that had been nagging at him. He couldn't see his parents wasting their time in some pathetic little cult. Wearing silly robes, cutting animal throats, and drinking blood or whatever, that wasn't his parents. Especially if it was all just dress up. But if there was some real power behind it, some truth in the myths, *that* was a different matter. He could easily see his amoral parents clutching at poky old superstitions to attain it. Whatever *it* was.

And now what? The questions floated from the cloudy depths of his subconscious. Jon was flummoxed. It would have to be . . . Well, no police. It might not be illegal. Freedom of religion meant just that. Legally, nothing he could prove at that moment meant anything. Maybe the tape? Oh, yes! If you couldn't go for a legal cure, then social ostracism would be just as effective. Worse really. The family might take a major financial hit and lose everything. That three minutes of tape and an explanatory note could easily be passed along to the local news. All three of the networks were so desperate to upstage the others that there was no doubt one of them would play it.

He grabbed a blank video tape from a high shelf, then connected two VCRs together. It was a trick Michael had taught him. If you connected the output wire from the first VCR and plugged it into the input jack of a second, then you could play the tape on one, while making a copy of it on the other. The two of them used to have their parents rent videos, then they would make illegal copies for later viewing. He copied the three minutes onto a blank tape and was just about to stash it away in his room when he caught himself.

That was no good. How did he know his parents didn't rummage through his room on a regular basis? Someone had slipped that tarot card into his notebook. He needed a place beyond his family residence. There was only one person he trusted enough to hold onto the tape. Michael.

The phone rang and he snatched it up, only now realizing that it was dark outside. Why was the house empty?

"Hello?"

"Hey," It was Michael. "You missed the game."

"Oh, sorry. I got sick. Been asleep all day."

"I understand, I was almost late filling out all these scholarships, then I had to run around and get stamps. My parents wouldn't give me any of theirs. Then I had to go to the bank to have money orders taken out of my account to send in for the college application fees. All of them have nearly wiped me out."

"Yeah." Normal world problems just couldn't make an impact today.

"You missed my announcement for the next game."

"Which is?"

"It's Halloween on Friday, so we're gonna have it in a cemetery."

"I don't know. Isn't that illegal?"

"This is a decommissioned cemetery. No one goes there anymore. We're gonna bring sleeping bags, pick up some snacks, game all night, then come back in the morning. It'll be so rad."

"How's a cemetery get decommissioned?"

"It's full. Been that way for a hundred years or so. They don't even have a caretaker. Everyone else is going."

"Everyone?"

"Louis said he'd tell his parents that he was camping with us, which is kind of true. His parents would freak out if they knew the truth. And Kathy's parents are out of town. They went on some dig to Mexico and won't be back for a couple of months."

"What? They just left her alone?"

"Yeah. She said it was your fault."

"Me?"

"Said it had something to do with stuff you showed her parents. Something similar had been dug up in Mexico and they ran down there to look at it and maybe find where it came from. Kathy told me she had never seen her parents so excited. She claimed it might be a breakthrough discovery that would cement their careers."

"What did they find?"

"I dunno. You'll have to ask her, since you two have been spending so much time together."

"All right. Knock it off."

"Kathy and Jon were ugly dumb lovers.
Especially in their hand-me-down covers
When he pulled out his trigger
She said, 'Not much of a frigger
Can't find the right hole to make me a mother.'"

"You are hi-fucking-larious."

"Are you in?"

"Okay, I'm in. Gotta go."

An odd thought just occurred to him. Was the find in Mexico the same bowl his parents had locked up? He flipped the painting and plugged the code into the hidden safe. The bowl was still there. The money, the guns, the genealogy also. He opened it up and took another look. Once again, the size of his family surprised him. But this time he focused on the top of the chart. Most the family seemed to emerge from 13th Century family with Jerome St. Fond as its patriarch. A man who sired thirteen children. Apparently, the name had originally been *de St. Fond* and changed sometime in the 17th Century.

Penciled in just above that, with a connecting line, was the name St. Fond and a small note in tight script stating, "See Roman and Gaulish records for more detail."

He folded the chart up and was about to put it back, when he spotted a small book in the back that had been previously hidden by a pile of money. He snagged it out. It was ancient, hand bound by a long dead craftsman. The pages were not paper, but vellum—the membrane of skin from a calf, soaked in lime and stretched to make it useful to write on. A process not used beyond the Middle Ages. There was no title, just a series of chapters written with a calligraphic hand. A leather bookmark, attached to the cover by a thin thread, was set to a chapter named Vita Beato Fond and a hand drawn picture of a saint, which looked remarkably like Mother. The actual text was written in Latin.

The lock on the front door clicked. Cold fear ran down Jon's spine. The panel to the secret room was open and all the machines were turned off. Shit, shit, shit. He threw all the stuff back into the safe and raced across the room as if the hounds of hell were nipping at his heels. Below, people were coming in talking, laughing, and being a loving family. No time to set the machines, he popped the panel back in and snuck over to his room, peering at those below between the bars of the upstairs railing as he did so. Mother, Father, and Catherine were all in the living room, licking frosty goodness from a waffle cone. Nonchalantly he walked down the stairs.

"We've got ice cream," Catherine yelled at him, thrusting her pink cone forward in a challenge. What she meant was *we did, but you get nothing.*

"Good to see you up and about," Father said.

Mother muttered something about Jon's laziness, but stopped to look from Father. "We had to take Michelle in. Turns out she's pregnant again."

"She gonna have another 'bortion," Catherine blurted between slurps of cream.

The parents laughed pleasantly. Mother dropped to her knees and hugged the little girl tightly. She was offered a bite of the little girl's cone in return, the ultimate act of giving for a young child. Father stepped up to Jon.

"Didn't get you any ice cream," he said. "Anything you want to say about that?"

"No," Jon replied.

Truth is, he barely noticed the injustice. He was too worried about the switched off VCRs. Father's yellow eyes burrowed into him. With a struggle he met Father's gaze, hoping like hell that his face was a blank. They locked eyes for a brief eternal moment, then the elder pulled away and went up to his room without comment.

Later that night, after it seemed the entire world had fallen asleep, Jon crept back into his parents' room. They had made a ruckus earlier, a lot of playful screams, but it all died down around two and he waited another hour just to be sure.

Over time, he had learned which of the floorboards in the old house would creak, so he took a weird route across the hall, stepping here and there, mostly sticking to the sides where the boards were thoroughly nailed in. Their door was slightly ajar, Mother's wheezing snore filtered through the air. Inside, their TV kept displaying some rather violent pornography on a tape loop.

Carefully, inch by inch, he stuck his head through the door. The stench of recently expelled sex mixed with some type of lubricant assaulted his nostrils. Mother and Father were passed out. The blanket only barely covered those anatomical pieces of his parents Jon hoped to never see again. Empty bottles of top shelf liquor lay scattered about the floor.

One step, two steps, three steps across the carpet. Someone waking? Stop. Pause. The telltale heart thumped hard. Sleep babble. Father turned over. Five more steps and he was in the closet.

He pushed the button and the wall clicked open. He twirled around, looking at the two bodies, waiting for some sign that he was busted. But no. The snoring continued, the porn played on, and Jon slipped into the secret room.

The machines were still turned off. He quickly flipped them back on, rewound the tapes, and started to record again. That meant his exit from the closet and his parents' room would be recorded as well, but it couldn't be helped. He looked around. Was everything in the right place? Had the chair been there? Or was it further back? He moved it. It didn't look right, so he moved it back.

Slipping out was easy and he crept down to the kitchen. The tape was good, but he wanted more. Perhaps a sampling of what was the milky stuff cooking away in the crockpot. Leaving all of the disgusting possibilities aside, it must be some concoction to help them with their rite. He rummaged through the kitchen. Looking in all cabinets for the crockpot, searching inside every nook for a hidden space, but it all came up empty. He searched the rest of the closets on the first floor, groping away for hidden rooms, but again came up empty. The item wasn't there.

He poured some tap water into a glass and sat down in the dim kitchen. The light from a full moon was his only guide. What was there left to do? Watch and wait. Keep an eye on what shuffled in and out of the safe. That seemed to be the best source of information beyond the video tapes. Tomorrow he would have to give the tape to Michael to hide for him. Jon decided that he would only use it as a last defensive measure. If his family was destroyed, then that meant he'd be out on the sidewalk too or stuck in some godforsaken foster home until he hit eighteen, then tossed out onto the cold streets. Even if he emptied the safe, it wouldn't last him that long. No, he had to wait and find a better way.

What the tapes had revealed was that his older sister was also a victim of these strange rites. Was there an ally there? Could she help in some way? Possibly. If he could ever catch her at a sober moment. Their relationship was practically non-existent. She was so addled with drugs, it was nearly impossible to have any kind of conversation with her. But he had to try.

He pulled down the drawstring for the ladder to Michelle's attic apartment and crept on up. It was cramped and smelled bad. He had to stoop slightly under the low ceiling. Most of the room was taken up by a large TV and stereo on one end and a bed jammed into the other, in-between lay a carpet of garbage.

Drug residue, clothes, beer bottles filled with cigarette butts, expended lighters, and various incidentals crunched under his feet.

There she was, similar to the other night with the hot dog, unconscious, naked except for a rubber tube around her left arm and a needle dangling next to it. He threw a ratty blanket over his sister and tried to snap her out of her stupor.

"Michelle. Michelle."

Her eyes half drooped open. A bubble blossomed between her lips. It grew to extraordinary size then popped.

"More?" she said.

"Michelle, do you know what they're doing to you in the basement?"

Her eyes held no recognition for her brother, but the words snapped some trigger in her memory. An idiot smile lolled cow-like on her face as she said,

"The basement is great. It's where they make me immortal. It's why I get more."

The heroin high claimed her and she nodded off to chase the dragon. Jon slipped down to his room, letting the ladder snap up. She was in on it. As much as her addled brain could take in, she agreed with whatever her parents' plans were.

CHAPTER 6

Blessed are the Bold

"**THE NAME MEANS** Hill of the Ghouls. Isn't that messed up?"

The black van clunked on through the fading light of day. It was All Hallow's Eve and rather than get drunk and steal candy from children like their peers, Jon and friends were bundled away in warm winter gear and passing around a bottle of scotch Kathy had stolen from her parents' liquor stock.

"How much longer, you reckon?" Louis asked.

"Soon. Maybe twenty more minutes," Michael answered from the driver's seat.

"You actually been there?"

"Uh . . ."

"That's what I done figured."

"Hey, I got a road atlas." He hefted up a massive spiral notebook filled with the finest AAA maps. "It's current. Came out last year. I know where I'm going."

Michael lapsed back into discussing the fanciful and grotesque history of Goodleburg Cemetery, their ultimate destination. Jon only tuned in with half an ear, since he knew the first thing Michael said was untrue. The place was named after one of the families who had settled the area and donated the land for the religious to plant their carcasses. Their name might actually translate to "Hill of the Ghouls", but that wasn't the intent of those who Christianized the place Goodleburg.

Michael went on about ghosts, fatal car accidents, suspicious deaths, satanic cults, desecrated graves, and mutilated children. All of these apparently were connected to the graveyard. Each account had been published in various ghost hunting guides available in local bookstores.

"You really believe all that?" Louis asked.

"I look at it this way. A few things you might be able to write off as coincidence, bad luck, or someone making up a tale. But there are just so many stories collected in this one place that you have to pay attention. I mean, it seems like *something's* going on."

Jon kept his mouth shut. His recent brush with the bizarre had tossed all his old objections out the window. *But*—he couldn't help yanking out that but— one of the reasons there were so many stories was that it was one of the first areas inhabited by colonists. The cemetery had some of the oldest graves in New York State. Thus it had more time to collect weird stories than in other places.

As for the larger number of car fatalities, the roads were barely one step above dirt paths. Add the icy winter weather and a Depression-Era alcoholism rate and you have a perfect recipe for large helpings of road pizza.

Jon moved to the back of the van and sat down next to Kathy. She had been keeping her distance on the trip.

"So, how is it my fault your parents abandoned you?" he began.

"Those damn pictures you showed them. It's all my mom could talk about for days. They called up everyone they could about it, all over the world, and no one knew anything. Dad said it was probably a hoax, but when my mother gets on a new idea . . . Where did you get them anyway?"

"It's not important."

"Well, she got some anonymous package in the mail with a broken bowl and a letter in Latin."

"Latin?"

"Weird, huh? That got them all excited and she got my dad to make a few phone calls down to some colleagues at the state university in Mexico City. Three days later, they had permits to do an excavation at an old site and they ran off."

"That was fast, wasn't it?"

"Yeah. That process is supposed to take months and the financing even longer. I guess some strings were pulled or whatever. My dad has a lot of connections down there."

"So they just left you alone? "

"They gave me money for food and other stuff. It's not the first time they've done this. 'You have to make work your greatest joy in life,' my father always says, 'otherwise you're just wasting time.' And they do."

"Sorry if it was my fault."

She touched his hand lightly. "That's okay. I'll be home alone a lot."

He stiffened up, in both senses. Damn it, why did his hormones have to constantly run wild? The invitation was open, right there for him to grab. Again he had an idea in his head of the movie-star hot woman he really wanted, and Kathy just didn't fit the bill. He'd heard plenty of his mother's feminist minions whining about men thinking with their cocks. He decided to take the opposite route for once and show them all. He pulled back. Kathy withdrew her hand and stared at the floor, saying nothing, cheeks a little red.

Michael's voice filled the interior. More ghost sightings. More creepy happenings. On and on and on. It seemed like he'd memorized the book. Louis turned to Jon.

"Is he fulla bullshit or what?"

"Sort of."

"No, I'm not," Michael protested.

"I've looked into it."

"'Course you did," Louis sneered. "You're a big nerd. Always lookin' shit up."

"And the only real thing corroborating these stories outside of the spook books," Jon said, ignoring Louis's barbs, "is that abortion doctor in the 1940s. Pregnant women would slip into town at night for the operation and he would bury the unborn remains in the graveyard. It was hinted that he paid off the local cops, because he was only stopped when the FBI stepped in."

"Shows what you know," Michael yelled, gleeful. "They don't have any cops. Place's too small for a department. It's patrolled by the county."

"Touché."

They hit the border limits for South Wales, a hamlet clustered in the poverty ridden towns south of Buffalo. It was an unincorporated township, hanging onto the ass end of the larger Wales. South Wales had been grandfathered in to modern New York because it originated from a time before local governments bothered to write stuff down. Pioneers went out, chopped down some trees, slapped up a mill near a creek and, voila, a new pocket of civilization blossomed.

The only thing in the colonial records about the place was its physical location. Rumors suggested that the place had been the scene of at least one unrecorded massacre. The area had originally been conquered by one of the Iroquois tribes and was then taken over by the unfriendly emissaries of the Holland Land Company. Later on, the company was ousted by English land grabbers.

It took them roughly five minutes to drive through the entire hamlet and another ten to locate the graveyard. Jon imagined it would be an image from an old horror flick. Iron railings surrounding the perimeter and a perpetually squeaking gate. Maybe a deranged groundskeeper with a lantern and rusty shovel prowled about the grounds. The ancient stones of the dead listing this way and that, and moss growing over everything. It was nothing like that. There was no gate or barrier, just some slate steps leading up to a raised area covered in graves that stretched out over an acre and a half.

They pulled their gear from the van and Michael led the way, waving about a flickering flashlight. It was a cold and biting night with a hint of icy rain on the wind. Typical late autumn in New York. The graves were old, low, and faded. Most were so weather beaten that their epitaphs had nearly eroded away. Many had been knocked over and broken in several pieces. Anarchy signs and swastikas were liberally spray painted about. A few beer cans and plastic six-pack rings spouted up here and there. Several graves looked like they'd been dug up as well, or at least recently disturbed in some way.

Suddenly Michael began running back towards the van.

"Where the hell you goin'?" Louis yelled after him.

"Forgot to lock the van door."

"Gawd damnit." Louis kicked a chunk of rock that used to be part of someone's headstone. A dearly beloved sister. "I ain't never gonna get used to this cold. That wind zips up and cuts you right to the bone."

The ones born in the area almost instinctively pulled their jackets tighter and stomped their feet to generate warmth. Louis looked at them as if they were crazy, then joined in after a minute.

"Where'd he get that van anyhow?" Louis asked.

"He said his uncle let him borrow it."

"Didn't know he had an uncle," Louis mused.

Neither did Jon. He'd known his friend since the fourth grade and the only uncle ever mentioned was one who burned up in a house fire in the early 1970s. Assuming the man hadn't come back from the dead and bought a van, Michael was lying. Maybe he stole it?

The little light of their driver's flashlight stopped, then became bigger as he returned. "All right," Michael said. "Let's get going. It's over this way, I think."

"You been here before?" Jon asked.

"Ah, no."

"Then how do you know where we're going?"

"Uh, well, I read about it, okay. It's the only mausoleum here."

"Where did you read about that? I didn't see anything on it."

"Guess you didn't read those books as thoroughly as you thought."

It took them a few more minutes of stumbling around to find the entrance. The door was obscured by a semi-circle of trees. It was a rectangular building with a locked gate in front of stone stairs that echoed down into the dead earth. The name above the entrance was nearly gone. Jon rubbed his hands across it and could barely make out the surname "Goodleburg", the family who had donated the land. An old lock had been smashed off long ago and replaced by a modern one wrapped around a thick chain. Louis jerked it.

"We ain't gettin' in there."

"Sure we are." Michael pronounced and fished out some lock picks. "My brother showed me how to do this. Only thing he ever showed me." He pushed forward and set to work on the lock.

"I don't like it," Kathy said. "We're literally walking on someone's grave here."

"Ah, it's not like we're going to dig them up or anything," Jon chided.

"Besides," Michael triumphed, holding up the jangling lock, "we're in."

Total darkness dwelled below. The kind that only the bowels of the earth can produce. Four flashlights illuminated the room, but still could not drive it away. Musty smells, rotting leaves, dust, dirt, maybe some old rat feces. A wide room opened up from the stairs.

Three stone caskets sat in the middle. The walls were lined with plaques where lesser members of the family had been interred. Michael was beside himself.

"Nice. Very nice."

"Creepy as hell. Perfect for Halloween. You can almost feel the weirdness."

And Jon could. Little by little, as he walked across the granite floor, the feeling crept up on him. The dread. The clench in his bowels. Just like in his basement. He stopped. What did it mean? *Did* it mean anything? Perhaps his mind was just playing tricks on him.

"What's the matter with you," Louis laughed at him. "You 'bout shit your britches."

"It's just dank down here."

Michael and Louis laughed harder. It meant being cast down to a lower spot on the totem pole. However, he'd been insulted enough by his parents to know how to handle it. First point, don't show any reaction. Second, hit back.

"Almost as dank as your mom's vagina."

The laughter turned. Even Kathy, who normally shunned the boys verbal roughhousing, joined in. Her eyes shined brightly at Jon, but that look went as quick as it came. They reached the far end of the tomb and laid out their sleeping bags. Little votive candles, dozens of them, swiped from Louis's survivalist uncle, were laid out over the floor and lit with a barbeque lighter. Their low flickering added to the mausoleum's sinister aura.

Jon suppressed the panic as best he could, but by God, that feeling would not evaporate. Doritos and Mountain Dew and little disks of sugar and chocolate called Fudge Rounds, were passed about. The game was unpacked.

Jon placed the image of Crixen Runeburner in its appropriate place, his stats laid out on loose leaf, and picked up the cards. He had honed his skills at the game down to an instinctual rhythm. He could almost anticipate each of the Game Master's actions and block with a corresponding throw and chant. It was a pattern, a mental dance, where the world described became a vivid gossamer waking dream.

Once the atmosphere tape was droning on a portable tape player, the game began. Jon, Louis, and Kathy dove into their characters, becoming Crixen Runeburner, Big Jim Umbrage, and Black Leaf. The scenario was spun out before them. To the east of the New Lands, where they had been adventuring for some time, on a ramshackle road in a derelict country, the heroes found a toothless beggar, dressed in black rags and waving a sack of coins at a crossroads.

"Steal," yelled Louis.

"Deflect," countered Kathy.

"Ask," demanded Jon.

Between bursts of bloody phlegm, the ancient beggar described a world of green and plenty that no longer existed. Because the world was so easy, a man, this man, pushed things too far. He poked into the membrane of the forbidden and released the beast. His fat, sheltered life, which he oh-so smugly thought inviolate, was cast to arcane winds. A ravaging beast, which sucked the land's life, was nearby in a dilapidated cemetery. The old man was too weak to travel.

"Go," they recited together and threw their cards.

When the heroes looked back, the beggar had melted into the earth. Iron railings, rusted and twisted from time's decay, surrounded the graveyard. A perpetually squeaking fence greeted them with ear piercing shrieks. The old tombs were crumbling and decayed, becoming little more than havens for giant spiders and other violent aberrations of nature.

"Kill."

"Kill."

"Kill," was repeated over and over.

Finally the erstwhile heroes found the grand tomb, whose bronze doors they hammered open. The three mighty heroes descended into an octagonal room. Shimmering before them was a lady silhouetted in white, cold as the winter's morn. Her black eyes absorbed them. Her idol was placed on the board.

"Attack," roared Louis.

"Repelled," replied the Game Master.

"Dispel," spoke Kathy.

"Absorbed," replied the Game Master.

Crixen Runeburner racked his brains. Which wizard trick would destroy the evil? Every attack was harmlessly passing through the enemy and she did not retaliate. Was this not the beast they sought? No? No!

"Speak," yelled Jon. "Speak with dead."

The card was thrown.

A flare. A flush. An explosion of cold.

The woman was there. An exact duplicate of the miniature, only seven feet tall and screaming. The party jumped back. How could they not? Kathy rolled over some candles and accidently set her jacket on fire. Louis smacked his head clean into a stone wall. A small trail of blood followed him down to the floor.

Her outline was pure platinum white, yet nothing filled in the borders of its form. Her black orbs grew into terrifying dimensions. They tore into Jon's soul, claiming portions of it for her own. An insect pinned to a card, he sprawled on the floor, limbs jerking about in rhythmic terror. An invisible foot crushed the air from his lungs.

And her shriek! Like razor blades across chalkboards. It cut deep. Into the soul. Into the psyche. Into the ear drums. Blood drops circled around the basin of his ear.

She ran forward on thin air. The tassels of her intangible shawl draped over him. Like a naked shower in the North Pole, the heat ran out of him. Then she was gone, up and out of the tomb. Jon sat up. After she passed, the cold air warmed ever so slightly. He rushed over to Kathy and helped her get the coat off, throwing the thing away to smolder in a corner.

"Come on," Kathy yelled and dragged Jon towards the tomb entrance.

Their voices echoed strangely in the hall, as if a new room had opened up in it. Footfalls followed them out into the star bright night. The Cold Woman was in the center of the cemetery, dancing on the tip of a pointed gravestone. Kathy clutched Jon close, and he held her back with equal intensity.

"Ah seen some messed up stuff," Louis's voice drifted in from behind them. "Once saw a kid get a pencil shoved right into his eye, but this beats all."

Her wails began again, dragging over them. The sounds had a tang, a flavor like old sins dredging up putrid blood. The world wavered. Shadows grew teeth. Monstrous feet shambled about them, unseen yet there. Hot breath with evil intent snorted, its origin a single microbe apart from the world. So close it could taste their flesh.

Louis broke. All that football practice aided him well in running from danger. Head still bloody, he dodged and weaved away from the unseen perils. His screams merged with the Cold Woman's, then disappeared among the grave markers. Jon only wished he could follow, but he was rooted to the spot. He pulled Kathy's head into his chest and held it. Eyes squeezed shut, tears dripped all over his shirt.

"It's coming. It's coming," she cried.

He felt it too. Though the true nature of "it" was an unknown. Just a supreme sensation of impending evil, of a calamity yet to happen. A nuclear winter where Jon and Kathy were squashed bugs, trampled and forgotten.

All he could do was stare at the Cold Woman without blinking. The world became worse if he shut his eyes. That's when things became real. All the evil in existence played out for him.

This site had always been a point of evil. Here, monsters were born and innocents died. It had always been so. They all danced through Jon's mind. Weird, blood soaked rituals, enacted by tribes whose existence had long been wiped away by the sands of time, created totem beasts of ferocious power and bottomless appetites. Bad magic had created a leak, allowing things from beyond the universe to sneak in. Over the ages, hordes of demons manifested from this cemetery had caused untold misery throughout the world. Witch doctors, shamans, old world sorcerers, even a few New Age gurus had exploited the weakness here to ferment evil.

Reflections of the magician's spirits increased, each presenting a foul offering to things beyond. While their garb changed significantly—feathered headdresses, shirts made of human skin, bloody lab coats—their intentions never did. Even a few kids, no older than ten, were part of the increasing horde. They ran about in knee pants, holding up a mason jar filled with something inky black and putrid.

Jon couldn't stand anymore. For the worst was to come, he knew. A primeval warning, dredged up from a thousand fear-filled past lives, told him not to look. To hold on. To do whatever it took to keep those lids open. Terror lurked about, absolute alien malevolence, that meant to steal his soul, absorb his being, feast on his karmic effluence. Formless, caught on the eddies of time, inscribed in antediluvian rock, the evil was there. And it could not be bested.

The Cold Woman turned and ran at him, shrill and covered in all the pain of the world. He screamed, but no sound emitted. Knees buckled, the frigid earth received his body. Kathy stood still, her own high-pitched wailing lost in the Cold Woman's cacophony. Her transparent face loomed over him, distorted in anger. The black eyes rolled about abnormally in her skull. Her shivering fingers reached for his throat.

Jon's willpower abandoned him. An instinct to close his eyes, to not see his own death coming, took control and he squeezed them shut. All he remembered was a pale glow. Sickly yellow with black splotches, fading in and out like a dying sun. His heart was grabbed and squeezed. Life in all forms sucked away to feed this beast. Then—

It was gone.

Jon opened his eyes. There was nothing there. He was still cold, but the woman had disappeared, evaporated into the ether. Kathy was stark still, whimpering. He took her hand and led her quietly across the graveyard, towards the van. Submissively, she followed, face half-buried in her shirt.

"Are you all right?" he asked.

"I . . . I don't know."

"What happened to that thing?"

"I don't know," she repeated. "My eyes were closed."

"Yeah."

"So what was that? What happened?"

"I don't know any more than you do."

"It looked just like that miniature."

"I know. Let's get a safe distance and—"

They had reached the stone steps near where the van was parked. Headlights flared up. Jon leapt down the stairs, leaving Kathy behind. For a moment, he thought someone had jacked the van, but it was still there. Its chrome reflected the moonlight. Twin brake lights trailed off down the road. Who the hell was that? Another goddamn mystery.

"Let's just go," Kathy whined.

He took two steps forward, realized his error, and ran back up.

"What?" Kathy whined.

"Michael's got the fucking keys," he yelled.

Their driver was still deep in the mausoleum, sitting among the empty soda bottles and sleeping bags. He was hunched over, rocking back and forth, game miniatures scattered about him.

"Yes, yes," he said to the air. "I understand. I agree."

CHAPTER 7

HAMMER OR ANVIL?

"THEY DO NOT listen, but they hear
Cowards who strut like a buccaneer
They're committed to evil,
Their soul's past retrieval; You're the devil's puppet, I fear."

That was Michael's opening line as they drank coffee and ate scumdogs at one of the innumerable all-night Greek diners riddling the area. After the coffee was dropped off, he had dumped twelve creamers into it and churned the mixture slowly with a spoon, turning the black liquid light tan. He refused to tear his eyes away from the vortex being created in the middle of the cup.

Jon bit into the scumdog. The specialty of the house. Onions, eye-watering mustard, hot sauce, and some kind of Greek glop were ground together into a lumpy greyish-brown paste and dumped over a lonely hot dog. It needed to be eaten fast as the concoction had a tendency to dissolve the bun into a sticky blob. The mixture sounded disgusting, but damn it tasted good. Hurt going out the end, though, especially after about five or six of them.

"So, are you—?"

"Shush."

After he had dragged Michael back to the van, they had taken off at a manic pace. Despite the cold, Michael had sweated through his clothes. The teen dampness turned into an uncomfortable funk in the van. He was nearly mute. An insane gleam had lodged in his eye, along with a bit of joy, some mischief.

Kathy was in tears. Jon had put her in the backseat, tried comforting her with sips of Mountain Dew, but it was all in vain. She would not calm down. Jon couldn't really blame her, but it still grated his nerves. They were all right, yet her whimpering increased.

They drove around the backroads of the hamlet, looking for Louis, but he was nowhere to be found. There was a lot of woods out there. Maybe he had tripped and was lying bleeding in the woods. Maybe he was hiding in a tree waiting for the safety of daylight to walk back to town. Any of that could be true.

They had no choice but to abandon him and head for home. A pang of guilt hit Jon over this, but what were they gonna do? Hang around all night? Besides, Louis had cut and run, left them to die. What kind of friend does that? Had he kept his nerve, he would've been all right.

They had dropped Kathy off at home. After an awkward hug with Jon, she left, disappearing into her prestigious home.

And now here they were.

"Why don't you tell me what happened?" Jon said.

"Hmmm?"

He kept stirring the coffee.

Jon grabbed his arm. "That was no coincidence,

our being there. You set that up, knowing it would happen."

"Hoping."

"Hoping it would happen. That the Cold Woman would—?"

"Appear? I didn't expect that."

"You've done the research like me. There have been reports of a ghostly woman haunting that cemetery for decades. It's the most common story. You must have set it up, since she looked a lot like the miniature."

"Not 'a lot.' Exactly." Michael thumped the table, eyes sparkling. "Her essence, spirit, however you describe the phenomenon, it was funneled into this world via our belief, our mantric actions, and adopted the miniature as its base representation."

"So, we created her."

"No. We influenced the spirit's form."

"And you knew this was going to happen? You used us as guinea pigs."

"There's been some speculation as to the nature of paranormal manifestations. Some say it's all ghosts. Others write about beings of pure spirit that never had a physical form. Angels. Demons. Valkyries. Mara. Aliens. What if it's none and all? What if the manner of this manifestation is based upon what we expect to see, and the creature latches on?"

"Uh?"

"Our mindset, our mood defines this thing," Michael said. "There has been so much talk about ghosts in that cemetery that I guessed it was our best chance to make an apparition happen. There's something about that place which allows such manifestations to occur with greater ease. Our game created the right atmosphere to cause its occurrence. The time, the mood, the chill. I just thought the whole thing would be less dramatic."

"Oh, it was fucking dramatic all right."

"What are you talking about?"

"The visions. The monsters and magicians. Didn't you see them?

"No," Michael's voice trailed off. Jon could see him bouncing around in his own head, trying to assemble the missing jigsaw pieces. "But then I was inside."

"How did you stumble onto this? I've never heard of anything like it."

"There's all sorts of stories of magicians in the stupid ages conjuring up the devil. Some of the old Kabbalistic and Cathar traditions even have rituals for commanding angels. There are many, many legends of such conjurations and just as many different 'spells' or rituals for it." Michael snorted in distaste. "If you strip away the superstition, it boils down to having the right people, the right emotional atmosphere, and the right place."

"The place means something?"

"You can't just do it anywhere. Certain areas, I don't know why, are more pliable, are softer around the edges for contact with—"

"What? What are they?"

"I don't know that either. The Beyond. There are plenty of labels, but we might not have a concept for what they actually are."

"How did you get started on this?"

"I've been researching for a while. Just digging through old books and the like. Looking for this Beyond and I came across a lot of ideas. A lot of local stuff. I didn't mean to use you guys, but I *had* to know if it was all lies."

"If what was lies? You're not being straight with me."

Michael downed the coffee in a single gulp like a shot of booze, then waved the half-asleep waitress over for more. He repeated the creamer ritual and shook the story loose from his past.

"When I was eleven, I had an experience. It was during the summer. Remember back then, we used to play outside all day and the only thing our parents would say to us was 'Come home when the streetlights turned on.' My parents usually didn't bother, so I just went home when everyone else did. Then one day I decided to stay out. It was my birthday and my parents had forgotten. They never really did much for it in any case. I think I got a couple of hostess cupcakes once, but nothing beyond that. I can't complain, they never remembered my brother's either."

Jon suddenly realized that it was true about Michael's birthday. He had never been to one celebration of the event. The date had never come up. Even Jon's own parents would spring for a crappy gift and cheap cake.

"I was just walking around, throwing pebbles at streetlights, when I wandered down to the old grain elevators. Before you ask, yes, it's same one we go to. I was used to old drunks and homeless prowling the area, but this time it was different. The area was filled with cars. Expensive, new ones. There was a smell of rotten eggs and burning rosemary coming from the building. A glow emanated from the ground floor, and I went to investigate.

"Inside, a low fire burned. Around it was a group of people, men and women, in red robes, holding hands, and chanting in a low murmur. Another one in black would occasionally toss something into the fire, then scuttle back watching them. It all came to some kind of climax, when they raised their hands together and began to shout. That's when I saw it.

"It was by the corner of the building. A shape, encased in white, like a reverse shadow. It was dressed in old school buckskins and carried a flintlock rifle, reminded me of those old movies about Davy Crockett. It looked around, pointed, raised its gun and vanished. After that the people stopped. They threw a bucket of water and a few bottles of bleach over the fire.

"Bleach?"

"It was something white from bleach bottles, so I assumed it was. But that isn't the point. I went back there several times at night and I never saw them again. They might've missed the 'ghost', we'll call it that for lack of a better word, but I've never forgotten. That's why I picked the place as our gaming spot. Hoping to see it again."

"And did you?" Jon asked.

"Yes. Three weeks ago. When everyone had left, I saw the buckskin ghost again. It was in the same place, going through the same movements. I tried to communicate, but it was unable to. It was just a thing, a spiritual animal, given brief form."

Three weeks ago, Jon mused. *After we started the new game.* Out loud he said, "What do you mean, animal?"

"If the forms they appear in are influenced by us, by our expectations, then what it actually might be is a fleeting wisp from a realm where life has no physical form. So trying to talk to it would be like attempting a dialogue with a mosquito or an eel. It just can't be done."

"It sounds like the ghost of an old frontiersman, not some wisp."

"Not necessarily. Perhaps the robed people influenced its form, and my expectations of what it looked like caused it to manifest in the same manner."

"A lot of perhaps." *And a lot still not said*, Jon thought.

"I didn't have much until today."

"You, or *we* really, influenced the form of the Cold Woman."

"Yes, but that was incidental. I made further contact beyond."

"With?"

"With an intelligence."

The next day was a Saturday. Normally a day of frolic and rest for the high schooler, but Jon found himself haunting the back of a rat's nest that posed as an occult bookstore called The Wizard's Zap. The married proprietors were a pair of leftover hippies who never bothered to mature out of their mid-twenties. Frequently, they'd pigeonhole a customer, boxing him in with banter and their foul body odor, and lament how so many of their generation had "sold out" by getting real jobs, having children, and taking responsibility for their lives. Often the entire store would empty when one of them uttered the preamble, "Back in the sixties."

The place was a disaster. Scores of books were piled up every which way. The building had been a cheap knock-up, slapped together in the 1940s and it looked as if the shelves had been hammered in shortly thereafter. Most of them had rotted through, meaning tons of paperbacks were plopped on top of each other in a series of wobbly stacks. The stacks were so close together that removing any individual book placed several of them in peril of falling over and burying a customer in an avalanche of cheap pulp paper.

Jon had begun the day with the college libraries, then the public libraries, then the major bookstores, and was eventually reduced to this place. He searched every time worn text, every ancient grimoire, every scrap of mystical garbage scratched out by an old weirdo over the last five hundred years. All to find a single name.

Calach.

Michael had clammed up after revealing the name the intelligence had given him. He said he needed to check on a few things before going any further. Then he had downed two more scumdogs and dropped Jon off.

That weekend, Jon's house was mainly empty. His mother and little Catherine were out competing in the Beauties of America pageant. If beauty were the major prerequisite then, to Jon's mind, his six-year-old sister would lose by a wide margin. Father had informed the household that he had "business" to take care of at his office all weekend. And Michelle, she seemed content to spend a few days burning holes in her liver with booze-and-pills milkshakes. She was incoherent the entire time. Not that Jon had anything to say to her.

The day had been taken up by this seemingly fruitless search, until in the dingiest part of the store, in a crumbling red book published in 1900, he found the name. *The Book of Sacred Magic of Abramelin the Mage* was filled with weird double-talk, esoteric terms, confusing graphics, and yawn-inducing florid language, but the name was there—as was his invocation.

Calach, "the milky backed", a minor legionnaire of the infernal forces. The creature was apparently connected to a larger entity in the form of Ariton, one of the eight Princes of Hell. This royalty was associated with dominion over water and took direction from the North, whatever that meant. Calach was used to invoke hexes on enemies and love charms on unwilling women.

Hexes and love charms. That had possibilities, if it wasn't all crap.

The old man at the front, a bundle of wild whiskers and armpit hair long enough to braid, wiped his nose on his Grateful Dead shirt and thumbed through the book. The image on the shirt caught Jon's eye. It was a skeleton in blue, carrying a bindle in one hand and a red rose in the other. Arms outstretched, head upwards, it was about to step off a cliff. There was something there. The red rose—

"This is kind of a collector's item," the old man said, distracting him.

The red coloring of its leather cover had faded almost entirely. The paper was stained with coffee and many pages had dog-eared corners. A few notes had been penciled in by previous owners. The stitching on the old fashioned binding was loose.

"Looks pretty beat up."

"You know, back in the sixties," *Oh Jesus.* "We got all into this sort of stuff. Everyone wanted to expand their horizons, man, beyond all the Bible stuff they'd been programming us with since like birth, or earlier even. So we did all this stuff, like with Crowley and those guys, to see the mystic side of life and take stuff to help us do it."

The old hippie picked up the book and stared at the cover. An illustration had originally been embroidered on it with some imitation gold leaf which had long flaked off.

"Not that this is Crowley," he continued. "I mean it is, but it's Crowley before he was *Crowley*, you know? This is Mathers, well Mathers translated some like old French stuff, but . . . No, it was like older, Hebrew, I think." Jon wished he had a watch he could check. "But this is Mathers in the Golden Dawn time, along with uh Fu Manchu?" *What?* "No, like who was it? Rohmer! He did Fu Manchu around then too and hung out with them."

"Well, isn't that something. How much?"

"Thirty-five."

A complete rip off, but the proprietor's hippy funk began to overpower Jon's gag reflex. He threw down the cash and retreated with his prize. Mutterings by the old man about this "slacker generation" and kids who "had no respect" and were "dumb as shit" followed him out the door.

Next stop was the local hobby shop, Choo-Choo Junction, where they bought their gaming supplies. The place mostly catered to the more traditional hobbies of the Boomer generation: model trains, car, and boat sets, associated miniatures, RC kits, archery sets, and plenty of yarn for the female crafter. It always smelt of model glue.

Apart from a small rack at the back of a chain bookstore at the mall, this was the only place for his friends to buy role playing materials, and the selection here was even skimpier. Weird off-brand titles haunted the single shelf of games. Role Aids, Flying Buffalo, Judges Guild. While waiting for the owner to help a customer, he flicked through a flimsy softcover, bound like a spiral notebook, named *Spawn of Fashan*. Jon took in its ugly layout, with bad art and densely packed text. Hideous. He threw it back.

The owner was an old man, sporting skinny arms and a fat belly. Cotton white hair stuck out of his ears, and rainbow suspenders held up a ratty pair of britches. He looked at Jon without interest.

"I was wondering if you could order a game for me or if you knew the company that put it out. It's called Dark Dungeons."

"It's one of them weird ones like Dungeons and Dragons."

"Yeah."

With a sigh, the old man pulled out a mammoth catalogue and flipped through it. "Got a card game called Dark Cults."

"That's not it."

"Then I can't help you."

"You have no information on it?"

The old man stabbed at the catalogue with an irritated finger. "It's not in the book!"

Jon left. The old man's mutterings about these "pansy kids with no money" tagging at his heels.

Strangely enough, the owner had been more helpful than the drones collecting minimum wage at the chain bookstore. They were incapable of telling him anything at all, even whether or not they could get a copy of the game.

This all was beside the point. If Michael hadn't gotten Dark Dungeons from these two places, where did it come from? Same place as the van? A non-existent relative? It was just one more thing for Jon to look out for. One more puzzle piece that didn't fit.

He churned it over in his head as he rode over to Kathy's, but nothing connected. She answered her door, pale faced and red eyed, last night's rank clothes still on. She let Jon into the foyer and slumped against the wall.

"I couldn't sleep," she said. "I close my eyes and hear the woman. It's the worst thing ever."

"Just wanted to—"

"I can't get ahold of my parents in Mexico. They must be off at some dig. Will you stay the night? I don't want to be alone."

"Uh . . ."

"Please?"

Baby blue pleading eyes. A desperate curl to her voice, one that was just about to drop off into tears. What man could resist?

His protective instincts kicked in and without thinking he uttered, "'Course I will. As long as you want me to."

They sat down awkwardly in the gigantic living room. Neither knew what to say and simply stared at their hands from opposite ends of the couch. She tried to fill the air by turning on the TV, but the roar of game shows and the vapid diatribes of Phil Donahue sank into the void. If anything, the noise made things worse. Kathy brushed back a few tears.

"How about something to drink?" she said and ran off before he could reply.

He was cold again, but the frost was ingrained in the spirit of the household. He looked around at the furniture, the coffee table books, the pictures, and felt the chill of fraud. This wasn't a place where a family lived. It was a waypoint for related strangers to catch up before they hurried on their way.

She brought back two cans of soda and sat a little closer to him. Her hands rubbed together in a fast pace, like she was trying to scrub blood out of them. Their thighs touched.

"It was all I could do to keep everything out of my mind," Kathy blurted. "She was a force of evil. I know it. When she screamed, Hell screamed with her. Didn't you hear?"

"Yeah, I did. I held you and your eyes were closed."

"Didn't keep out the screams."

"Yes, but what did you see?"

"The Cold Woman?"

"No, no. When you shut your eyes, what did you see?"

She simply blinked at him, uncomprehending, and he let the matter dropped. If you hadn't actually experienced the visions, it sounded insane. To hold back the stem of tears he saw swelling again Kathy's eyes, he gave her a quick pat on the shoulder. Taking a mile to his inch, she latched onto his torso in a death grip and nuzzled up close to his chest.

"I can hear your heartbeat," she said.

In for a penny, in for a pound. He put a comforting arm around her. Things stirred below. The uncontrollable hormones of a seventeen-year-old cascaded and filled his genitals, jamming it tight up against his jeans. Could he? Should he? Would this be the moment? The pivot point that would destroy his virginity and finally cast him as one of the have-nots and not haves.

He was pretty sure he could, but inexperience grabbed his throat. A lot of childish *what ifs* and *maybes* scared him from acting. She would probably be amenable, but that probability was not a certainty and that held him back. Fear. Irrational fear. Fear of looking a fool. Fear that he'd somehow misinterpreted all of her obvious gestures. Fear that she would laugh at him and he'd never be able to recover. Fear that she'd blab to everyone about how disgusting he was. Fear that he would be terrible at the act.

Most of all, fear that she would tell everyone. Even though he liked her a lot, she wasn't the fantasy girl that his mind craved. His body would've taken anything, but his ego wanted that perfect woman to flash around and show up all the other assholes. His broken virginity needed to be shouted out and lauded over and Kathy Lauder was not the kind of girl you bragged about banging. Maria Maleventum on the other hand . . .

Kathy's snore interrupted his lustful thoughts. Drool from her mouth soaked into his shirt. That ended that. He'd spent too much time fretting about it and poof, the virginity fairy had departed.

She obviously needed the rest. He pulled out the red edition of *The Book of Sacred Magic of Abramelin the Mage* and spent the rest of the afternoon boning up on Victorian Era interpretations of magic and its uses.

Sunday. A day of rest and worship for the good Christian. The start of a drudging work week for the Muslim and Jew. For the observant high schooler, it was a day of great ambivalence. You were off from school, but the knowledge that you must soon return to the hated halls loomed like Damocles' Sword.

This Sunday found Jon knocking on the Dutch family's door at one in the afternoon. His mother answered in a frayed robe, sticking a sippy cup into the mouth of a toddler. She looked at Jon without a hint of recognition.

"Is Michael home?"

She nodded angrily. All these annoyances. When would she get some *me-time*? A bellow was sent up the stairs. A gesture was tossed at Jon to either come in or fuck off. She wandered back into the kitchen and crooned along with a sappy song blaring from the radio.

Michael bounded down from his room in two mighty leaps. Sunshine sparkled from his face. He punched Jon's arm playfully.

"Life is good, but I'm better."

"I've been looking into this and—"

Michael shushed him and pointed upwards. The pair retreated to his room. Jon plopped on his friend's bed, while Michael stood in the center of the room. He seemed to have grown three inches overnight.

"So, you're ready to do this?" Michael asked.

"I'm not sure."

"Why the hell not? This is a major threshold we're crossing. Contact with the Beyond. Think of what we could learn. What we could gain."

"That's the other thing . . ."

He tossed his copy of *The Book of Sacred Magic of Abramelin the Mage* at his friend, bookmarked to the appropriate page. Michael looked at the page. His eyebrows raised sharply when he came across the passage describing Calach.

"That's interesting," Michael said. "But all it means is that we're actually onto something. It's already been done. We can do this again."

"It's not that. You seem really unprepared for this. This book talks about all sorts of pitfalls that can happen."

"Books can't actually talk," Michael interrupted, smirking.

"Don't be an asshole. You know what I mean. It *states* that months of spiritual and physical purification is needed, along with various sigils and magic squares, and very precise ritual presentation."

"And yet we did it without any of that crap."

"It seems incredibly dangerous. Apparently without the correct wards it leaves a body open to spiritual possession."

"Which is why you won't be summoning this thing. Crixen Runeburner will."

"What?"

"You obviously didn't listen to a thing I said last week. It's all about being in the proper mindset. If bullshit rituals and incoherent mumbo-jumbo puts you there, great, but it's about you, not them."

"How can Crix—?"

"Names have power. Power to shape and mold. We can't define this contact without it, but it goes in the opposite direction as well. They can use our names against us and probably will if given a chance. So we hand them a different name, a false persona to focus on."

"That's very weird."

"No weirder than the actual game that created the persona. We've gotten rid of the random elements, the dice. Crixen Runeburner might have begun life on a sheet of graph paper, but now he's entirely in your head. He's a fully formed personality that you slip into when the game starts. I've seen it. Your face changes. The inflections of your voice alters. You know him intimately."

This was true. He didn't even need to look at his character sheet anymore. Crixen Runeburner was a part of him, an easy mask to slip on.

"Think of it as an ego shield," Michael continued. "If the entity believes you're something other than what you are and you believe it during time of contact, then the real you is safe from attack."

How tempting this was. To see beyond. To grasp secrets only a handful of people in the world had ever understood. To have power over others. He rejected the idea. Shook it from his brain. What Jon really wanted to understand was what his parents were up to. If he could learn along the same lines as them, then he could ward off any malicious moves his family made against him. It would be purely for defensive purposes, nothing else.

But along with that, Michael had some explaining to do.

"How do we do this?" Jon asked. "I mean, do we have to use like virgin's blood or—"

"No, no. We just play the game as normal, until contact is made."

"I'm not sure we can get the others to go along with it. Louis has disappeared and I saw Kathy yesterday and she was still scared half to death."

"We don't need them. Just you and me, buddy. As it should be."

"And where do we play? Back in Goodleburg? Can you get your uncle's van again?"

"N . . . no. We can do it at the grain elevator in the midget room."

"Why there? It worked at the cemetery."

"A little too well. I'd like a lower burn, until we're really sure."

"You said you were sure."

"As much as I can be, but we're still walking into darkness here. Let's go slow and take sure steps."

Jon stopped. Now was the time. Michael was hooked, ablaze with the idea. Excitement twitched all around him. He was nearly hopping up and down at the thought. Perfect time to pump him for information. All he had to do was threaten to pull the rug out from under his plan.

"Where does the game come from, Michael?"

"What? I— I got it at the hobby store."

"No, you didn't. I checked there and at the mall. They never heard of it, couldn't find it listed anywhere. Who gave it to you? Was it the same people who were at the cemetery on Friday? There was a car waiting by the van."

Michael was silent for a long time. Each second

compounded his guilt. What exactly he was guilty of remained to be seen, but there was something there. Michael had palmed a few of the jigsaw pieces and needed to cough them up.

"Dude, if you don't tell me, I'm gonna walk."

"You gotta believe me—"

"I don't gotta do anything. Who was it? Who? Was it my father?"

Michael was taken aback. Genuinely so, Jon could tell.

"What would your . . . ? No! This doesn't have anything to do with you, man. I wanted you in on this because we've always done everything together, but—" He shook his head and his tongue darted in and out of his mouth like a nervous tick. He growled, "This is my story. *My story*. You're just along for the ride. A bit player to swell the progress. You're not fucking Hamlet! You're not fucking Hamlet!"

"What are you going on about?"

"*I* set this all up. *I* arranged it. And *I'm* allowing you to come along."

"And *I* so much love being your fucking canary."

"It wasn't like that."

"Man, you're acting crazy. With all this insanity, I'd like a few answers. Please?"

Please must have been the magic word. Michael calmed down immediately, gratefulness and triumph flipping back and forth over his face. He sat down on the carpet and sighed, then sighed again. Was he stalling? Or calming down? The outburst was something new. Jon never knew his oldest friend harbored this bizarre resentment against him.

"While I was looking into this stuff, I started where

anyone would. The occult bookstores, the New Age dives, the herbal and fragrance stores, and by reading the flyers off their community bulletin boards. That's the best way to find stuff, right? Well, I came across a flyer advertising classes in 'thelemic mediation techniques.' That set off some triggers and I went to a few classes, met some people, then got invited to a secret place where they all congregate. It's called Snakeland."

"Snakeland?"

"It's not that far from where we game actually. An open patch in the woods where the religious cast-offs of modern society congregate to practice. All sorts go there. Wiccans, Druids, Pagans, you name it. Most of them are poseurs, but there was one guy . . . Brian Elder. You know him?"

"No."

Michael stared at Jon's face for a few moments then continued, "He knows his stuff and used to be part of a group that operated in this area. He hooked me up with this game. If there were people following us out at Goodleburg, they might be connected to him."

"What kind of group."

"An occult one."

"That could mean almost anything. It's like calling yourself European. Were they Satanists?"

"As far I could tell, yes. Brian Elder didn't come out and say it, but it was pretty obvious. He's also the one who loaned me the van to Goodleburg."

"Sounds like he was using *you* as a guinea pig."

"I paid him for both. So, I didn't think twice about it. This group he was part of often contacted demons or so he claimed. He never demonstrated it to me. Told me to 'find my own path.' However, he did sell me the copy of the game."

He should walk away, Jon knew. Hitch a ride out to California and become a surfer. But he couldn't, a force pulled him back, something stronger than his flight impulse. There was a possibility to grab some actual power here. It was an opportunity he didn't want to pass up.

"All right. I'll help you. Just you and me. But I'm gonna want to meet this Brian Elder guy and size him up. Maybe he isn't as disassociated with the Satanist group as he made you think."

"Agreed. To Snakeland then."

CHAPTER 8

SNAKELAND

MICHAEL CLAIMED HE was fatigued, so they agreed to meet after school the next day to attempt contacting Brian Elder. The school day stretched on at an agonizing pace, until that blessed final bell released them all from captivity.

The day would've easily been forgotten, tossed into the lump of other boring days in their memory, except they were about to leave the building with a gaggle of Italians, led by the snarling Gabbaducci. As usual, the girls followed. Jon's nightly fantasy girl was among them.

"I heard you've been telling people that I'm a faggot," Gabbaducci yelled at Michael. His nose bumped Michael's.

"I . . . I didn't."

And of course, he hadn't. It's just that the boy wanted to fight and rather than find a reason, he manufactured one to justify his assholeishness.

Gabbaducci slammed Michael's head into the wall.

"You want to fuck me in the ass? How 'bout I do it to you and we'll see who's the queer." He punched Michael in the nuts and sent him sprawling. "You'd probably like it, too, you fucking homo."

Hunched over the now crying Michael, Gabbaducci turned to garner laugher and kudos from his fellow thugs. His face was the textbook definition of stupidity.

Father's words flooded Jon's brain. *It isn't 'nice guys' that finish last. It's weak men who do so.* And before he knew it, Jon had stepped up to Gabbaducci and pushed the bully off his friend.

"Leave him alone, jerk."

The bully actually backed up, incredulous that an invertebrate like Jon would dare step up to him.

His buddies mockingly chanted "Ooh."

Gabbaducci glanced at them. All of Gabbaducci's bully instincts tingled. Jon was an unknown quantity. He hadn't been labeled an easy mark, so the bully was unsure of his success and might be beaten up, but if he backed down, his buddies would spread the word that Gabbaducci had pussied out. His tough guy image would forever be tarnished. Then no respectable Italian girl would fuck him. He had to act but decided on a tactic of ridicule.

"Look at this fuck," Gabbaducci mocked, jabbing a finger into Jon's chest. "You think doin' this means my girl is gonna bang you? I seen you look at her."

From the gathering crowd, a loud "Ew," escaped the lips of Maria Maleventum. This hurt worse than any blow from her boyfriend could have. It reinforced every one of his doubts and kicked his heart into the gutter. Gabbaducci saw this and his laugh grew crueler.

"Jesus, I didn't lay a finger on this guy and he's going to cry."

One of the others shot out a warning, "Mr. Sobel, Mr. Sobel," and the crowd dispersed. The almostbrawlers separated. Jon helped Michael up, the latter wiping tears away and led him towards the bike racks. When the teacher walked past, it was as if nothing had happened.

"You're fucking lucky," Gabbaducci called.

" . . . think I'd want to have sex with him," Maria Maleventum's voice drifted after him. "He doesn't look Italian at all."

They were silent on the ride to the old grain elevator, only slightly grunting to each other as they hid their bikes and negotiated the treacherous way up the fallen stairs and into the midget room. Michael had come prepared with everything needed.

Candles were lit. Dark Dungeons was laid out. The pair took one long look at each other before beginning. A new horizon was before the friends. They started a solo adventure. One where Crixen Runeburner ventured alone into the depths of a tomb brimming with horrors.

Attack, defend, heal, harm. With each action, each command, Jon slipped further into Crixen Runeburner's skin. He stopped considering what his character would do and simply knew. The elf mage's mind coalesced in Jon's frontal lobe.

His mind populated an ethereal world conjured by Michael's words. The sights of the ancient resting place filled his eyes: Cobwebs, opened graves, crumbling brickwork, traps, shambling undead, carnivorous monsters, poisonous scavengers. All the while, the sickening feeling, same as his cellar and the defunct cemetery, grew in his gut. Smells of dirt and rot and animal scat crept up his nose. He was there! He was there!

The last chamber was breached. The final enemy spirit was dispelled back to Hell. The idol, the goal of his quest, was before him. It shined white, unmolested by the taint of ages. Hammered into its base was a bronze plaque bearing the phrase, *Speak the name of whom you seek.*

"Calach."

And it was so.

A voice slithered out of nowhere, faint, like a low wind, but distinct. Each vowel curled around Jon's brain. Each consonant an ice cube down this throat. Yet, he kept on.

"Who be there?"

"I name thee Calach," Crixen said.

"And Calach I am named. Who does so? Who calls me forth?"

Names have power. Names have power. "Crixen Runeburner calls you to treaty."

"Crixeeenn Ruuuneburner," the bodiless voice rolled the name around. "Stilted way of speaking. Not many alive know the name, Calach. You smack of fiction. Your face waivers like a heat vision."

Fiction? A warning look from Michael. The low spirit, the demon, the entity from beyond, was trying to break through his persona.

"Hear and obey. I have summoned and named you. Calach, milky backed, you are bound."

"Bound am I now?" it snickered.

"You are here to answer. You are here to obey."

"Answer what? What can Calach tell you?"

The voice had grown in the air. Like crystallized syrup, sickly and sweet, it poured into Jon's ear. All the while they spoke, both boys maintained the image from the game in their minds. It was just another NPC encounter.

"I wish to know about the human, the pater familias, of the St. Fond family and his wife."

"Calach doesn't know things. Calach does things."

Hex's and love charms. He knew this yet had hoped there would be more. Well, if the ancient mages like Mather and Crowley couldn't coax out more from the demon, what chance did he have?

"Who's that poking out behind there? Does it have a name?"

Damn it. This was harder than he thought. Crixen Runeburner was mage extraordinaire, greater than any *human* mage. If anyone could get more from Calach it would be him.

The vision shook. The world lost mass.

"Are you there, Runeburner?"

Don't lose focus. Don't lose focus. But . . . but . . . what did he want? Knowledge. Knowledge.

"You will tell me. I command it."

"There's nothing I can say. Calach is a lowly name. It knows nothing. No one tells it anything."

Was this true? If not Jon . . . Crixen was at a loss of how to compel the entity to cough up more. He looked helplessly at Michael. The ethereal world supported by their brains waived once again.

"A test then," Michael said

"Who speaks?"

"I am the Game Master."

"One among many. I see a blank face, an imprint of nothing, with the swirling universe as a cloak."

Michael blinked, his face grew pale. Was the

demon defining him instead of vice versa? Could it get the upper hand this way?

"If you know nothing," he said. "We will test your limits. A hex and a charm."

"Pity poor Calach. He's cold and he's mad," was the sarcastic reply.

"Answer," commanded the Game Master.

"Answer to what?"

"You will do these things."

"That's not a question."

"Can you?" Michael faltered.

"Oh, yes. That is what Calach does. Tee hee hee. Who to be hexed?"

They looked at each other. Jon nodded to the Game Master. His mind was almost completely gone from the image now. It was all too real.

"Vincent Gabbaducci."

"And who is to be charmed?"

"Maria Maleventum. She is to fall in love with a person named Jon St. Fond."

Sweat dripped from Jon's forehead. Passions stirred and the red haze of desire rode over his brain. Could this really work? The girl he wanted so much, the focus of his primal lust, would soon be his. And so easily? He became so excited he made himself sick.

"Jon St. Fond," said the entity. Sneering curiosity. A treasure uncovered. Jon's blood froze. His name was now known. "Is that you?"

"Calach doesn't know things. Calach does things. And he will do this," stated the Game Master.

"Oh, and he will. Once he's been paid."

"Paid with what?" Jon blurted.

"Don't you know, mage? If you are what you claim.

Calach needs something of the target of the hex. Something he's touched. So Calach can focus. Hair from those to be charmed. Where it's ripped from doesn't matter."

Jon wondered about how necessary it was. Perhaps the creature needed a DNA signature to home in on. Some psychic radar guidance system. Or was it just a shit test to see if those conjuring the creature were serious.

"And blood." Calach finished.

"Blood?"

"Fresh blood, straight from the victim's veins."

"Uh."

"Human. Animal. Matters not to Calach. Complete the rites. Spill the blood and it is yours."

"We'll give you your blood and hair, but don't waste my time on rites and that crap."

"Oh, you do know something, Game Master. Much more than your elf mage flunky."

Michael turned the game over, severing the connection. The vision, barely a foggy image in Jon's mind, erased completely. The dread ebbed slowly from his bowels. Contact broken. They were alone.

Michael leapt over the scattered game pieces and hugged Jon. Lingering sexual excitement charged through him. Jon could read him like a book. He was proven right. He could make deals. A glint of hunger for power sparkled in the eyes. This was just the beginning to him. Murky plans formulated in his brain. Right now, the achievement was enough. And for Jon, perhaps more in the days to come. That is the only reason he didn't walk away immediately when Michael asked,

"Where are we going to get the blood?"

"If we do."

"What do you mean? You can't back out now. This—"

"I can if I want to."

Give me a big enough lever, Archimedes wrote. The modern world was built on leverage. It's just how you got things done.

"Why would you?" Michael asked, his voice was soaked in whiny pleading that made Jon want to slap him.

"Because you haven't held up your end of the bargain. Take me to Snakeland."

Another day had to stretch by in slow motion before the journey to Snakeland could happen. His mother and little sister had returned, basking in the glory of a second-place trophy. From a little devious eavesdropping, he discovered that Catherine wasn't expected to place, but it seemed two of the other contestants had gotten sick from food poisoning. Mother and Father both laughed heartily at that.

"Whatever it takes to get ahead," Father declared, patting the grinning youngster who hugged his leg and slipping her a hundred dollar bill.

Later she taunted Jon with it, waving it at him and jeering. "Father loves me. He hates you. He told me so."

All he could do was slam the door in her face. She spent a few more minutes yelling muffled insults through the wood, then left. The problem was Jon couldn't really disagree with her.

At school, he saw Kathy, still bleary eyed from lack of sleep. Her clothes were dirty and wrinkled. Hair matted and face unwashed, she tottered about like the walking dead. He tried to say hi, but she just brushed past him, entranced.

Louis still hadn't returned by that Monday. A worrying prospect. Was he still wandering out in the woods? People tend to think of New York as one huge asphalt jungle, nothing but high rises and slums, but there's a lot of forests between the urban centers. It was quite possible to wander for days without seeing civilization. Jon and Michael debated whether to call at Louis's house on the way to Snakeland. Jon felt it their obligation.

"He wouldn't be out there if not for us and we just left him."

Michael disagreed.

"As far as he knew, he ran off and left us to die. Besides, if he was missing wouldn't his parents be calling us? They seem to be a pretty tightknit family."

Fair enough point. Jon gave in.

It's odd to picture that a significant amount of foliage, nearly enough to be classified as a small woods, could exist in the middle of city, but it did. This wasn't the result of urban planning, but rather nature reclaiming the land.

When the steel plants died, so did the transportation industry attached to them. Long stretches of land that once held railroad tracks on top of artificial hills had been abandoned, leaving plenty of land for rogue vegetation to creep in and spread.

Under the ruins of a dismantled trestle bridge, in an area of twisted plants and rusted out vehicles, they met. Snakeland, the witch's burrow, was a circular area where three fires burned in old fifty gallon drums. The grass had been worn away through constant foot traffic, leaving only the bare brown earth glaring out. Figures in odd clothes danced by the fires.

Why did they meet there?

"Last woman in America was hanged for witchcraft right on this spot," some patchouli stain of a man stuttered at them. "Goody Smith."

"Well, goody for her. Hell of a way to become one of history's footnotes," Michael sneered.

Jon nudged him and whispered for him to be cool. Overnight Michael had become arrogant and condescending. Contact with the beyond and a half done deal with the devil had put unwarranted lead in his pencil.

The people gathered in Snakeland had been strangely welcoming. At first, Jon assumed that was due to Michael being a familiar face, but many introduced themselves to both the boys. Michael didn't seem to be as much a regular as he had let on.

"Lot of new bodies here," Michael whispered. "Lots of poseurs."

Jon could see that. Though friendly, each person always made sure to throw whatever occult bullshit they touted at the pair: Crystals, charms, and kindergarten interpretations of complex philosophical trains of thought. Buddhism, devil worship, Taoism, Wicca, generic paganism, UFO cults, all were mixed together in this group. Each discourse was dispensed in-between puffs off a bong or slurps of beer. All of it was cribbed from other sources with no variation or originality.

Each person present was just looking for an audience to show off how "different" they were. Whenever another person spoke, the poseurs' eyes trailed off and their minds sprinted ahead to the next talking point where they could butt in and demonstrate their plagiarized "wisdom." Many of their personal egos rested on being *the* person of great knowledge, even though their learning only extended to a couple of half-read paperbacks.

There was no rhyme or reason. A completely mixed bag of beliefs, like a gang for Unitarian misfits. If you stripped away the jumbled religious crapola, it was just a party for the pretentious.

There were some nice people wearing wizard hats, glitter makeup, black fingernails, mohawks, ripped jeans, heavy metal T-shirts. Cheap beer, pot, acid, whippets were communally passed about. A few slipped behind car wrecks to indulge in harder substances. Some teens with safety pins in their heads futilely spray painted pentacles over the dirt.

A scrawny reed snuck up behind Jon and snaked a wilted arm in front of his face.

Jon started.

"How doin'," the face attached to the hand said. "I'm Brian Elder."

A withered man, fitting his name, somewhere between seventy and eighty, though still spry. He was nearly hairless, with a close-cropped crown of white that blended seamlessly into his alabaster skin. The rest, eyebrows, nose, ears, cheeks, and chin, were scraped as clean as they could be. So white was he that it was nearly impossible to tell where his teeth began and gums ended. He might've been mistaken for an albino if not for his deep black eyes.

Deep was as good a term as Jon could've thought up, for the orbs seemed to dwell on and on, like an echo through a dark hallway. They reflected obscure secrets and cryptic answers to which even the questions had been forgotten. Something sinister was in the brain connected to those eyes, something strange and alien.

"Come on. Come on," the ancient said and hustled a little ways away from the others.

The trio sat in the dirt, the light from one of the barrel fires played across Elder's face. Unlike most men his age, he had no problem squatting. He moved like a man of twenty. He pulled from his pocket an open bag of gummy worms and extended it to the others. When those were refused, he sparked a joint and offered that. Again, both boys declined.

"I hope you're not going to have a cigarette," he said to them. "I despise tobacco. Smoking it is a perverted habit for degenerates." He raised the bud. "This is all I need."

The thick white smoke that poured from Elder's nostrils and lips had a thin line of red running through it, like a peppermint vapor. Both the boys coughed heavily as the smoke tried to climb up their noses. There was something else mixed with the marijuana. Jon had smelt pot enough times, mostly when it emerged from his sister's room during her sexual romps, and this was an entirely different stench.

"Do you know why we all gather here?" he asked.

"Yeah, Goody Smith."

"And you know her story? In detail?"

They had to admit no. Without prompting, the old man went into a well-practiced spiel.

"The first wave of pioneers did a good job. Most had thrown off the shackles of a life where their fate was predetermined—poverty, back breaking work, early death. In the old world, the class system was the immutable law of God. No wonder Calvinism was so popular. But here was an unspoilt world, where not every piece of land had been snatched up by some noble prick. They hewed out a decent life and made what they could.

"It's the second wave that brought civilization and all its leftover evils dragging behind like an uncut afterbirth. They arrived running from tyranny, only to become tyrants themselves. Nearly a century before the revolution, when the hamlet of Black Rock grew to a township, came the near destitute Goody Glover and her daughter. She told a weeping tale of being deported with her husband and child from her native Ireland by Cromwell's invading forces and how they were sold into slavery on a sugar plantation in Barbados. There, her spouse was executed for not renouncing his Roman Catholic faith.

"Goody escaped the slavers and made her way here, to the good Protestant land of plenty. She became housekeeper to a rising family in the textile trade. Rumors say she drank. Others that she whored. Whether or not it was true, what has been universally accepted was that she had a gorgeous singing voice. One that, due to the strict religious laws, she was not permitted to use. So, she did so only at night. They say visions danced in the moonlight when her golden voice graced the night. Men would sneak around the corners of their house to listen in, and the air would grow light like a fairy story.

"Though she did not flaunt it, her Catholic ways raised eyebrows. Despite vicious rumors by other women to the contrary, she spurned all suitors. This led to much grumbling, much talk of her haughty ways. In all things she lived as a decent woman should.

"The fateful moment came after the young daughter had been accused of stealing a pair of stockings by the mistress of the house. A terrible fight ensued and, later that night, the mistress and her three daughters became violently ill and started to act strangely. They talked to the air and inanimate objects but refused to discourse with actual people. They couldn't walk normally and instead had to stride about as if a hoop was between their legs, or else they would fall over.

"The local doctor, if you could call him that, examined them and proclaimed they had been bewitched. Suspicion fell on Goody and her papist ways. Several small dolls were seized from her room. The kind used to curse, her accusers claimed. In reality, they were just representations of saints.

"Goody was seized and thrown in the local jail. There she stopped being able to speak English, though she understood it, and could only communicate in her native Irish tongue, which at first was misunderstood as a demonic language.

"At the trial, all sorts of things were brought up, her 'stubborn idolatry', the weird effects of the women, though modern physicians might recognize them all as brain damage caused by ergot poisoning from spoiled wheat, c'est la vie, and her inability to recite the Lord's prayer from memory—a sure sign of Satan. A few others claimed they had dreams of her riding broomsticks. Two men, former suitors, came forward and claimed that she had stolen their penises after being pulled into passivity by her golden singing voice. They had to ransom their cocks back by performing blasphemous rites in the church. They testified she kept the genitals all writhing around in a bird's nest like giant maggots.

"With that sort of damning evidence, the judges were quick to order her death. On that fateful day, November 16th, 1688, she was taken to this spot and hanged until dead. The mocking shouts of Black Rock townspeople ushered her into Hell.

"In her last words, she stated that executing her would not heal the children. This was taken to mean that either she was innocent and someone else had cursed the family or that the damage was done and couldn't be undone."

Jon stopped him there. Elder had become more and more agitated and was tearing up clumps of turf and whipping them around. The joint smoke was completely red at this point. All the poseurs gave him a wide berth, fearfully glancing over shoulders at the three of them. They pointed at Elder and whispered warnings.

"But she was innocent," Jon said.

"Course she fucking was," the near albino laughed. He licked his gums in an obscene manner. "But the family *was* cursed and whoever did it got away scot free. In these cases the innocents are always hurt. In all the witch trials in America only one ever got the right person, Bridget Bishop."

"You're very sure."

"Oh, yes," he said. "It was mostly about hurting the

husband of the family. He was a real prick, poking his nose in everyone's business." Black eyes sparkled. The grin dropped to a leer. "He had to go. Had to be distracted."

Elder stubbed out the dead joint, then settled in cross-legged, dragging in his feet so deep that they disappeared. His demeanor changed, his face twisted up into disgust.

"Now what do you want?"

"I want to know why you're helping Michael."

"Because of all the dead presidents shoved in my face."

"Just for the money?"

"I like money. I require a lot of it."

Rumpled T-shirt sporting a logo for a band that broke up a decade ago, jeans so faded the knees were nothing but threads, scuffed shoes that had been re-soled at least once, with a broken shoestring tied back together. No cash spent for clothes, and really, how much could he have wriggled out of Michael?

Jon turned to Michael for confirmation, but his friend was in his own world. Sitting upright, he stared at the strange man as if Elder was the ultimate riddle, a lock with no key, a missing link in a forgotten chain. His lips kept muttering something inaudible, just below the range of human hearing. Sweat clustered at his temples. No help there.

"Tell me about the game, Dark Dungeons."

"Back in the old days, I ran with a pretty wild crowd. Satanists and occultists, as you like, they mixed and matched that shit up for whatever hit their funny bone. Often they'd just shoot up cocaine, drink their gin rickeys, and summon up a spirit as a party favor.

Then one of them wondered why the rituals worked only some of the time, why there were so many different rituals, and why the same spirit could be yanked to the world on different dimes as it were."

"Because it's the people not the rite," Jon interrupted. "We're past this."

"Don't step on my story, prick," yelled the old man.

A "whoa" came from behind his back. Jon tilted his head and saw everyone, all the poseurs, had backed up to the other end of Snakeland. They stared at the ground, at the sky, to the east, west, south, anywhere but them.

"Yeah," Elder continued. "Some became more attuned to making contact than others, and some places were better than others. Right, Jon?"

Those eyes took him in and Jon could only nod.

"There are soft spots in the world, where the beyond is just one step away. The universe is still young, still a growing boy, hasn't reached its full maturity. And, like a baby's skull, some parts are more malleable than others."

Yes. That made sense, he guessed. Not in a scientific way, but if you ignored physics, it might be real. Jon found that he was suddenly dehydrated.

"The game," he croaked.

"What an ornery cuss. Fine, the game," he sparked another smoke, the same peppermint curl flowed from it. "Certain parties weren't satisfied with the will-they won't-they outcome of these rites and tried to come up with a way to standardize it. Dark Dungeons. An elegant and versatile system, which can be altered to fit the needs of the players, yet structured enough to force all minds down the same rabbit hole."

"And it even works when the people playing have no idea what it's all about," said Jon.

"It works better that way sometimes, especially when the world is soft. You know that, Jon. You can sense it. Your guts twist up whenever you're near a spot. It's your special gift. The only thing interesting about you."

Elder's flat lips twisted up. He seemed to be tasting the air. Nostrils flared, little white hairs shook inside of them. And those eyes! They deepened, went further into the unknown.

"How—?"

"It's my job to know. I'm a psychic assassin."

Jon laughed. Michael's breathing slowed down. In the corner of his ear, Jon heard the posers making their goodbyes.

"You pay me money. I crawl into the victim's head and destroy his life. Suicides often follow."

Jon found it hard to swallow. The lack of moisture was even worse. He worked his mouth to wrangle up saliva, but nothing came out. Had it all been sucked into this madman's eyes? The thought grew stronger. He suddenly believed everything Brian Elder said.

"Who—?"

"The game was manufactured on a limited run. Only a few hundred were made. I've grabbed the stray copy over the years. Some guy named Gygax in Pervertsville, California got hold of one and made the knock-off, Dungeons and Dragons, but it just wasn't as good."

"And who were these people that commissioned it?"

"They called themselves The Order of the Bright

Dawn. Operated out of New York City. Long gone after the crash of 1929. Most of them cannibalized each other during the Great Depression. The leader was a Limo Brightson, made a fortune in linseed oil. Lived well until he spontaneously combusted on the same day Pearl Harbor was attacked. Don't know why, so don't ask."

"So, if they're all dead, who is producing them now?"

"No one. It's a relic from an old time."

"That box looked brand new. The pieces were all plastic, not something created in the 1920s. The papers were crisp and white, no age at all. Someone made it in modern times."

"Okay, a few more were run off by some rinky-dink outfit in Mexico. All the original sets were too damaged to be of much use. So, last year, one of the last disciples of the Order, a woman named Charlotte de Courrière had a few more manufactured. During the rush to get them distributed, I snagged a few. Michael here was the beneficiary of my larceny."

"Rush? Why a rush?"

"I don't know. Something big seems to be stirring up the occultists down south. It happens. It's why I came back up here."

"How . . . ? What is the price for playing the game to its end? I mean, when dealing with the demon, or entity? How much does it cost a person?"

"What you're really asking beneath it all is, 'Will I damn my soul to Hell for dealing with these creatures?' You won't."

"Because Hell doesn't exist?"

"Oh, it does, but making a few extra-curricular

deals isn't how you damn your soul. Especially if the other bastard really has it coming. Remember, you make it a demon in your mind. It doesn't have to be one."

"Then what are we dealing with, if not demons."

"Kings of dead universes, crotchety spirits wanting to walk again, the leftovers of an alien race, the memories of physical beings cast aside, some zeitgeist aspect made real, ancient watchers frozen in stone, entities of pure spirit who have never known flesh. Take your pick. Though, I hazard the last is probably what you've been describing. What name did you give it?"

"Calach."

"That's a loser. Really fucking bush league. Go big or go home is what I say. You know some big demonic titles, use them. Or try an angelic name, that'll give you some weird results."

"Are you saying Calach can't do anything?"

"Oh, no, sure it can," Elder spat. "But not huge things, which is the most fun."

That suited Jon fine. He was just dipping his toe to test the waters in any case.

"You lent Michael the van to go to the cemetery."

"I rented him my kick-ass van. He asked for it. Had no other way. Blah, blah, blah."

"There were others there watching us."

"Nothing to do with me. I don't speak to other people much."

Sure he didn't. The old bastard knew something, but how much was spin Jon couldn't suss out. The conversation dried up with his body. While there might have been more to ask, his head was suddenly empty.

"I think we're done here."

"Good. I got a bottle of Mad Dog yowling for me at home. Time to mosey."

They rose. Michael snapped out of his torpor and shook Elder's hand. Even though the three barrels still burned, they were the only ones left in Snakeland.

Just as they were about to leave, a question popped into Jon's head as if from nowhere. A stray thought that would not go away. He called to the departing figure of Brian Elder

"Which saints were they? If you know."

The man stopped and yelled from the field.

"What saints?"

"The saints that Goody Smith had images of."

"Why, Saint Patrick, patron of Ireland. Saint Jude, patron of lost causes. And the last . . . "

"Yes?"

A crooked smile. "Saint Fond, patron of falsely accused women."

He knew he was going to do it. Despite the hemming and hawing, despite all the leveraging with Michael and the odd man at Snakeland, Jon always knew he was going to make the deal with the demon.

The prize was too sweet to pass up. The power, his first ever taste, was too addictive. He had to see. He had to know. Anything else was just procrastination. All roads led him back to the midget room.

The only hesitation was the blood. Neither of the boys relished the idea, but they had to do it. After a long and exhausting debate, they went to the city pound and picked a cat slated to be put down the next day.

It was an old, foul stray. A feral creature all its life, it had been finally trapped after it grew too sickly to run any more. It was too ill to groom itself properly, giving the feline a sickly sheen over matted hair. One eye was milked over. Half an ear had been chewed off. Numerous scars crisscrossed the body.

They got weird looks from the pound people when they selected the near-dead cat, but no one objected. It was one less carcass for them to incinerate. The animal barely stirred in its crate as they navigated up the treacherous passages of the old grain elevator to the midget room.

For the items related to the victims, school provided the best opportunity. They waited until school was out, hiding away in the science lab until after even the janitors had gone home. Jon took a crowbar and broke into their lockers. For Maria, they plucked stray hairs from a brush she stored there. For Gabbaducci, it was a pair of stiff and stinking gym shorts that hadn't been washed since his freshman year. They broke open a few other lockers and threw the contents around just to cover their tracks.

The instrument of death was a kitchen knife Jon smuggled from his home. Though he supplied the weapon, he couldn't bring himself to use it. Thus, it was Michael who held the animal aloft, after they had re-established contact with Calach, and slit the cat's throat.

Its blood spilled over the center of the game, almost being absorbed by the plastic board. The hair and shorts were then thrown into the mix. A disturbing sound of pleasure, like a pedophile achieving orgasm, filled their heads.

How? Jon thought. How did the blood benefit them? What did Calach really gain from this? The blood didn't disappear. It just stained the floor. Or was leaving a stain on the world the actual point?

"The pact is sealed," the voice said.

Both felt the entity break contact. Jon didn't realize they could do that. He assumed the spirit was trapped until they let it go or lost concentration. None of that occurred to Michael. He was too giddy.

"Now all we have to do is wait," he said.

CHAPTER 9

DROWNING THE CEREMONY OF INNOCENCE

ON THE WAY OUT, Jon was subjected to all the nocturnal haunts exactly as what happened at Goodleburg Cemetery. With every blink, a new horror filled his sight. It was so ghastly he nearly fell through a hole in the floor. Michael needed to guide him down the treacherous stairs. He asked questions all the way about what Jon saw.

As had happened at the cemetery, visions of evil clouded his senses. Up and down the structure, people from different times and fashions committed vile acts. Beatings, thefts, rapes, and murders viciously played out around him. Dark creatures with indistinct features floated all around. Dark tendrils, rippling with profane power, rubbed over the evil doers, transferring a joy of sin to the men.

A spectral Brian Elder was on the bottom floor of the grain elevator, dressed in the style of the 1920s. He had pinned down one of the demonic things and was sucking power from it via a paper straw punctured into its skull. The magician's shade somehow recognized Jon and waved to him before evaporating into the ether.

Jon was pulled the last hundred feet as Michael's mythical frontiersman appeared and shot a pregnant doe. How much of that was real? How much actually had happened in the past? They had the consistency of dreams or nightmares, yet there was a pungent earthiness to them. The visions weren't just bits of nonsense.

"I don't know what's going on," Jon said, after he had laid in the dirt for half an hour. "Every time we contact—"

"But that's incorrect," Michael interrupted. "This didn't happen when we first contacted Calach."

True. Why hadn't he thought of that? Jon stared up at the twisting stars. All the answers lay out there somewhere. All the evil, horrible truths. Perhaps he should start a policy of willful ignorance, then happiness would be his.

Michael was still going on. "If what you say is accurate, then it seems you have a reaction whenever something changes as a result of contact. The world shifts or some muck at the bottom of the spiritual pool is stirred up, and you have a psychic allergic reaction."

Did they only occur at such times? He remembered the hallucinatory episodes at his house. They were wilder, but still vivid. One had definitely happened during some bizarre ceremony at his house, but Michael didn't need to know about that.

"Yeah well, it was all evil. Doesn't anything nice ever happen? Why don't I see that?"

Michael had no answer, so he sidestepped it. "The point is that this is a good sign. It means the entity has done something in the world."

If Calach had affected a change, the results weren't seen immediately. They expected Gabbaducci to spontaneously explode in horrific fashion across the school cafeteria, or die in an ironic way, but nothing.

He and his cohort of greasy stooges still stomped around talking of their standard 3 Fs: fighting, football, and fucking. Maria still hung among them. Still attached to her man. Nothing had changed.

Sitting through class became a contest in endurance. School and school work almost didn't exist in Jon's mind anymore. He took nothing in. All efforts to penetrate his brain was wasted. It was as if he had graduated to a world beyond the mundane.

Through the school grapevine, Jon heard that Louis's parents were at the school office. All of the football team were pissed off. They roamed the halls taking random shots at weaker males.

"That dumb hick is gonna fuck everything up."

A bruiser dented his knuckles against a locker.

"We had a shot, a real shot, this year."

What happened?

"His inbred parents pulled him out. They're filling out all this paperwork to home school him. Fucking weirdos."

Home school? Wasn't that for religious nut jobs living on a hidden mountain compound or spastics too unstable to handle normal high school interactions— or for his older sister, supported by his parents for whatever reason?

Over the following two weeks, while they waited for the curse to ferment, things became weirder at home.

Jon's parents swapped roles. Mother was gone most of the time on "business." Snatches of eavesdropped conversation placed her in New Orleans, Los Angeles, and Victoria, British Columbia, among some obscure others. The specific nature of her trips were unknown, but on her return Jon spotted some deep bruises on his mother's arms and legs, which she tried to cover up with long pants and sleeves.

While she was gone, Father took charge. He spent nearly all day at home, making phone calls in weirdly accented French and jotting shorthand notes in a beige leather notebook that he hid in the safe. Jon snuck in and read them, but it was unintelligible.

Father didn't like to cook, so most of the meals were takeout—burgers, wings, and pizza—the unhealthy trio of junk food that plagued the city, not that the kids complained.

As much as he provided for their material needs, toys and pretty clothes for Catherine, booze and sundry drugs for Michelle, Father gave them nothing emotional. No support. No love. No hate. Simply a void. Even when he punished Jon or praised Catherine, there was no feeling behind the words. It stuck out more during this time. Catherine began to whine for her mommy and, for the first time in her life, no one rushed to solve the problem.

During this time, two things happened which set Jon's mind ablaze. He came home one day, very anxious and hopeful, to find his sister topless on the living room floor, yet again soiling the antique rug. Her floppy breasts slid off on either side, their lack of movement indicated the girl had stopped breathing. An annoyed Father was kneeling over her, filling up a large cardiac syringe with an orange liquid. He saw Jon and smirked.

"These junkies just can't help killing themselves."

He jammed the needle into her heart with a vicious thud. Michelle's eyes shot open. Each orb was nearly filled with blood. They waggled about uncomprehending for a few seconds, then the lids slowly closed. Breathing resumed.

"Have to call the doctor again," Father sighed, then commanded Jon, "Give me a hand with her."

The pair hauled her thin, yet surprisingly heavy body, up the stairs. Michelle snored away, oblivious to ever having been in peril. Jon found himself voicing a question that had never occurred to him before.

"Why do you encourage this?"

"There's a method to my madness, don't you worry," Father chuckled in his deep baritone. "Each step is taken with absolute purpose. How did Crowley put it? 'Do as thou wilt shall be the whole of the law.' Actually, I think he stole that from Rabelias. However, most people think it means to become a beast like your sister here, but really—"

They deposited Michelle into the attic drug den she called a bedroom. Through the dim light came all the horrid smells of pleasure gone sour. The natural debris of a wastrel life, where the enjoyment of "now" meant more than anything else. Father picked up the thought when they had crept down.

"—but really he meant, make your will into the law. Make sure each step is done with precision and the depraved humans of this society will surrender to you at every turn."

"So, you turn her into a junkie for some power play?"

"Are you that stupid?" Father's yellow eyes turned Jon's guts into a squirming bag of rats. Yet, he put his blank face on and stood his ground. "Do you know your tarot? The major arcana?"

"What do you mean?" Jon asked.

"Yes, you do. All the decisions and possibilities in the world are spread out in those cards. Do you know which one you are?"

"Um . . ."

Slam. The door to little Catherine's room shut. She had been privy to all of the ongoing actions but preferred the company of her imaginary friends and dolls. Now she was angry because real life had intruded into her domain. Both the males stared at her door for a second, then Father started right back up.

"Zero. The Fool. You're stumbling about blindly looking for answers, looking for purpose. That's fine for a bit, but one cannot remain the fool forever or else you step off a cliff. You must make your next move or die."

There seemed little doubt now as to who slipped the Devil tarot into his journal before, but what was the purpose? These cryptic messages, these little taunts and odd discussion points indicated something deeper. What was underneath the words? There was something there, Jon could smell it. A formless lump of meaning without definition. A riddle that only time could unravel.

"How do I do that?"

"The fact that you ask means you're heading in the wrong direction."

"And where are you? What number do you think you are?"

A laugh, deep and sinister. "Wrong again. Who cares where I am, it's where I'm going that's important. Your sister up there has a very important part in my future. That's all you get."

Jon was dismissed with a cologne-clogged wave of Father's hand. Fine by him, Jon had something to do. First he biked over to a payphone next to a dilapidated convenience store. There was only a 30-70 shot the thing was working, as ripping out the receiver by the cord was a popular pastime of the local pre-teen potheads. He had little other choice, though. Jon didn't trust the phones at home anymore. If there were hidden cameras everywhere, a tap on the lines was not out of the question.

He dropped a quarter in and called Michael.

"You still got that video tape?"

"The one I'm not supposed to watch? Yeah, it's here under my bed."

"Good. You *haven't* looked at it, have you?

"No." A little defensiveness in his tone. "Why are you asking? Do you need it?"

"Not right now. I'm just . . . just making sure."

"Okay. Let me know."

As he hung up, Jon noted an uncommon lack of curiosity by Michael about the tape. Well, either he's seen it by now or not. As long as he kept quiet and the tape was safe, that's all that matters.

That idea flitted from his mind, as did everything else Father had said to him. It was the same thing that had been distracting him since school that had made him so anxious and filled with hope. By itself, the event was a little thing, but it filled Jon with wondrous and beautiful anticipation, and warmed every inch of him with love and lust.

On his way out the door to unchain his still borrowed bike from its post, he had spotted a group of Italians all yelling at each other by the cars their parents had bought for them.

The cause of the argument was lost in the furor of the two males butting into each other, and the others loudly cheering. Among the horde was Gabbaducci, who was thoroughly enjoying himself, screaming for blood to be spilt. He looked pale, tired. Maybe the beginning of something bad happening, Jon prayed.

Next to him, as usual, was Maria, beauty glowing off her, watching the yelling. Then she turned and stared at Jon. Not just looked, but openly stared. And when their eyes met, she smiled—a sweet, welcoming smile that stirred every molecule in his body. It was the greatest feeling ever. A moment indelibly stamped on his soul. Romeo and Juliet's first dance.

Gabbaducci caught her looking and snatched her away, but that didn't erase the moment. The breath caught in his throat. Was this going to happen? Would she be his?

Reveling in the sweet anticipation, he rode over to Louis's house. In the daylight, the place seemed even more cluttered with weird garden knickknacks and a partially disassembled motorcycle in the driveway. Louis's father and two younger brothers were on the lawn trying to fix a gas mower that had conked out halfway through the lawn. Each had their own opinion.

"Told you the durn spark plugs been disconnected."

"No, it ain't."

"Well, it's dirty then."

"I tol' you the grass is too high." And it was high.

"You can't have the gauge so low or else it's gonna keep clogging up the system."

"Hit the carburetor. Make sure the gas is flowing in."

"Hey there, Jon," Mr. Norton, Louis's father, greeted him in a friendly manner. "Been a while. You looking for Lou?"

"Yes."

"Go bang on the door, his Mother'll get him."

They went back to spinning theories about the mower. Jon stepped onto the sagging porch. It was so rickety that every time he had done so in the past, he was afraid one of his feet was going to break through the old wood and get torn up on rusty nails or ripped off by a snarling animal underneath, but the structure held and he negotiated through a collection of discordant wind chimes. None of them blended musically with the others. Louis's mother had collected them from dollar stores in the five different states that the family had drifted through.

His mother cheerfully said hello and called up the stairs for Louis to come down.

"I'll let you boys talk," she said.

What came down was not Louis Norton, or not the same teenager that Jon knew. Streaks of white shot through his once bountiful head of blonde hair. His movements had a listlessness to them. And there was something else, something he couldn't put his finger on.

"Hello, Jon," Louis said flatly.

"Hi," Jon paused. How should he broach the subject of what happened at Goodleburg. "Some kind of time the other night, huh?"

"You could say that, but in a way it hasn't ended for me. We called up a soldier of Hell with our satanic game and paid the price for it." He eyed Jon up and down, really looking at him for the first time. "Or I did, at least."

"I know it was weird, but—"

"It wasn't just the spook. Off in the woods where I went for safety there were things. Things old and awakened. Things waiting for the end of the world and becoming impatient. They got senioritis, because it's soon to happen."

Jon remembered. He remembered the sensations of doom emanating from the cemetery visions. There was no arguing it away.

"What kind of things?" he asked.

"Things with ragged shapes, like half-torn shadows puffed up with poisonous gas and sickly yellow spots of light puncturing through. That's all I could see. There was more to them, I could feel it, but my eyes couldn't take it in."

His head shook compulsively as he spoke. As if he were fighting some primeval instinct to suppress the evil events.

"I fell there," he said, "into their world. One step and one half of my brain. Like melting between molecules. They circle in an endless loop, the lights and shadows, looking to strike out, to grab life's form. They are all minds and spinning energy embedded in rock. They whispered weird secrets that I am only beginnin' to understand. And they are anxious to come here."

"I see."

"No, you don't. They want to come *now*, because later they won't be able to. Judgement Day is near."

"Ah. With the Antichrist and Armageddon . . . "

Louis nodded gravely. He was a believer.

"That's why I dropped out from that school. It's full of sinners. I left part of my soul behind in that half space, Jon. I have to atone and get it back before the Rapture, when all good Christians are called to Heaven before the final battle between Jesus and the Devil. My parents agree."

"I've never heard that before."

"It's there in Revelations. Look it up if you think I'm a liar."

'I didn't say that."

Louis stared at the screen door for a long time before blankly saying, "You get out of here, Jon. You done bad things, but you're not a bad guy. Try to save your soul if you can, but you need to go and don't come back."

Louis went back upstairs and that was the last Jon ever saw of him. The entire family up and moved two months later.

"I'm sorry Jon. It's for the best," Louis' mother called after him as he left the house.

Half a block away, it suddenly dawned on Jon what was bothering him the most about Louis. It wasn't what he had said, but how he looked. His eyes! Somehow his friend's eyes had changed color and shifted from steely blue to dark brown.

The next day at school, a balled-up note was tossed at him in a crowded hallway. Inside, scrawled in a woman's hand, was Maria's name and phone number. Was this real? Was this a sick game? He looked around, all breath sucked from his body. Neither she, nor anyone from her group were about.

Did he dare? Did he dare disturb the universe? Make the call? Are you kidding? Hell yeah, he dared! This is what he'd been waiting for. The rest of the day, he found it difficult to walk, he was so stiff with anticipation.

He biked with difficulty to a payphone after school, still afraid of bugs at his own house, and gave her a ring. After an agonizing eight seconds, her mother answered and called Maria to the phone.

"Hello?"

It was indisputably her voice. Breathy and brash mixed in a seductive tonic that he couldn't resist.

"Hi, it's Jon."

Dead air.

Oh shit! He was an idiot! Had he fallen for a prank? Was someone fucking with him? Who? Who? Must be Gabbaducci, that asshole. Blood burned inside his cheeks. The world could crumble to a mote of dust and all life swept away into a black hole, and Jon would welcome it to hide his shame.

"Hi," Maria said at last, very happy. "I'm glad you called."

All that negativity fell away like a snake shedding his skin. The world bloomed into bursts of bright color and light. You could get drunk on the air and Jon felt as if he had.

"I'm glad I did too."

"Yes."

Now it was Jon's time to fill the line with dead air. His mind hit a blank. Everything drained away. Christ, he was going to come off as a spaz, a loser, a dope with a tied-up tongue. Say something! Say something!

"Sh—should we go out sometime?"

"I'd love that."

"Great. How about—?"

"Tomorrow. I want to see you."

Very nice. "Tomorrow."

"And you got to take me to some place nice. I'm not some cheap whore, you know."

"I never thought you were."

"Good, because I don't like cheap guys. There was one prick who took me out to that hot dog stand on Sheridan, you know? Thought he could get into my pants with a foot long and some greasy curly fries."

"Heh, really?"

"Yeah, then he tries to make a move on me and I'm like get your fucking hands off me, creep, or I'll bite your dick off."

"I'm not cheap."

"Good. I want to go to Lombardos."

The woman had expensive tastes. While not the most ostentatious of restaurants, Lombardos had the reputation of subtle elegance and such atmosphere did not come cheap in the world of fine dining. However, was he going to say no with the prize in sight?

"That's doable."

"Great. Pick me up around seven."

Now all he needed was a lot of money and a car.

Michael wasn't all that excited about his friend's success. In fact, Michael seemed damned angry that his friend's wish came true and his own seemed stuck in limbo. Maybe it was the fact there was much more strife in his household. Apparently, several letters from colleges had arrived for Michael and his mother had thoughtlessly thrown them out, thinking nothing of them, uninterested in whether her son had been accepted by his choice of colleges. They were screaming at each other when Jon approached their screen door.

"I didn't know," his mother yelled.

"They were addressed to me! That's all you needed to fucking know."

"Watch what you say to your mother," Michael's father butted in. "It was a mistake."

"One that could ruin my life!"

"Ah, please, gettin' into college, big fucking deal. You're not going to get anywhere with it, so stop wasting everyone's time."

"You don't know."

They both just laughed at their son, who burst out of the house and ran into Jon, sobbing. They went around back, past a pile of half-filled paint cans that Michael's brother had been sniffing, to a trio of trees, their adventure spot from younger days. It took a while for him to calm down, which he did by throwing pinecones at an old shed. Then Jon's pronouncement riled him back up.

"When's mine gonna kick in?"

"I don't know. I thought you'd be happy."

Michael only grumbled and smashed a pinecone against a tree. Jon offered up how pale Gabbaducci looked the other day as a peace offering.

"So what?" Michael fumed. "You got a hot girl lusting after you, what did I get? Oh, he feels a little queasy. His fake tan needs touching up. He has the sniffles. Big fucking deal."

"Give it time. That's all I'm saying."

Michael sullenly nodded.

"I need your help to get a car to pick her up for the date."

"What do you want me to do? I don't have one."

"You got one before. The van from that Brian Elder guy."

"Ah. I don't know how to get hold of him, except at Snakeland. I don't know where he lives or even that much about him. He had his own reasons for helping me."

"I guess I'll ask around there then."

"He seemed kind of dangerous. I don't know how exactly, but he had that aura of being capable of great evil. Didn't he?"

Jon thought about it, but every argument was overridden by daydreams of Maria's curly hair, scented with female attraction. Phantom sensations tantalized him: Of his hands running over her perfect skin, her shapely breasts, moist mouth. All other ideas were driven out.

"Don't care. I'm doing it."

CHAPTER 10

BLESSED ARE THE VICTORIOUS

LOMBARDOS WAS NOT a small place, but it was carefully designed so that every table felt intimate. It was close, warm but not hot, with tasteful, but not distracting, art about the room. Taken as a whole, each room in itself could be considered a work of art, so elegantly did every table, chair, color, and painting swirl together.

Jon did not notice any of this. All he had eyes for was the young lady across the table slurping down lobster ravioli. He picked at his salad, filled with odd vegetables he'd never heard of and sipped a diet Coke, served to him in a wine glass to help make him seem grown up. As he did so, Jon mused on what it had taken to bring them both to this spot.

After Jon had told him of the success the previous day, Michael had stormed off up to his room, predictably reciting one of his foul limericks.

"There died a young girl named Maria,
Well known for slutty behavior,
When the priest thought her shriven,
And fitted her for heaven
He cried, 'Go on and fuck the Savior!'"

Sour grapes. Michael would just have to get used to the taste of them. Jon had bigger things to worry about. Maria. Eventually he would get back to figuring out what his parents were up to, he told himself. Right now, he needed to take care of this. In fact, it was all he could think about, no matter what else happened. Jon took stock on what the date required. Even if the girl was charmed, that didn't mean he shouldn't put his best foot forward. First was money.

Well, that was easy. He waited until the old man was busy elsewhere, then snuck into the "hidden" safe. So much money was piled up that his parents wouldn't miss five hundred. Or he hoped they wouldn't. Father seemed very busy this week, disappearing for fourteen hour stretches and Mother had come and gone. She was now dragging little Catherine around to another set of beauty pageants. Oh, screw it, this was his chance. Even if he had to pay off Hell afterwards, it would be worth it to fulfil his wet dream fantasy.

Several new documents placed on top of the money had caught his eye. It was a deed, an old land registry on top of a modern reiteration of the same information, and a transfer of title and bill of sale to a company called Bright Dawn Cleaning Supplies, Inc. The title was for Goodleburg Cemetery. Could you buy a cemetery? Jon had never heard of such of thing. He guessed it might be possible if the graves were on private land. Goodleburg was one of the oldest cemeteries. It had certainly been around before any current laws on the books. Maybe its private status had been grandfathered in.

Was it Father who had been spying on them that night? Either him or some flunky, like that man

Absolom, who had disappeared after that day. What had he and Father been talking about? Memories of their three-way with his mother had driven away the rest of the details of that afternoon.

As to why it was bought, that was easy. They needed it for its soft properties to better contact the beyond. Guess the basement wasn't big enough, or malleable enough, for whatever Father had planned. It must be something big. Jon knew Father wasn't an idle boaster. The old man was up to something.

That was all the thought Jon had given the mystery. He was a man with a mission. After closing the safe, he had snuck back into the secret room to rewind the tape just a bit. Inside he saw that the old bottle of whiskey had been replaced with a new unopened one.

Then came the vehicle. He had his license, but there was no way to borrow Father's BMW. The St. Fond patriarch kept the keys in his pocket at all times, and Mother was still gone on her trip.

He was forced to go with his first inclination and get Brian Elder's van. This had been daunting. It meant dragging himself off to Snakeland and listening to dull people pretend they're clever, until he could drop the fateful question on where the old man might be found.

Most of the poseurs turned pale at the question and refused to talk. They started like they'd been slapped and changed the subject. One fellow with a forgettable face and a pink mohawk just shook his head back and forth until he vomited. There was only one person, a rotund woman, who liked wearing operatic Viking gear, who whispered, "I heard he rents a room over on Windspear in the University Heights area."

That was a jog. The area was in Buffalo proper, near the massive state college, where all the Ivy League rejects ended up. Once a proud Irish working class neighborhood where everyone knew each other, the whole of it had been renovated into transient apartments for the college crowd. As the occupants tended to move after a year, the absentee landlords let the houses fall apart, doing just enough to keep the lazy building inspectors off their backs.

Without knowing exactly where Elder was on the long street, Jon rode up and down it endlessly. Whenever he tired, the vision of a naked Maria spurred him on to keep pedaling until he spotted the same van Michael had gotten.

He strode confidently on to the house porch, the building was a duplex, and banged on the front door. Thick curtains flickered on the ground floor and the old man appeared at the door, dressed in a sauce-stained T-shirt that bore the legend "whip inflation now." He walked outside in flip flops worn down to its last layer of foam rubber.

"Why, it's the melancholy douche. How fares Demark?"

Jon brushed off whatever the hell that meant. "I want to hire—"

"Oh, that's different!" Elder squealed and hustled him inside.

The first thing Jon noticed was that the curtains weren't actually curtains at all. Both the walls and windows were covered with thick sheets of linoleum, while the hardwood floor was bare, except for pizza boxes.

Everything in the place was hand-me-down and

makeshift. Instead of a table, there was a giant spool that used to coil industrial strength cables. Milk cartons substituted for chairs. A bunch of old gym mats and flat pillows were his bed and sofa. A little black-and-white portable TV rested on the floor. Jon noticed it was the same type he had in his room.

"Uh, nice place."

"Don't pay any attention to it. I got taken in by a linoleum salesman once and didn't want the stuff to go to waste." He plopped down on the mats. "So, who's the mark?"

Jon remembered Elder gave his profession as psychic assassin. "Oh, no, no. I just want to hire your van for the evening."

Elder was disappointed and mumbled into his chest for a while until Jon threw a c-note at him. That perked the old man up and he ran into a back room to root about for the keys.

"You have to fill it up with gas," he called.

"Fine."

Jon peaked at the backroom. It was filled with antique oddities tossed about on cheap fold-out card tables. Weird devices of smoked glass and metal and ancient bronze astrolabes, used in older days to navigate the seas, lay cluttered together like the discarded science that spawned them. Yellowed papers, pieces of parchment, vellum documents, and what looked like papyrus codices were heaped around a state-of-the-art Commodore 64 computer and at least fifty square floppy disks. The monitor was propped up by a large book made of several thousand pages, with a thick leather cover and sealed by a brass clasp. Anatomical charts covered the walls. Little notes were taped all over them. What they were specifically about was a mystery. The alphabet used was unknown to Jon, assuming it wasn't just gibberish.

Brian Elder jangled the keys.

"Got 'em. I need it back tomorrow. Also, don't get pulled over 'cause there's no insurance."

It was a stretch and a haul and a pain, but finally he got the girl and made it to her dream date. He only hoped that it would translate into something more at the night's end. There was a little hiccup when he first picked her up. Maria wrinkled her nose at the old van smell as she got in.

"Jesus, where did you pull this wreck from?"

Jon didn't respond. His every impulse kicked him to try and please her, to apologize, and hope she would be placated, but Father's words floated in his head. *It isn't nice guys who finish last. Weak ones do. You've all been brainwashed to assume that being a submissive to a woman's ever-shifting wants is somehow being a 'good guy.'* He wasn't going to fall for that. Still, he couldn't bring himself to say something back, afraid she would walk. Even with a spell on her, she seemed pretty strong-willed. Silence was his middle ground.

The van needed new shocks and brakes, making it a rocky ride. She "eeked" and "ooped" at every bump and jolt and whined about the ripped leather seats, but Jon kept his mouth shut. Things got better at their destination. He let her order whatever she wanted. That impressed her.

And as she gobbled away, he drunk in her beauty and the anticipation of later made him dizzy. So intoxicated was he that he overlooked all the red flags her personality kept tossing into his face.

Like the fact that she dropped f-bombs as if they were commas,

"I fucking love the fucking scampi here. It slides like fucking butter down my throat. That's what they're fucking known for. That and deserts. I'm going to get the fucking crème brûlée."

Or that she gossiped incessantly.

"She fucked at least half of the school. Margie just can't keep a cock out of her mouth. I heard that she even did one of the janitors, the one with the lazy eye. I mean, I don't know, but I believe it. She gets around."

Or that she didn't have a nice thing to say about anyone.

"Margie's my best friend and all, but after lunch her breath always stinks. I can't fucking stand it. I'd tell the bitch to brush her teeth, but she can be so touchy. I hate people like that."

Or that she felt she deserved to be taken care of by someone for the rest of her life.

"My father only makes $60,000 a year, so he's kind of a fucking loser. I don't know how my mother stays with him. He's always saying, 'That's too expensive' or 'We gotta save money for retirement.' If a man can't keep you in this year's fashion, why fucking bother with him? Move on to someone who's got the goods."

None of that mattered. None of it registered. Especially as the moment this evening revolved around inched closer and closer. The bill was paid. The generous tip—only slapped down to impress her—was shelled out. As they reclaimed the rickety van from the valet, she rubbed against him and whispered the magic words,

"Let's go back to your place."

Bump, bump, roll, shake, and rattle. Pothole. Car crash. Kids playing street hockey. Red light. Red light. Red light. The city itself conspired to slow him down. With that delay came anxiety. Would he be any good? What *was* good? He didn't want her running around talking smack about him like she did with everyone else. Could he even get it up? He never had a problem in the past, but doubt lingered now that the crunch was on.

The moment arrived. He lurched to a stop in front of his house. He fumbled with the front door key. Suddenly the mechanism was an intense puzzle. She tackled him as soon as it cracked an inch.

They tumbled across the antique carpet. Lips locked. Ass grabbed. Her hair fell across him. Gorgeous curls, all filled with sweet pheromones. Her breasts, firm melons of perfection, pressed hard against his body. His member pressed hard in return. No problems there.

Thump. Grind. Thump. Kiss. Was anyone home? Could anyone hear? Jon didn't give two shits. Let them enjoy the show. The moment came. She reached down into his pants and grabbed him. Oh, mama! He almost lost it right there. He rolled her over and slid his hand beneath her jeans. Quivering. Moist. Dripping. Just waiting for it.

Clothes hastily pulled off. Tossed here and there. Bra across the couch. Briefs atop the lamp. Naked bodies in fluid motion. Pulled together hard, as if they were trying to absorb each other. And then—

"We're home."

Mother and Catherine stood in the door, back from the pageant circuit. Both stared down at the naked teenagers. The younger one was goggle-eyed as she peered at their genitalia. This was something beyond her world view. A defining moment in a young person's life and not in the way you want it to be.

"That's my grandmother's Oriental rug!" Mother screeched. "You lousy little fuck."

Maria leapt up, snatching up what clothes were in arm's reach, and bolted into the night. Jon was about to run after her, but—

"Cover yourself up, please."

By the time Jon pulled his pants on, Maria was long gone. Last he saw, she was hopping down the street, one leg in and one out of her jeans.

"What are you doing? What are you doing? What are you doing?" she yelled at herself all along the way.

He drove around, but she had vanished into the wide labyrinth of side streets. Blue balls assailed him. The pressure was incredible.

Back at the house, Mother yelled that he was going to have to hand scrub the carpet to remove his stink from it. Never mind that her oldest daughter had vomited and drunkenly urinated on it repeatedly over the years. Jon brushed past her. She was a gnat on his windscreen. Catherine leered at him from her doorway.

"I saw your thingy," she said. "It's ugly and small."

"So's your fucking face," he snapped.

Catherine's face registered a satisfyingly shocked expression. He slammed his room door. Manual relief once again tonight. It didn't take long, though he begrudged the entire world for having to do it.

Jon spotted Maria the next day at school. She was across the hall with her usual guido gaggle, staring at him. The girl just stood with them, not interacting. They asked her something to which she didn't reply. Then one of her friends, Margie the skank, caught her gaze and saw it led to Jon. All the girls sniggered. Jon was going to approach her, but the bell rang and he had to scamper in a different direction.

The next time he caught up with her was during lunch. They passed close by, Maria still with her cackling foul-mouthed friends. She rubbed a hand clandestinely across his chest. The sensation nearly drove him crazy. He walked funny the rest of the day.

Michael was angrier than ever over the development. He kept repeating, "When's it gonna be my time?" Then snarled profanities at his friend. They sat at a lunch table across the room from Gabbaducci's tribe.

The Italian was there laughing and sneering in his regular manner, but he was even paler. Band-Aids covered his forehead and his eyes had a sunken hollow look. A couple of times he nearly doubled over with coughing fits. Michael cheered up a little at the display, but it still wasn't enough.

"The demon gets the blood and all I get is a case of the sniffles."

"It wasn't a very big cat," joked Jon. A smile snuck over Michael's face in spite of himself and they both laughed.

They stopped when Kathy seated herself in front of them. Each day she looked a little worse. Her eyes were as red as rust. She was unkempt, hair sticking out every which was. The girl looked as if she'd only been washing her face in tears.

"Jeez, Kathy," Jon said, worried, "is that stuff at the cemetery still bothering you that bad."

She tried to choke up a few words, but nothing came out except a low wail. He skirted around the table and gave her his arm to rest on. She sobbed into it for a few minutes. Michael rolled his eyes.

"Hey, it's over now," Jon said to her. "You'll never have to deal with it again "

"It's not that," she sputtered. "My parents . . . No one's seen them in days."

"Are you sure?"

"Of course I am. What a stupid question. The other people they were with said that they went to bed one night and . . . and—They just disappeared. All of their clothes and money were in their room. Only their notes and photos and cameras were missing."

"Are the police doing anything?"

"Pfft. The Mexican police? Might as well hire Mr. Magoo to find them. Oh, God. Oh, God!"

Jon held her a little bit. He could offer no other comfort except empty clichés on how everything would be all right.

An uproar from the other table startled them. Maria had begun staring at Jon as he comforted Kathy and her friends poked some fun. Gabbaducci had grown jealous, or maybe just angry, and slapped the girl. She spit in his face and he punched her again. The lunchroom attendants jumped in and Gabbaducci was hauled off kicking and swearing.

Thus ended the entertainment for the period. After school, he drove Brian Elder's van back home. The old man seemed surprised, as if he'd forgotten that he had a vehicle. Purely out of curiosity, Jon asked how much it would cost for Elder's psychic assassin services. The rest of the money in Father's safe gave him ideas. Elder quoted a ridiculously high price.

"You don't get many to take you up on that offer, do you?" Jon asked, waving at the dingy apartment.

"Only people of quality. Way above your shithole station."

Jon left the old charmer without a retort. He might need the van again. It was a good thing he held back, for later on that night Jon received a phone call that made him seriously consider taking up the crackpot's services. It was dark and Jon had dropped off early in his room. He was awoken by a violent shaking from his mother.

"Call for you. Don't be all night."

He grabbed the receiver off his desk and gave a greeting.

"Is this fucking Jon?"

It was Gabbaducci. What the hell? Some other weird background noises came through the line. He couldn't quite make them out.

"Yeah. It is."

"Oh, yeah, Jon. Heard you've been giving my girl a hard time."

"What? No."

"Don't fucking lie to me asshole. Ugh. I know it."

"Look dude—"

"Don't fucking dude me you piece of shit. She's my woman! You understand? You try to talk to her again and I'll blow your fucking chest out. I got a gun and I know how to use it."

A squeal in the background and some more grunting, then evil laughter from Gabbaducci.

"You know what else I'm doing while talking to you? I'm showing this bitch who she belongs to."

"If you hurt her . . . "

More laughter. Another squeal.

"Lookie at the white knight coming to rescue the fair maid. Forget that shit, pussy. Ugh. I'm not hurting her. I'm fucking her. Fucking her hard. Right, baby."

Maria's voice floated in from the background. "He's fucking me hard."

"And you love it!"

"I love it."

She didn't sound like she was being forced. Just the opposite.

"I've got my cock right in her ass as I'm calling you a faggot. The only thing hurting her is how big my dick is. It's tearing her up. Blood and everything. First time. Anal virgin. But she can't get enough, right?"

"I can't get enough," she moaned. "I want more."

"So, stay away, or you're a fucking dead man. I'm hanging up now 'cause I got to blow my load in this bitch."

Click. Dead air.

Jon just stood there stupidly holding the phone. The surrealness of the call numbed him. He dropped the receiver back in it cradle and plopped back in bed. The phrase *that was weird*, kept repeating in his head. Course, what did that mean in the context of the charm? Had it worn off? Maybe Gabbaducci had cast one on her as well. Or maybe the jerk was full of shit and that had been a different girl. Sure had sounded like Maria, though.

However, even if Gabbaducci wanted to back up his threat, he was in no shape to. Next day during gym, he collapsed climbing a rope. He had shimmied a quarter of the way up, then fell unconscious. From what Jon heard, he had hit his head pretty hard. The ambulance took him off with Michael snickering in evil glee. Jon couldn't really blame him, but he felt his friend might've hid it till they were alone. There were still buddies of Gabbaducci lurking about who enjoyed causing fights as much as the bully did.

Later on at home, a minor crisis erupted as Michelle nearly died again. While watching the TV through a haze of various illicit substances, she must've snorted one drug too many. One moment she was sitting, unsuccessfully trying to light a cigarette, the flame bobbing back and forth in front of the paper cylinder. The next, she keeled over.

Seems to be the day for that, Jon thought. How long until they attended her funeral? As they all wrestled with her body and ran about trying to revive her, a task so often repeated now that it had become mundane, the doorbell rang.

Catherine joyfully yelled that she would get it and, as they were connecting the IVs into Michelle's track-laden arms, she called out, "Jon, that naked girl is here."

Maria was indeed standing at his doorway, though she wasn't naked. He looked around the porch, checking to see that there wasn't a violent guido just out of sight. A sleek yellow Chevrolet Corvette was parked in the driveway. He was about to ask whose it was when he noticed the license plate, "MARIA1". That was her car? Why the hell had she insisted that he drive on their date? More nonsense.

"Don't worry," she said. "With Vinnie in the hospital, no one cares what I do . . . or about you."

He stared at her, almost in a new light. The lust-tinted goggles had slipped after the other night and all of her flaws shined through. He saw how she slouched on one leg in her skinny knee-bearing skirt with bulky pink sweater. He finally saw the dull stare in her eyes that looked on everything with disinterest. Even the way she popped her gum smacked of self-indulgence. The world was there to serve her.

Something changed in Maria, however, whenever her gaze alighted on his face. It became hungry, fanatical even, then it darted away and returned to its bored and detached view of the world. She seemed to be trying to keep from looking straight at him.

"Some phone call last night."

"Yeah, that's like what I wanted to talk about. I feel kinda bad."

"Oh, do you? I thought you were done with him."

"Why do you think that?"

"We went out on a date and almost . . . you know?"

"So?"

He honestly didn't know how to respond to that. Mark the sign of the whore, boys. You deal with one, you should know what to expect.

"I don't—"

"Look," she interrupted, unsure how to continue. She wasn't used to dealing with things. Didn't like it. She'd always had Daddy or some loud idiot to handle the hard parts of her life. Now, she was on foreign territory. "I don't know what's going on with me. I mean, you're not the kind of guy I go for. You're not really good looking and you don't work out so your arms are ropey and you don't have any real money, though you pretend you do, and your van's a joke and you don't like any cool stuff or listen to cool music. I mean, do you even know who Madonna is? Or the Bangles?"

Jon did and couldn't have cared less.

"Their music speaks to me. It defines what's going on in my life. You have no idea how important it is to me. It's like everything. You don't know."

No, he didn't, but he knew enough womancraft by now to pretend he did.

"I like it too."

She snorted. "Yeah, right. Jon, you have nothing that appeals to me. I mean Vinnie's got a way bigger dick and he knows how to use it good. But somehow, I can't stop thinking about you. Every time I see you, something pulls at me. It tells me to have sex and that I should be in love with you, even though I don't want to and never really could."

This wasn't what Jon had bargained for. He assumed that she would believe her feelings to be real, but this artificial insertion into her soul was grotesque. She was repulsed by him and never would be otherwise.

"So, I think we can just do it," she concluded. "We're never gonna be boyfriend and girlfriend, but we can bang and like get it out of our systems. Okay?"

Well, that sounded reasonable. A perfect equitable arrangement they could both live with. He knew it was sleazy, might even be considered rape on some level, but the goggles slipped back on and the only thought bouncing in his brain was how much he wanted to have this woman.

The door creaked open and Mother stuck her head out. Catherine crept behind her legs, giggling at the teens.

"Oh, good," Mother said. "You've both got your clothes on. There's a phone call for you, Jon."

"I'm in the middle of something here."

"Go ahead," Maria said. "I've got to think some more anyway."

"Can't blame her for needing a break from you," Mother snipped as he passed.

He pulled the receiver from the wall-mounted phone in the kitchen. Michelle was flopped over the table. Lines of fluid nourishment crisscrossed over her. Michael was on the other end, practically frothing at the mouth.

"Did you hear?" he laughed. "Today is the most beautiful of days."

"Hear what?"

"So, you didn't hear?"

"I'm real busy, man. Let me—"

"Gabbaducci's got AIDS! That's what he was hospitalized from. He's isolated so he can't infect other people. The family tried to keep it quiet cause of the shame, but it got out. His pals couldn't keep their mouths shut. It worked! It worked!"

Jon hung up without saying goodbye. AIDS. That was the big one. They'd given that asshole a death sentence. There was no coming back. Unlike Michael, he couldn't revel in Gabbaducci's downfall. They'd killed a man, as surely as if they'd shot him in the face. Even though the guy deserved it, even if he was the biggest asshole in the world, the gravity of it made Jon sick to his stomach. It was so much better when it was just a dream, a dark wish. Now that the dream was reality . . . part of his soul withered and dropped off.

A further thought smacked him. If Gabbaducci had

it, then— His head snapped up. His feet flew across to the porch. Maria was still there, smoking a cigarette.

"Did you know that Gabbaducci has AIDS and that's why he's in the hospital?"

"Yeah, so?"

"So, you've been having sex with him."

"It was only in the ass that last time."

"Are you kidding me?"

"You can't get it that way."

The term flabbergasted would be a mild version of Jon's reaction. Was she *that* dumb? "How do you think all these gay guys are giving it to each other?"

"What?" Clueless look. "I don't know, because they do like gay things to each other or whatever."

"Including anal sex!"

"Oh." Confused and a bit nervous. "But that doesn't mean—"

"And you've had sex with him before, even after he started to look sick. He probably infected you a dozen times over."

Catherine crept about the periphery of Jon's vision, smiling her evil smile. Maria still didn't seem to get it. He shook her. Those curls of hair he loved fell all about, but now her beauty was gone. All Jon could see was the disease loitering at the bottom of her vagina.

"You need to go," he said. "Go home and get to a doctor. See if there's anything that can be done. Hopefully—"

He let it drop. She stood there for a moment, mouth opening and closing, like a fish gasping for breath. Then she booked for her yellow sports car and zoomed off at a dangerously high speed. Catherine began jeering at him the moment he stepped inside.

"You had sex with her and got AIDS? You're gonna have a baby and it'll have AIDS. You're gonna have an AIDS baby."

"*Shut up.*"

Stomach sinking, all his hopes and dreams turned to ash. He ran up to the second story. She was right behind him the whole time chanting, "*AIDS baby! AIDS baby! AIDS baby!*"

At the top, something snapped. This was too much. The final straw. Every humiliation, every disappointment, they piled on and on and now his reserve was broken. Jon backhanded the little girl as hard as he could. Catherine's body tumbled down the stairs, hitting each individual step. Her head veered over and knocked out a few of the railing spokes, making nasty cracking sounds that hurt just to listen to. She hit the ground face down. Catherine's left arm bent back up behind her with the hand facing the wrong way. A thin cry rose up from the little girl.

Mother dashed out to cradle her child. She let out an inhuman wail, filled with all the sorrows of the world. The motherly she-beast was unleashed. Anyone who came close to her would've been torn to pieces. Mother was so out of control, she couldn't muster up a coherent threat against Jon. All she did was bark high-pitched screams at him.

Someone gripped his shoulder from behind. Father. Jon prepared himself for a scolding, a beating, some other terrible type of punishment. None of that happened. Instead what he heard was, "Looks like things are going to be tense here, son. I've got some business down in Mexico. Why don't you come with me? And when I've got everything settled, I'll take you to a whorehouse to lose your virginity. Would you like that?"

Jon didn't feel that he could say no, even though for the first time in a long time, sex was the furthest thing from his mind.

CHAPTER 11

Vaya Con Diablos

TIJUANA, MEXICO—The rank scrotum sack of North America. Named after someone's syphilitic aunt—or tía—who had been run out of Spain after her whorehouse was burnt down for allegedly holding occult rituals in the wine cellar. The woman, Juana, ran to the New World and opened a trading post, offering hospitality and cheap native pussy to leftover conquistadors and Jews escaping the Inquisition.

The city would've ended up a cum-stained husk if, by luck, the American border hadn't been slapped right in front of it after the annexation of Texas in 1845. Since then, it's thrived on offering flimsy goods and illicit services to every gringo wandering into the country.

None of this was on Jon's mind as he flew into the airport attached to the region. The gravity of his actions still weighed him down, still clutched him like a tumor on his conscience. Father had been right to suggest he take this trip. For some reason, a change of scenery made all that horror seem part of another world.

This new world brought its own horrors, however, beginning with the seven-hour flight from Buffalo to Mexico. Jon had never been on a plane before, never really been on vacation before, and the sensations of taking off scared the shit out of him. White knuckled, he gripped the seat as the world dropped out below and he took to the sky. It was like that first drop on a roller coaster, only in reverse, where there was nothing else but the thin floor supporting your body. His belly floated and colon felt ready to empty. It was a horrible, bumpy, violent ride.

Father, seated next to him, had taken it all in stride, of course. This was a common interlude for him and he dealt with it by taking full advantage of the frills of the first-class passenger. Once the plane leveled out at cruising altitude, he dangled a glass of whiskey in front of Jon's face.

"Not bad," he said, "but not my preferred brand, as you know."

Yes, he did know. Glenlivet Nadurra. The brand of the bottle in the little surveillance room. Apparently, the elder St. Fond knew of Jon's snooping and let him in on the gag. Once again, Father toyed with him. How did a man gain such confidence? His whole livelihood might hang in the balance, but Father would never show an ounce of concern.

At first, this trip seemed like a reward for breaking his sister's arm and giving her a concussion. He didn't really need it. Jon had to admit the act itself was reward enough. The sensation of power was intoxicating, and he would be lying if he claimed he didn't want more. His brain, on the other hand, was still clouded over in guilt due to Gabbaducci's eventual fate.

Now he had this dangling barb about the whiskey jabbed at him at 30,000 feet. Did Father know, or was he trying to rattle Jon to give up the goods? Silence was probably the best defense.

Father tried again.

"I heard a good one the other day," he chortled into his drink. His third one so far.

"There was a young man from Tijuana,
Who declared, as he wallowed in guano,
'It may seem imbecilic,
To be coprophilic
I indulge in it just 'cause I wanna.'"

A limerick. Michael's little creative endeavor. Again, this might mean nothing. Father knew Michael. He could've discovered his friend's poetic habits through his surveillance of Jon. Father easily might be just shaking the tree to see what dropped out of Jon's mouth. Enough of that. He was going to do some shaking back.

"Do you know a guy called Brian Elder?" he asked.

"A sensible question at last. Yes, yes, I do."

That was more honest than Jon expected. Maybe the alcohol was loosening lips. "How do you know him?"

"He's been there all my life. I've never not known him."

"All your life? He must be—"

"Incredibly old and hasn't aged a day for all that time. Always had the face of a scrawny old man with black eyes. He was good friends with my great-grandfather."

"What is he? He's not really human, there's something—"

"Missing, yes." Sip, sip. "He commands himself with much more grandness than he actually possesses. Those who go beyond can snap at greatness, thrust oily hands towards the golden bead, and occasionally become a power unto themselves. Brain Elder tried, and what we see is the wreckage of a cosmic failure, or the residue of a monumental success. I've never been sure which. I don't think he knows either."

"But can he do things?"

"He has power of a sort, but he's crippled mentally and physically. What we see could be just the leftover humanity that a power beyond doesn't need, that was flaked off like a scab and tossed behind. We'll talk more about this after we touch down. There's someone I want to show you."

"Hold on. One last thing. Is he what he claims?"

A chuckle. "What's he claiming?"

"He says he's a psychic assassin. That he can get people to commit suicide by crawling into their heads."

Loud boisterous laughter. Father wiped his eyes and thrust the glass out to be refilled, which the servile steward quickly did.

"I'd say that there's a possibility that it was once true. Great-grandfather and he were sorcerer criminals in arms. They stole. They killed. They conned. They molested. Whether it is true *now* is up in the air." Sip, sip. Sip, sip. Father slammed the glass down in frustration. "Stop pussyfooting around. Time to connect the dots."

It was the moment. The one that had been brewing for months. The confrontation between father and son, but the moment had no dramatic feel. It was more of an anti-climax. A mystery that a two-year-old could figure out by now. No need for a pretense.

"You've been watching me through surveillance cameras in the house," he said.

"And."

"And Michael's been spying on me, too. You got Elder to give him the game and directed him to take us to Goodleburg Cemetery. Which you now own," Suddenly he remembered the conversation with Absolom at the dining room table, before the pair tag-teamed his mother. "Which you purchased from the Osborne Canning Company."

"Well, you know more than I believed you could work out. Very good. Your friend said you had no idea."

"How long has Michael been reporting on me?"

"A while now. I needed to direct things in a certain way and he was the easiest instrument."

"What did you offer him?"

"Michael has ambitions beyond that trash family of his and he had started poking around in areas that I keep abreast of. I offered to show him a way to power. And I did."

"He snapped it up with gusto."

"Thanks to you."

Jon turned and looked into Father's yellow eyes. Once again, he had to wonder what the older man knew. Why had he been manipulating Jon? He was about to ask but held back. It could be a trap. Or something he was supposed to figure out on his own.

Instead he asked, "What's going to happen to Michael?"

"What do you do with a tool that's no longer useful? Whether you remain friends is your decision, but I wouldn't want someone around who's betrayed me."

A fair point. However, Jon couldn't conjure up the energy to care. They had been friends, a team, surrogate family, for so long. He found it almost impossible to really blame Michael. His friend was desperate. With such useless parents, his dreams of getting away wasn't going to happen without outside help. Plus, with all the other surveillance Father had on him, it wasn't much of a betrayal at that. It was all beside the point. There was something else Jon wanted to know.

"I'm going to ask you a question," Jon said, "and I want a straight reply."

"Oh, very good! Ask away."

"Why don't you care about me?'

"I feed you, clothe you, and make sure you're educated. Would I do this if I didn't care?"

"You have to do that."

"No, I don't. I could throw you out. Plant drugs on you, and then report it to the police and make sure you're sent away for a few years. There are a number of possibilities. But I don't."

"Then why do you treat me—?"

"Because I am not a crutch for you to prop yourself up with. Follow your own path. Figure out your own problems. Be the solver, not the whiner. Be the man everyone wants to be, not the sidekick. That requires you to be strong. The more you can do on your own, the more confident you'll be. The more confident you are, the more people respect you."

"But—"

"There's no but. Everything your mother and I have done, the way we treated you, was designed to make you stand on your own and fight back. I've been waiting for you to retaliate for some time, hoping every day that this would be the time you lashed out and took control. Finally, my prayers were answered when you gave Catherine that concussion."

"Jesus, that's—"

"That's how the men in our family are raised. To be strong, to take command, to demand what they want. There are many who strut about with puffed-up attitudes, but are weak on the inside, writhing in pathetic self-doubt. The St. Fonds have long realized that to achieve the strength we desired in our younger generation, their personalities must be forged from struggle. From that struggle, true character would be seized."

"And what if I hadn't?"

"What do you do with the runt of the litter, with the undersized vegetable? You throw it away."

"Glad I could measure up."

"You haven't yet. A first step is just that, singular. It's promising, but a lot more ground needs to be covered."

With that proclamation, Father downed another drink and passed out for the rest of the flight. Jon did nothing but contemplate the false serenity atop the cloud line. The vapor thin peaks and valleys soothed him, lulled him to believe in a cotton-candy view of life, simple and peaceful. But he knew, all it took was one step beyond this plane and everything would fall to pieces.

The airport, like most airports, was a nightmare of waiting for some slouching oaf to actually do their job at a reasonable rate. Need the bathroom, stand in line. Need a quick snack, stand in line. Need to exchange money, stand in line. Need to check a passport, stand in line. Need to make a bribe to smuggle in contraband, stand in line. Luckily, Father's fluency of Mexican Spanish cut down on the red tape.

The airport, built in a futuristic style in the 1950s, hadn't been refurbished since that ancient decade. Everything was rundown and frayed around the edges. Occasionally, an advertisement featuring smiling Mexicans was slapped over mildew-covered walls, but it was like painting a dying plant green. Outside, a driver was there to escort them around and took Father's suitcases with disgusting servility. Jon's expectations had been low when he stepped out into the blistering Mexican sun, but as he observed this lawless city, he realized with shock that his sights had been way too high.

Tijuana was not an example of Mexico putting its best foot forward. Unshaven men ran around bartering gasoline for food. Toothless old women gummed week-old candy bars. Children with practiced sorrowful expressions sold individual sticks of gum at 1000% markups. Cheap goods were hawked from teardown stalls, their proprietors hurled every insult under the sun at those who didn't ogle their crap merchandise. Drugs of every sort was offered by seedy men with runny noses and faded jeans. Vines had grown through abandoned vehicles on sinister side streets. Beggars lined every street and crowded each corner, all of them had mastered the fake pathetic whine. All of them needed your damn money urgently.

Everywhere, tourists stumbled about. Wearing loud clothes and clean socks, they were all over: Drinking, buying drugs, haggling with prostitutes, marveling over the "handcrafted" native goods, dodging panhandlers, paying off corrupt cops, and gawking at the poverty and general degradation.

Father instructed the driver to pull over by a crumbling curb and got out.

"Time for a teachable moment," he said.

He approached two beggars sitting in the shade. Each was dressed in ragged clothes, with bellies exposed. Both held out feeble hands, asking for a donation so they could live.

"Por favour. Por favour," they screeched in unison.

Father sympathetically looked down at one and handed him a hundred peso note. The second beggar gawped at the charity and redoubled his entreaties, hands flailing for the generosity of this great man. Father once again looked concerned, then kicked the second beggar in the head. Blood and teeth fell out of the man's face. Father stooped back into the car and told the driver to continue on.

"What's the difference between my two actions?" he asked Jon.

"The first was good. The second evil."

"Wrong. The first took my money and gave me nothing in return. The second cost nothing and made me laugh. By my definition, the second was the good act. Do you see my point?"

"Laughs can be cheap?"

"No. Good and evil are subjective. A programming of society. Why am I supposed to feel good about handing my money to some human detritus? How do I know he's not a pedophile and I've accidently supported his filthy habit? We've been brainwashed by flabby liberals to feel guilty about wealth and success.

I don't. I never will. With a lack of guilt, you also lose your need to cleanse your soul by throwing money down the toilet."

"Some people like it."

"My point exactly. They give charity not out of a desire to help others, but because it makes them feel good. They pay for that sensation like any other vice. It's a rush, same as gambling, liquor, drugs, or loose women. The only difference is that it's the only one which allows people to be sanctimonious afterwards."

"But if these people are in genuine need?"

"Then they need to fix themselves. Look at the Mexican Stock Index. Financially, this country is doing great. The reason it hasn't filtered down to the lower classes is because of massive corruption. No handout is going to fix their shitbag country. I need to fulfill my genuine needs and *my* genuine need is to spend *my* money on making *me* happy."

They spoke no more on it and finished the ride in silence.

A massive water fountain bearing the legend, "Lomas de Agua Caliente", dominated the entrance to the neighborhood of their destination. It was immense with water shooting from the top to fill two successively large bowls, which spilled out into a beautifully blue-tiled pool beneath. Or it would have been beautiful, if the water hadn't been green.

They drove up to a spacious villa surrounded by high white-washed walls with elegant iron spikes and armed guards at the gate. The car breezed through after a brief conversation at the gate. The villa's rooms were large and airy, and tiled immaculately in brown and red. The furniture looked antique, while the guard's weaponry was very modern. They were met by two middle-aged twins, a brown haired male and female. Father introduced them as distant cousins to the St. Fond family, Arlo and Lola de Courriere. They were tanned but had a European tang to their bodies. Definitely descended from old conquistador stock. Both had hungry eyes that rarely blinked. A malevolence hung behind their irises.

"You have the nganga, tío?" asked the male, Arlo.

Father shooed away the servants and with magnificent aplomb produced the bowl that had once been stored in his private safe. The same one which had made Kathy's mother more excited than any sexual act. The one both her parents had come to Mexico to find copies of and then disappeared. That raised suspicions. Was Father involved? Jon had no idea how much clout the old man had in this country. It could all be a coincidence. After all, Kathy's parents had gone missing in Matamoros, literally on the other side of the country. Jon had checked.

The twins snatched up the bowl and probed it with cold fingers. They licked their lips and nodded as the artifact was inspected, practically swaying with serpentine hisses as they did so. Jon was about to ask a question when Father shot a finger to his lips.

"Absolom already inspected it and gave it a thumbs up," Father told them. "But take your time. We're going to get settled, maybe take a dip in that magnificent pool, then I'll introduce Charlotte to my son."

The twin's gaze lifted to regard Father as he said this, then stared into each other's eyes. Some indecipherable communication passed between them and they nodded. Servants came in and took their bags.

"She is in the wine cellar," Lola informed him.

"I think I'll bring her up for some fresh air."

"As you wish, tío," said Arlo. "The client's people informed us that he and his woman will be here tomorrow. No reason to delay."

"Indeed not."

At his room, Father informed Jon to save any questions until later. Jon didn't argue, jetlag began to hit him. The suitcase was thrown in a corner. He didn't see the point in unpacking. They were supposed to only be here a few days.

The room itself was large, dark beige, and filled with old credenzas and various knickknacks common at the beginning of the 20th Century. A four-poster bed dominated the room. Upon further inspection, he found that the frame was an antique, complete with silk drapes around the sides, but the mattress was firm and modern.

There was one creepy thing. All of the decorations consisted of photographs of the twins and a woman Jon guessed was their mother. Each was in the exact same pose, but the ages varied from photo to photo. The twins on the edges of the picture, holding hands, eyes downcast. Their faces almost obscured as they stared at the floor. In the middle was a plump older woman with dark curls and a pallid complexion. As an adolescent she must have been beautiful, but her looks had faded by the time the pictures were shot. Fat folds, wrinkles, and sagging flesh had chased away most of the beauty, however its shadow still lingered under the skin. An evil smirk, filled with contempt for anyone else, was chiseled on her face.

The only break in the pattern was the very last one. It was the same pose, but both the twins' heads were up and gleeful smiles painted their faces. The woman was there. There was something wrong, though. Something not properly conveyed in a still shot. The smirk was gone. Her face drooped even more. An oddness drifted about the eyes. They looked almost near-dead.

He heard a splash through the window and stepped out onto an outdoor balcony. Below, Father, well-toned and muscular, was swimming in a massive pool the shape of Mexico. The air was beautiful, languid, a universe away from the rest of the city. He lay down on the bed and succumbed to blessed sleep.

His dreams were more vivid than usual. He was in a giant concrete maze, being chased by two monster rats whose tongues whipped acid into the air. He could smell the rancid meat on their breath. Did one normally smell things in dreams? Jon, as he huffed and puffed away, couldn't remember doing so before. Then he stopped. If this was a dream, then these things couldn't really harm him.

The rats pounced. He was knocked down. The smells grew worse. Huge incisors bit into his shoulders.

Wake up. Wake up. Jon ordered himself, but that didn't happen.

The rats dragged the squirming Jon over to a blue pentagram, which lit up in electric lines. The monsters let him go and backed away, dragging their noses across the ground. A giant hand reached down from the swirling heavens above and grasped him.

A massive thumb pressed against his face and it

popped back like a Pez dispenser. There was no pain, just incredible pressure on his head. Another hand descended, holding a screw and a screwdriver. The screw was twisted and twisted into Jon's exposed upper palate until it punctured his brain.

The hands and rats blurred and washed away as if they were watercolor stains. He drifted in the warm embrace of a milky galaxy, eventually coming to rest on a plane of glass. Brilliant stars twinkled about him. Twin shimmering creatures, like showers of light with blue glowing eyes, floated to him. They took in his soul, measured it against a featherweight of love, and then cast him away.

Jon was poked awake by a decrepit maid and told, "Meester Fond ess downstares."

The smells of the dream still lingered in his nostrils. He changed clothes, tossing the dirty ones back into the case with the clean, and hurried down curving stairs to a sparsely furnished living room. Father was there in a plush leather chair. The woman from the photographs sat beside him in a wheelchair. A red blanket was tossed casually around her. Father rose.

"Jon, I want you to meet your great-aunt Charlotte de Courrière. The last of the Order of the Bright Dawn."

The Order of the Bright Dawn. The occult group which had created Dark Dungeons. Jon had tried researching them, but there was nothing. From the library, down to dark nooks where fact and myth blurred, there was no information on this group. After learning of Father's connection to Brian Elder, he assumed that the old man had lied about everything anyway. This revelation made him reconsider.

"Hello?" he said.

The old woman shifted, unresponsive. Jon stepped closer. She was sallow, pale, and deflated. There wasn't much going on inside, but she wasn't a complete vegetable. Her eyes would not look at anything directly, certainly not another human's. They seemed to seek out the middle distance between objects and gaze at nothing. She hadn't visibly aged since the final photo from upstairs, while her children certainly had. Another ageless wonder. His life was starting to get crowded by them. Father poured some brown liquid into a snifter.

"You're looking at the great magical failure, just like her organization," Father began. "She reached beyond to pluck power, to realize herself in totality, to become the one—the magus—and walk between the raindrops. This lump of flesh is the result."

"And she did this on the day Pearl Harbor was attacked."

"December 7th, 1941. A day that will live in infamy, but for a different reason to our family. It was the natural conclusion to a failed experiment," Father took a sip, then asked. "Who told you that date? Brian Elder?"

"Yes."

"You have an excellent memory. A trait to be nurtured."

"He also said the founder of the order, a Limo Brightson, exploded on that day."

"Limo Brightson was the name of the Dark Dungeons character of Limo de Courrière, Charlotte's husband. He took it on as his magical veil, his protective ego. She really ran the show. For some reason, Charlotte loved him, or so I was told. They attempted to ascend together by repeatedly using ancient rites to journey to the beyond, the world of symbols and dreams. One blew up. The other is *this* bag of flesh."

"What was this order?"

"It was a sign of the Roaring 20s. Magical societies were quite the thing and the upper crust couldn't get enough of them. Let's not forget, this was the age of Aleister Crowley. His Thelemite Society and the Hermetic Order of the Golden Dawn were big hits. Charlotte here wanted to recreate that success in America and become a mystical celebrity herself, which is an anathema to what the family teaches. Essentially the Order was the public face for our family's private life. Charlotte convinced the others that it was a chance to bring those with magical talents into the fold and those with the greatest would be allowed to marry into our line."

"From your face, I assume it didn't happen."

"There was a brief flare, which made the whole debacle look good for a moment, but it was blown out by the Great Depression. She and her society faded into obscurity, not even worth a footnote of history. A complete waste."

"You keep calling her a failure, but how do you know? Like Brian Elder, she doesn't age. Maybe *he's* the failure and *she* succeeded. This creature in the wheelchair could be the leftover bit of herself she shedded. Maybe her husband succeeded, too."

Father swirled the liquor in the glass. His yellow gaze flicked back and forth between Jon and the aunt.

"Hardly matters," he said finally. "Either way, I'd call it a failure."

Jon walked the dead streets of Tijuana. The place smelled worse at night. All the stale beer, vomit, and outdoor toilets let loose their collective stench after sundown, as if the city itself was expelling bad air from its lungs.

He stomped on broken pavement and kicked spare bits of debris into the gutter. A three-legged dog limped across the street, sniffed at a half-eaten taco and howled its joy to the moon. If only trash could make him so happy, Jon mused. But it would not do. Not do at all.

Earlier at the mansion, Jon was all posed to grill his father over this "family business" and their "private life." A secret which he seemed to be the only family member excluded from. One simple statement drove it all away.

"I promised you a trip to the whorehouse. Best time to go is now."

With the tastiest carrot ever dangling before his nose, Jon tossed everything else. Everything seemed good at first. The driver stayed on the luxurious side of the city. Mansions and villas, which stretched over a quarter of a mile. Large gates. Only masters and servants allowed. The pigs of the lower orders were shut out.

The brothel was the same. Comfort and luxury shone through with every stick of furniture, every velvet drape, every bra strap, and crystal glass. Top shelf liquor flowed like mother's milk. Cocaine was offered around on trays like canapés.

The Madame knew Father well. She twittered

about him as he dropped hundred dollar bills and made outrageous demands. They chatted away in Spanish as he felt-up delicious prostitutes, all willing—or faking with incredible skill—to please.

Father had two luscious senoritas on either side. They were coffee-flavored, firm-breasted, sharp-chinned, and slim-waisted. He said something to the Madame and waved to Jon. The woman's eyes widened. The other whores tittered and stared at him with practiced wanton eyes.

"Come with me, niño," said the Madame. "Eye geeve you wat you need."

He was led along a back part of the ground floor to a green door. The woman motioned for him to go through. Jon complied, then wished he hadn't. Beyond the door was the most disgusting woman Jon had ever seen.

Completely naked, she was bloated beyond human proportions. Skin ruptures and purple streaks of bubbling flesh crisscrossed her body. She looked like a bag of skin leaking human fat. Both her arms were gone, sheared off in some accident. All that was left were a pair of stumps and puffed out scar tissue.

Her face lit up on seeing Jon and she waggled her stumps and licked black crud from her lips. Various growths had sprouted like toadstools on her face. Only two teeth held their grip inside her maw, both at the very front, giving her a mole-like appearance. Bloodshot eyes beckoned him.

The excess body mass strangely ended at her knees, the gams beneath were thin and sheer. Might've been beautiful were they not attached to the rest. They were a snake charm for these two specks of beauty, the only to be found in the room, led to a foul rat's nest lurking between. It was evil-looking. Dank and greasy. Untrimmed and unwashed. Profane odors drifted about and grew stronger as one neared the fateful hole. A voice spoke up behind Jon.

"Some peeple like her, si?"

"No!"

Laughter. Lots of laughter.

Behind the Madame, many of the house's patrons had snuck up behind to witness Jon's dismay at the grotesque whore. The look on his face filled them with joy. Father was foremost among them, his top-dollar prostitutes still beside him. Only now one was on her knees, fellating him.

"What's the matter? I offered you a way to pop your cherry and there it is. Don't be rude and turn it down."

"I don't want that thing," Jon yelled.

He could feel frustration tears welling up.

Fight it down, Jon. Not now. Father wants you to fail. No matter what he says.

"It's a test of endurance," Father smirked. "If you can fuck that, you can handle any dirty job. An ultimate exercise in manhood."

"Oh, you're so full of shit."

"Maybe you're a fag. Would you like to take her place? Asshole into vagina?"

"Shut up. Why can't I get one like you got?"

"That's because it's *my* money renting this hole." He slapped the kneeling woman hard on the face. "If you beg for table scraps, don't complain when they're rancid."

"Fuck you. You're the biggest asshole in the world."

He took a swing at Father, something he had never

dared in the past. The defiance had bad results. Father jerked aside, his cock slapping out of the whore's mouth, and grabbed Jon's arm, then used the forward momentum to toss Jon down the hallway.

"If getting a hot woman to bed you is so important, you should've taken care of it yourself. Gone after it with your own resources. You'll always get less-than from others."

Jon ran from the room, knocking over an expensive prostitute. Then ran from the house, kicking aside an end-table filled with cocaine. Then ran from the neighborhood, knocking over several garbage cans. An act of childishness, maybe his last one ever. He had no money and nowhere to go, but he recklessly threw himself into harm's way to demonstrate his anger.

He wandered for hours, his mind darting from one impossible idea to another. Delving deeper and deeper under the poverty line, he withdrew into his mind trying to figure out his problem. He ignored his surroundings, preferring to mope, until Jon found himself surrounded by a horde of grinning Mexicans. A car pulled up, headlights blindingly bright. A pipe hit the back of his head. He was tossed into the car's trunk and driven away.

CHAPTER 12

DEAL WITH THE DEVIL

IT HAD BEEN DAYS. Most of it was spent in darkness, as his captors kept his head covered by a stinking burlap sack. After he first was kidnapped, the villains had surrounded him, licking their lips, each wielding a knife, a gun, a chain, or a broken beer bottle. They all had cheap clothes adorned by some bizarre accessory above their social rank. A ruby ring, a diamond stud, a glittering belt buckle bragging about the size of Texas. His shoes were taken, along with his leather belt. The crooks seem very interested in his teeth, and whenever a new member of the gang came in, they delighted in showing them off.

Only one spoke actual English—sort of spoke it.

"You money, eh?" the man asked, scraping a bowie knife across Jon's throat.

"I don't have any money."

"You *money*!" the man thundered, then reconsidered. "Papa? Daddy? Daddy?"

Jon nodded vigorously. "Oh, yeah, he's loaded. Money all over."

"Good. Good," the man smiled, showing an upper row of rotten teeth. "Where?"

He provided them with the address of the villa. That sent a wave of joy and whistles around the room. This was a fat catch. Their ticket to the big time, away from cheap piñatas and toilet water beer. The bag was dumped back over his head.

And that's what his world became. Pure darkness, tied to a chair, bored to high heaven. He could feel madness creeping around the edges of his mind, sliding in through unknown angles. Lights with no earthly origins sparkled, spelling out arcane words in alien tongues. Put together, they presaged secrets not meant for the human mind.

About how the original color of elephants was orange. About how the devil had been dethroned by ruthless businessmen of the modern age. About how rocks can talk, but you have to wait half a century for each syllable. About how the footfall of doom was edging to make its first toehold in the world. About how the spirit of the Universe, Spiritus Universum, had been thrown down and supplanted by the specter of the previous universe. All sentient races spawned after that were cursed as interlopers and doomed to be spiritually exiled. Humans were the first example.

Then the bag would be ripped away and the real world shone in, chasing off the sensory deprivation dreams and malformed stories. Food and water were dumped down his throat. The sack would be replaced over his head and the world of unbelief claimed him once again.

Over and over, his perception of reality shifted one way and then another to the point where he couldn't tell what was truth anymore. Eventually, the day came when they pulled the hood off for good. The whole gang was around him, smiling smugly at their fatted calf. Fifteen low-rent peasants, ready to rumble.

Strange as it sounds, even in his obviously vulnerable state, Jon felt superior to them. He looked at the scum, most we're in their late thirties and had done nothing with their lives, could do nothing, would never do anything. They could barely think. Give each one a million dollars and they would still be nothing but peasants in snazzy surroundings. Each would probably blow through it in a year.

"Your papa give dinero. Lucky you. He pay today and we send you home. Comprende?"

Jon just nodded. His throat was parched and raw. He was afraid speaking would hurt.

"You should say thank you to us for treetin' you so good, sí?"

A trickle of blood slid out of the talking Mexican's nose. The others laughed arrogantly at his words, once they had been translated. Blood then started to run out of another's nose, then another, then another, till they were all bleeding.

In the first few seconds, they were pointing it out to each other. Then they realized it was happening to them all. Terror gripped them and they jabbered in their native tongue. The blood poured out thicker and faster. They started screaming. Some ran. Others dropped to their knees clutching crucifixes and pagan fetishes. The rest were too stunned to react.

As they panicked and their hearts pumped faster, the blood flushed out of them at an increased rate. It flowed from every possible orifice. It leaked and leaked until they fell to the ground, shaking and shivering, then stopped moving altogether. Jon was left alone, tied to a chair with a room full of glassy-eyed corpses and a lake of blood.

For half a day, he sat like that. Watching rigor mortis set in. Smelling the rot churning in the dead men's guts. Scared beyond all reckoning that he would die there as well, only slowly from dehydration. He sent pleading deals to all sorts of unseen entities, begging for release, until he heard footsteps outside the hovel and Father kicked the door open.

"He's in this one," Father called.

The twins rushed in. The male snipped his bonds, while the female looked him over. Her fingers probed his head and body with the same sterilized lack of empathy she had while examining the bowl.

"It's fine," she said to Father.

It? Maybe he'd be better off with the kidnappers.

"Release *him* then," Father said. "I don't want to spend any more time around here than necessary. Feels like I'm getting a rash just standing in this dump."

At least five other dead men lay about outside, having blown their lives out of their nose. A warm can of Coke was shoved at Jon, then he was bundled off in the twin's car.

"You get kidnapped by the worst people, son."

Jon silently sipped his drink, too much in shock to register anything beyond the sugar water and stink of dried blood on his feet. As in response to Jon's thoughts, Father took off his own shoes, hand-tooled Italian leather loafers, and tossed them to the buzzards. The twins kept theirs on.

"Just bought the pair last week. What a waste."

The contents of the Coke can brought him around

a little. He shook off the mental cobwebs and looked outside. The kidnappers must've taken him to some abandoned cattle ranch in the wildlands around Tijuana. The land was desolate, bleached to nothing under the sun.

As they began to reenter civilization, he spoke up. "Was all that you?"

"No," came the sarcastic reply. "They all had fatal hemorrhages at the same time by coincidence."

"How?"

"We have ways," Father said.

"We have ways," the twins repeated simultaneously.

"More bargains with demons?"

All eyes, even those of the driver, turned and stared at Jon. The glare from the sun through the windows made these gazes look yellow. They were outside the skull, outside the soul, creatures beyond the sacks of flesh attached to them, exhibiting alien menace and evil contemplation. Then all of the occupants began laughing and returned to the human race.

This wasn't a mocking laughter, or an insane cackle, but one that expressed disbelief at Jon's ignorance. There was an aspect to it all that he missed, a puzzle piece not revealed. Once again, he was the fool walking toward the cliff's edge.

They arrived back at the house and Jon saw there were several more cars parked around. These were of poorer quality than anything the twins or Father would drive, yet they were still a cut above the average vehicle Jon had seen littering the streets of Tijuana. Inside the foyer, the scraping maid whispered something to Father.

Then the man did something Jon had never seen him do before. Sweat. He took a handkerchief from his pocket and dabbed it across his brow. Father pulled Jon close.

"Go take a quick shower, then come back down. We have business."

"Is he too tired, tio?" Arlo, the male twin asked.

"That doesn't matter. He just has to be there. We can't put these people off anymore. It's now or else the entire deal swirls down the drain."

"I'll just make sure he doesn't disappear again," Arlo said.

He grabbed Jon under the armpit and frog-marched him up to the room. Once there, he refused to speak again. As Jon cleaned up, the twin simply stared with blank intensity. Jon didn't think he saw the man blink once. Once ready, he was marched back down in the same manner, then into the cellar, then the wine cellar below. The wine cellar was odd in that it didn't contain any actual wine. There were racks and vats available, but they were all empty. A stack of twelve mattresses were piled on top of each other in a corner. They were well maintained, each had clean sheets attached, but he had no idea who they were for. The servants all went home at night, leaving just the twins and their vegetable mother.

Arlo pulled on a wine rack and tripped a hidden door catch. A fake rock wall, indistinguishable from the real thing, swung open and revealed a further flight of stairs. Soft lights and soft conversation drizzled up from below. The pair went down.

The sub-sub-basement was not much more than a hole. It looked half-finished. The floor was dirt and support beams propped up the ceiling. Dozens of black candles, shaped like human skulls, illuminated the pit. The sickening sensation grabbed Jon the moment his toe crossed the threshold. This was it. One of the soft places of the earth. The power was stronger here than he had ever felt before. He nearly vomited. Arlo had to help him down the final steps.

In the hole was Father, the other twin, the non-responsive aunt, a man and a woman, and two further people tied hand and foot on the floor with bags about their heads. The new man was in his early twenties with squinty eyes and a fashionable mullet. Wearing jeans and a leather jacket, he took in everything with a haughty air. The woman was dark-haired with an oval face and full lips. Although she was attractive, her body language was off-putting. Something about her radiated evil. Her tongue darted in and out and her thighs rubbed together sensually as if she were aroused. Both had their eyes on the cryptic bowl in Father's hands.

"Now that we're all here," Father said. "I want to present to you, Señor Constanzo, the ultimate find, the Holy Grail of your religion. Stolen by the conquistadors and now re-stolen by us. The nganga of Montezuma himself!"

Jon remembered Kathy's mother telling him that a nganga was a personal, spiritual altar, filled with bones and debris meant to give power to the shaman. What was the religion again? Palo Mayombe. Were these two strangers practitioners?

The woman's thighs rubbed even harder. The man's cynical expression hardened. He was no fool. Arrogantly, he gestured for the bowl, which Father offered up gingerly.

"Do whatever tests you wish. The bowl, the skull top, the paint—all of it will carbon date back to the time of that noble Aztec."

The man nodded and kept looking. The woman peered hungrily over his shoulder.

"As we told you, your religion is far older than you have been led to believe. It is part of the lifeblood of this land. It is integral to its nature. Palo is the one true religion of South America. All of the others are false. The ancient Aztecs used it to build an empire."

"But Montezuma fell," the man called Constanzo said.

"That's because he made the mistake of believing Cortez was a god, allowing the man an opportunity to steal this item. Had he not, the results would have been very different. If you add this power to your own nganga . . . Well, use your imagination."

The woman whispered fiercely into the man's ear. Constanzo nodded and placed the bowl on the ground. The Aztec symbols etched into its bone bottom shone out. Constanzo pulled a large pocket knife out, unsnapping a jagged blade from inside the hilt.

"I'm sure, Mr. Zanzibar," Constanzo said to Father, "that we could send away for all of these tests and they would say this-and-that in language no one understands, but there is only one true test."

"Oh, yes," Father replied, nonplussed about the wrong name he had been called, "but to get this power, you must embrace the old ways. All these Palo practitioners use less acceptable vessels to build their spiritual power. They are too scared to seize true might as the Aztecs did. Animals are fine for lesser men, but in the old times one built their might by human sacrifice."

Constanzo nodded. "That is the old way."

"And before I sell to you. I have to be sure you have the cajones to use this sacred bowl as the ancients did, as all the spirits of the land *demand* it be used."

Constanzo hesitated, then glanced over his shoulder and saw the woman staring at him, gauging his manliness based on his next words.

He hiked up his pants and said, "I have no hesitation. Bring me the creature."

"You brought them with you from Matamoros. Those packages we asked for."

The tied up woman was dragged over and the hood torn off. Though he had a sinking suspicion before about their identity, shock still smacked Jon in the face when he saw Kathy's mother trussed up below. A gag was still tied around her mouth, eating up her pleas.

"Say the rite, splash some blood around. See the power for yourself," said Father.

"I want her intelligence, so save parts of the skull to add to my nganga."

"But of course. You might want to take her tongue too. She was always making phone calls, waggling it about, asking dangerous questions."

Without further thought, without the slightest trace of humanity, Constazo straddled Kathy's mother. Chanting away in some forgotten tongue, he pulled her hair back, forcing the head up, and readied the knife. The woman, silently orgasmic, held the bowl under the victim's chin. The voice reached a crescendo. One practiced slice across the neck produced a torrent of blood. It hit the bowl and the world turned. This time Jon did vomit.

The lights below didn't move, but the shadows

around them did. The air grew thick and noxious. It wasn't wet, but had a weird dry humidity as if the air pressure suddenly doubled. The thinness of the world was weaker than he had ever felt before. It was only a slight sheet, a mucous membrane, away from some horrible place. He could feel things pushing, fingertips rippling on reality's skin, trying to break the seal.

Jon flipped back from one nightmare after another. Eyes open, he had to watch his friend's parents butchered. Eyes closed, scenes of evil shot all about his brain.

Kathy's mother flopped about like a fish out of water. Her mouth opened and shut, lips half forming objections. How could this be happening? It was her first taste of life far from the Ivory Tower. She believed the people of Mexico are of a quaint, spiritual variety, not prone to violent superstitions like the bigots said. This was all very different from what sociologists had assured her was the truth.

Echoes from creatures of darkness raced around the cellar. Dogs with thick spikes instead of hair. Bat creatures hunting for souls. Ghoulish ruddy-faced things that spat out precious stones and drank children's tears. Constanzo sniffed and licked his lips, as if he could taste the evil in the air.

Crowded around Constanzo were reflections of human monsters from the past, committing almost the same ritual, using nearly the exact same gestures. Aztec priests, dark Spanish peasant women, leftover Mayan tyrants, occultist serial killers, and barely human mutants, all slathered about. Each offered up a foul sacrifice, a symbol of innocence betrayed.

The husband, a figure who was mostly a blur in

Jon's memory, was hauled forward and the bag ripped off. Gagged like his spouse, he spotted her corpse and struggled. Constanzo just laughed and chopped into the man's neck, roaring with power. He yelled something about two skulls being better than one. His female companion laughed/screamed, hands rubbing furiously down her pants.

It was over. The academics were dead. Their skull caps harvested by a machete. The rest were tossed aside. A plastic bag was provided for the transport of the gory items. Constanzo stood triumphant, gazing adoringly at the blood-stained bowl. The woman, having seemingly orgasmed multiple times, curled serpentine-like around his feet, whimpering in submission and pleasure.

"Are you satisfied?" Father asked, as if the answer was in any doubt.

"Yes. You can claim full payment. One phone call and it will be delivered."

"Ah, not here. Let me give you an address to drop it off."

The men went up, Constanzo made a rude comment about Jon squatting on the stairs. The twins stood absolutely still, staring at the woman on the floor. She was still moaning, a ripple of pleasure occasionally ran through her. Jon could do nothing but clutch his stomach and marvel at the volume of vomit he had disgorged. He hadn't eaten that much with the kidnapping and everything. It was unpleasant to look at, but he needed a distraction from the corpses of his friend's parents not twenty feet away.

Eventually the woman rose, covered in freshly fallen blood. The twins became animated, offering a towel and directing her to a shower on the second floor. Jon, not wanting to be alone in this evil place, could only pull himself up the stairs and roll through the door. All the while, he panted like an overheated dog.

The breathing remains of Catherine de Courriere were left with the corpses. A few moments out of the corrupted atmosphere below was all it took to restore Jon's strength, though the horror still weighed on him. Constanzo and his woman were departing. A few goodbyes were spoken in Spanish, Father still erroneously being called Mr. Zanzibar, and they zipped off, back to wherever they practiced their foul religion. The twins and Father waited a breath, then two, then three, then—cheered. Champagne was produced. Corks popped. Glasses clinked. Jon was offered a flute full. He took it, but not happily.

"Relax, boy," Father said. "We did it."

"Did what? That bowl thing wasn't real, was it? Some lost relic of Montezuma?"

"Of course not. We had it especially made to pass any tests, but we shouldn't have bothered. That dumb peon snapped it up easy enough. The family has always thrived on such idiots. Too stupid to even know his own religion."

"So, we sold this fake in exchange for—?"

"A pallet of pure cocaine. Once cut, it should garner about a hundred million on the streets."

"So we're drug dealers now?"

"Only in the short term. The grand plan we're embarking on requires an influx of cash beyond our current reserves. This will tide us over for quite a bit. And it felt really good. Even great-grandfather never pulled a score like this."

The twins laughed. Now they were childishly giddy. They poured champagne on each other and threw pillows in mock-fight. Lola, the girl, jumped up and down on the couch, slamming harder and harder until the frame broke. Her brother hooted. Jon downed his drink, not expecting the bubbles to run up his nose like it did. He sneezed out half of it and a servant refilled the glass.

"What grand plan is that?"

"The great concordance. I can't tell you more, you haven't yet been fully tested into the faith of the family. The wheels are in motion and once that occurs everything will be made plain. You see here a small part of our dealings but you can't know the rest."

"Why did you bring me down here then?"

"Because we couldn't have done it without you. Why do you think your mother hates you?"

That was an abrupt detour. Jon was flummoxed, the bad taste of the champagne didn't help. "Because you're raising me to be manly in the family traditions and—"

"No, no, no. She hates Michelle, too. You might not have noticed, because there's little more we could do to ruin the girl. As you may know, your mother and I are third cousins. She knew the deal when our marriage was arranged. Any males would be brought up in the tradition. She accepted this and the first girl— Well, she has a special purpose as well."

"Then why the hate?"

"The one thing your mother always wanted, her deepest soul's desire, was to *be* a mother and have a baby. One that would be hers alone with no strings attached. She has that in Catherine. But until she was born, there was just the two of you and bitterness set into her heart. I'm afraid she vented her frustration on you children."

"I never saw it with Michelle."

"That's because you're a self-absorbed teenager, but trust me, it's there. Also, she was very upset about the manner of your conception."

"What?"

"You were bred to be special. We call it The Opener of Ways. Why do you think these things affect you more than anyone else? The soft spot is strong in this cellar, but no one else lost their lunch. You were born to be a living conduit. We performed the ritual in our basement at home and, while swirling between worlds, I shot my semen into your mother's ripe womb. The transition was not pleasant to experience."

"I don't need all the adjectives. It's weird."

"That's why you are attuned to the beyond so wonderfully."

A deafening crash from the other room. The male twin had knocked over a mahogany curio case stuffed with antiques. Porcelain pieces and wood splinters scattered across the floor. The female twin laughed and hacked into a rosewood dining table with an axe. Jon was uncurious about all this. The revelations, the head games, and murders fully occupied his mind.

"What makes you think I'm gonna help you with anything? You just committed two murders of innocent people right in front of me and for what turns out to be a fraud. Those experiences would have happened no matter what they did down there, correct?"

"As long as they thought it would produce a result, yes."

"Then why have them killed?"

"Because some dumbass went around showing them pictures of an object that couldn't be true, potentially queering up our hundred million dollar deal. They were asking questions among the Palo sects down here, collecting statements about the bowl's inauthenticity, getting the wrong people interested. The bitch even called up our house about the polaroids you showed her. Too stupid to live. You might as well have cut their throats yourself."

"Her daughter is my friend."

"Yes, so?"

"What am I gonna to tell her?"

"You can't say anything."

"How are you gonna prevent it? Murder me, too? Then I won't be able to open stuff for you anymore."

"You're not the only opener the family has bred, son. Each house of long-standing owned by a St. Fond was built on a soft spot. I want you around because you are my son, but you're expendable. Anyway, that's not even what I meant. You physically *can't* tell anyone about the family. We've made sure of it."

"How?"

"A little geas from our friends beyond when we were arranging the fate of your captors. The twins insisted upon it after you got kidnapped and I agreed."

Rare china was pulled from ornate chests and flung around the room. A pair of pistols was produced and the twins took turns shooting the plates in midair. Waterford crystal glass was smashed next, then finely-wrought silver was tossed and shot at. 18th Century portraiture was torn from the walls and set ablaze in the backyard.

"You have a point, however," Father said, popping another champagne bottle. "I'm not going to bully you into this. You either join us or you walk away. No cries of foul play and no hard feelings, at least not on my part. I won't stop you from leaving, but I will give you incentive to stay."

"And what's that?"

"A million dollars. To spend as you wish. With the way people are snorting up cocaine back home, we'll soon be rich. It's only fitting you get a share."

One hell of a carrot. No doubt the money would come with a horrible twist like events at the whorehouse. Jon didn't trust that Father would let him walk away. Even with the limited knowledge he had, the man couldn't risk it. For now, Jon had to appear to give in. Later, there would be a reckoning. Even if their curiosity had gotten them killed, Kathy's parents didn't deserve to die, and his friend didn't deserve the pain of their deaths. Father would pay. The image of his patriarch had shrunk a few inches in Jon's mind.

"There's still the police down here. Are they gonna cause trouble?"

"The Mexican police? Are you serious? If they are looking for these academics at all, it'll be on the other side of the country where they originally went missing. Even if they arrested us, I wouldn't be worried. William Burroughs shot his wife in the face and walked out of prison after a minimal bribe. We could afford much more than him. Besides, we have a solution."

The doorbell rang. Arlo rushed to answer. His sister was now upstairs, throwing breakable heirlooms out the window. A large vehicle had backed up right to the front door. Rough men dawdled at the doorway.

"The mixer is here, tio," Arlo sang.

A cement mixer rumbled on the driveway. A long series of chutes were set up, leading from the front door down to the sub-basement. The lights were retracted down there and all anyone could see below was darkness. The vehicle turned and the cement flowed, slowly sealing up the scene of the crime.

"That old lady, Charlotte, is still down there," Jon said.

"We're burying her along with the evidence and the spot. Maybe this will finish the old bag off. She hasn't been fed in over forty years, but still hangs around. We're selling off the place after this deal, in case the man comes back. It's better not to leave soft spots around. Brings in ghost hunters and all manner of occult wackos. Then they track down the original owners and start connecting dots."

"Every family house was built over a soft space. They're all underground. That's interesting."

"Or built up to one. Very few of them are actually level with the ground. Millions of years ago, they may have once conformed to the contours of the land, but things change. Mountains are ground to dust. New formations are vomited up by volcanoes. Continents are severed, then rearranged. Land sinks. Land rises."

Filling the sub-sub-basement with cement took the rest of the day. Five times the cement truck went and returned, pouring its contents down into the earth. The twins demolished a good deal more furniture, drank themselves senseless, and as dusk crept over the sky, ended up nakedly groping each other in the pool.

"Now, that's sweet," Father said, a slight drunken

slur slipping in under his breath. "They really love each other.

Jon downed a bottle of champagne and passed out. Next day, a groggy Father nudged him awake. Jon had a blanket of scum residing on his tongue. He was thoroughly dehydrated. A pounding headache had taken residence.

"Time to go. The cleaners are on their way to spiff the place up to sell. We need to vamoose."

Jon stumbled upstairs to grab his suitcase. He found that the contents had been tossed about along with the rest of the room. Father kept bellowing for him to hurry or he'd be left behind. He only had just enough time to briefly soak his head under the tap before running down with his gear.

The twins were there, crisp and ready to go. Father handed them a pair of passports, driver's licenses with fake names, and a key.

"Enjoy New Orleans until your place is finished in Navarra," he said.

They both shook his hand enthusiastically, grateful and hopeful, and left. Neither acknowledged Jon in any way. Father and Jon left a few minutes later and flew back to the "civilized" world of Black Rock.

CHAPTER 13

THE CONQUEROR WORM

JON WAS BURNT OUT. The world didn't spin on its axis and his attempts to find out the ways of his family made him feel more and more the drone of some sinister hidden ant queen. Father had allowed him to drink on the plane, shooing away the disapproving flight attendants so the trip quickly became a blur.

"It'll take a little time to work out your trip to the ancestral family estate. Our sanctum sanctorum," Father had told him on the cab ride back to Black Rock. Jon blinked and suddenly the old man's yellow eyes were in front of his. "That is, if you're still interested."

Drunk and emotionally exhausted, Jon nodded stupidly. The world was a blackout nightmare. The alcohol did help make him not care, though. It pushed all the problems into a tiny box on a far-away island. Even if he tried to focus on his fears and worries and the evil deeds of the last few days, they wouldn't come closer. He was happy for that.

Back at their home, Mother stared darkly at him. Catherine, her arm in a cast, a few scabbed over scrapes still visible on her face, snarled and clung to her mother's leg. Her chin stuck out in defiance, but there was an underlying fear in her manner that Jon found delicious. She knew he could harm her and get away with it. The little girl resented that fact, but all those who normally protected her were suddenly powerless.

"How's the arm?"

This provoked a series of sputtering, almost incomprehensible, profanities from Mother. He walked away in the middle of it, giving her a big fake yawn to rage-choke over. He flopped on his bed and fell asleep. Father woke him up to say that a physician associate of his had written a medical excuse for Jon and he wouldn't have to attend school for a month.

"I think it's for whooping cough or yellow fever. Something like that. Either way, relax for a bit while the wheels are in motion."

"It isn't a fake AIDS claim is it?"

Father laughed. "Not at all."

What to do? He got up, then lay right back down as the hangover jumped him again. In Jon's reckoning, hangover was a misleading term. They should call it "the drag", because he felt like his entire body was just dragging along for the day. Every action, every thought, took twice as long. A further vacation, one where he hopefully wouldn't be stuffed into a car trunk, would be nice.

The best he could do was pull himself down the stairs and slowly eat a bowl of sugar blasted cereal, then back to bed. He flipped on the black-and-white TV and passed out watching some old film about bigamy. Father woke him up again much, much later by slapping a newspaper across his chest.

"I think you'd better have a chat with Michael," he said, as the fog cleared in Jon's brain. "Make sure he keeps his idiot mouth shut about us if nothing else.

The paper was folded over to an article proclaiming, "Slaughtered Animals Found in Abandoned Grain Elevator." Uh-oh. Jon leapt up and devoured the contents. A bunch of little kids were throwing things at each other in the head house of the old grain elevator when they discovered seven dead dogs hanging from the ceiling in a small room. Their throats had been cut and the blood drained. It was then used to paint "occult symbols" on the wall. Luckily the story was buried on page five of section C. From the descriptions provided, there was no doubt the dogs had been killed in the midget room, their old gaming den.

What had his friend, his betraying friend, been up to? What sick deal had been consecrated in those animal's blood? It had to stop. After the display in Tijuana, Jon knew the family wouldn't tolerate a hint of exposure and Father could easily order Michael put down like one of those murdered dogs.

Before that, Jon felt compelled to visit one other person. Out of guilt. Out of shame. Out of pity. He didn't know what he could do for her, but the pilgrimage to Kathy's house must be made. It was like a ritual cleansing. The evil magic might prevent him from telling the truth, but he still had to try. If he were honest, Jon was secretly glad for the magical restriction on his tongue. It divorced him from responsibility, allowed him to sidestep a messy scene without guilt. If he failed to tell her, it wasn't his fault.

Michael must've taken his brother's bicycle back,

so Jon had to hoof it for miles over to Kathy's house. All the leaves had fallen, creating a carpet of dead vegetation down each street. There was no way to avoid the rotting plant smell.

She must've just gotten home, her school things were still in the hall. Her eyes, ones which always used to light up around Jon, were dull and shaded heavily by dark rings. She let him in without a word, then slumped into the kitchen. His footsteps echoed like dead church bells around the empty house.

"I don't think there's any hope," she said to Jon's unasked question. "I think they're dead. What am I gonna do?"

Jon tried to talk, tried to tell her how her parents died, or just where they were buried, but whatever spell, what geas, his family cast on him caused the words to stick in his throat. Nothing, not even a croaking gurgle, emerged. Finally, he suppressed the urge to do penance and simply asked,

"Don't you have any relatives that can help?"

"My aunt said she'd look into things after the semester ended. She's a professor in Boston. It might take her a while, because of all the cats she has. She said she'd maybe help me if someone could be found to look after them for a bit."

Why did he come here? What did he hope to achieve? There wasn't really anything he could give her. No hope. No retribution. When he looked at her, Jon no longer saw the overweight teenager. He saw the beautiful soul dwelling inside, one that didn't deserve to be hurt. There was only one thing he had to offer. Something she'd wanted for a long time now.

Jon grabbed her face and laid a long passionate

kiss on her lips. She melted. Nervous exhaustion sparked a sexual explosion in both of them. Their bodies flowed together. One kiss overlapped another and then they slowed down. He led her into the bedroom and they slowly undressed each other.

Neither of them had any real sexual experience beyond some childish fumbling, so they took a while to figure out exactly where each thing felt best and how to create a good rhythm. The world beyond the bedroom door with its problems and murders faded into the ether, and all thoughts and sensations were directed into exploring each other's body. Licking, sucking, fucking. The first time was good. The second even better. By the third, he felt like a champ. And the fourth made him want to sleep the sleep of the just.

They fell asleep one on top of the other and Jon awoke to her snoring into his chest hair. The world began to creep in along the edges of the room. He tried to block it out by waking her up and going in for a fifth time, but it was no use. Even as he plunged into her, thoughts from the outside invaded his brain. Time to get out and deal with things.

As he was pulling on his socks, Kathy lightly touched his back.

"Thanks," she said.

That hung in the air. Thanks for what? Could be a good many things. It was just a non-committal generic idea. There was a sweetness wrapped around the way she said it that Jon didn't want to destroy. Any further examination, any discussion, couldn't add more to the sentiment.

"Will . . . will you come back later?"

"Maybe. I'm going to France soon."

She didn't ask anything more, afraid of the answer. So they left it and Jon pulled the long slog home.

Here he was, walking in a virginity-less world. Didn't seem any different. No problems were solved, probably a few more added. It was something he wanted over with for so long, but the spiritual numbness of his life had ripped away any long-term satisfaction. The planet came to claim him, as did Michael.

His friend pulled himself from the bushes in front of Jon's house. He wore shorts and a thin T-shirt despite the cold. A backpack was slung over his frame. He rushed over, literally salivating at his friend's return.

"There you are. Finally, finally."

Michael was gaunt. His lips were cracked from lack of liquids. He must've dropped at least twenty pounds since they last met. That was nearly physically impossible. Something else must be working on him. There was a blip in Michael's eye. An abnormal yellow light. Whenever Jon blinked it remained in his vision. Opaque and inhuman.

"You didn't think I could do things without you, did you?"

"I saw something in the paper about the dead dogs. That was you, huh?"

"There is so much power, it's incredible. It's in my brain, up my nose, crackling through capillaries, folding along the edges of my fingernails. And I did it myself. I didn't need you or . . . or anyone else who thought they were hot shit. I am the man alone. Clint Eastwood. And I can fuck up the world."

"What are you talking about?"

Michael grabbed him, bending Jon's wrists

backwards. His skin had a strange odor embedded in it, like old urine. "I got to show you. It's gonna be great. Come along."

"Show me?"

"Come along. It's not done yet, the icing has to be added, but you're my oldest friend. I really want you there. Come."

"Alright, Jesus. Just let me get a coat. It's getting colder."

He ran to his room and pulled a thicker jacket from the closet and capped it off with a baseball hat. He could tell it would be a frigid night, the air had already started to nip at his ears. On his desk, he saw the tarot card of The Devil lying there sideways. The indecisive route or the path not yet chosen. The material seduction or the man chained in fear by the world. Why hadn't Father taken the card back?

Michael grabbed his arm and leaned in close when they walked away, whispering directly in Jon's ear. A casual passerby might've mistaken their body language for those of lovers. Michael led them down familiar streets. Jon tried to bring up the sacrificed animals again, but it just brought out more raving.

"Oh, fuck them. A means to an end. Everyone is so limited by their fear, by what society tells them they shouldn't do. You take that step beyond and everything becomes wide open. Don't kill animals. Don't play the game by yourself. Have a well-developed personality in front of your mind. Absolute bullshit. Play the game and do your taxes and you can come out ahead. Hogwash, to paraphrase myself earlier. Ahead isn't a place. You come out in the middle and are forgotten by the next generation of middle seekers."

"I know about your spying. Father told me."

That shut him up for a minute. He glanced guiltily over at Jon, a slinking texture slipped into his gait. It reminded Jon of a weasel, or ferret, or some other domesticated rodent. A contempt for his friend, never been there before, was born.

"When he caught me sniffing around your family business, we made a deal. He offered me power and knowledge. A way to get beyond. You know my family. If I want to get ahead, I need to make good contacts . . . "

All the kingdoms under heaven will I give to thee, if thou shall fall down and worship me. Yes, the role playing games had all been Michael's idea . . . or rather Father's. How much of his life had been directed by that man? How many ideas had been subliminally implanted in Jon's psyche?

"And now I've finally made it."

"That video tape I gave you to hide. You handed it over to him, right?"

"Yes."

"When did you do it? How long after I ask you to keep it?"

"The next day, after I watched it."

Goddamn. Father had been playing with him all that time. Just jerking his chain, making Jon jump.

"So, you watched the tape of my basement," Jon said.

"It was fascinating, everything I wanted to see. All sorts of ideas floated up and connected dots. I was able to complete these rituals based on what I saw."

"Did you contact the creature Calach on your own? You managed the rite?"

"Hell, yeah! You and your father must've thought I

couldn't succeed on my own, but I did. I did everything. I got into Stanford. Did I tell you that? Well, I did. Acceptance. Fucking A. While the rest of you are pumping gas for a living, I'll be up, up, and away. Sipping champagne with a hot woman to do my bidding. And she'll want to. She'll want to do everything I say. Gladly give up her soul. Now that I know the means. I called to Calach on my own. I don't even need to do the rite anymore. We talk all the time, right inside my skull."

Inside his skull?

They stopped. Jon hadn't been paying much attention to their destination and found himself outside of Michael's house. Last one on a dead end street. The front door was open, despite the cold. The mesh from the screen door still was half fallen out. Faint music played inside.

"There's just one problem, though," Michael said. "Calach and I have discussed it at length and that's tuition."

"Tuition?"

"I can't afford Stanford. Even with loans and grants and things, it's just too much. My parents refused to give me any money, but there is a way they can fund it all. Insurance."

"Insurance." Jon felt like a Mynah bird.

Michael pulled a .45 automatic from his backpack and gleefully licked it. Instinctively, Jon jumped back, hands covering his genitals.

"Where the hell did you get that?"

"Does it really matter at this moment?" Michael said, bobbing the gun with every syllable.

A reply stuck in Jon's throat. His friend was gone,

really gone, and he sensed that the wrong statement would loose a bullet into his chest.

"How are you gonna get away with it?"

"The man up here," Michael tapped the gun barrel to his temple. "He knows how to type in the cheat codes of the Universe. He's got it arranged. He gave those two people . . . what were their names . . . those people AIDS. He can do the same for me. Together we can do anything."

Michael bounded up to the screen door. Manic energy pumped through him from beyond, yet his body shook as if about to collapse. His hand gripped the door handle. Jon didn't know what to say, didn't know what to do, hoped it was all just a dumb game, but he knew it wasn't. Michael's parents were lazy dicks, but that shouldn't be a capital crime.

All he could think of was to say, "What about the limerick?"

Michael stopped, thumb pressed on the door lock. "Limerick?"

"You always have a limerick ready. What's the one for this situation?"

"No . . . I don't think so." Michael flung the door open and bellowed, imitating Ricky Ricardo, "Lucy, you've got some 'splainin' to do!"

Bang . . . query, bang, bang, scream . . . . Thump, thump, thump, bang, yell, bang, bang, scream, thump, thump, thump . . . smash, scream, bang . . . roar, bang, bang, bang, bang, bang, bang, bang, bang, bang, bang.

He must've emptied the clip. Jon ventured inside. The stink of gunpowder was thick. They were gone, all gone. Michael's older brother was sitting hunched over in the front of the TV, a Road Runner cartoon playing on the screen. A hole the size of a human fist had been punctured into the back of his head. What was left of his brains dripped onto a pinhole ridden shirt.

When he entered the kitchen, Jon slipped on Michael's mother's blood, the one who could never remember his name. He fell and came face-to-face with her corpse. Though, it was more like face-to-lack-of-face. Jon screamed and ran the fuck out of there. The last he saw of Michael was his former friend standing on the second-floor landing, where he presumably had killed the rest of his family.

He was waving the gun about and screamed, "Everything's comin' up roses. Michael Dutch is the ten spot. The wheel of fortune's got my number and I'm riding it to the good life. You wait and see. You fuckers, you slugs of the earth, you scum who rule. High aces and red roses."

And he ran. Jon tore away from the dead end house as fast as he has ever run in his life. Blood smeared on his jacket. The devil nipping at his heels. Lungs burning and squealing in rage. Sirens in the far distance. Strangers glancing at him fleeing. All would be well. All would be happy. He just had to reach safety, home base, like a game of hide-and-seek. There it was. For once, his family house was a beautiful thing of solace. A place of medieval sanctuary.

No one was home, thank goodness. Jon stripped off his jacket. Bloody. That could be cleaned. His pants. Bloody. Toss that in the same load. Shoes. Bloody, not good. That would take some soaking. He imagined himself having left a literal trail of bloody footprints up to his own front door. On the other hand, his shirt was fine. Socks unsoiled. Cap . . . Panic. Panic. *The ball cap was gone.* Must've fallen off his head in Michael's kitchen.

Time to kick furniture. Time to scream at the world. Hit the wall. Blame the universe. Why did this stuff happen? Why couldn't life be simple? Was this the end of Jon St. Fond? Would he be convicted as an accessory to murder and sent to prison, there to be passed around for a pack of smokes? Boldly, Jon opened the secret door in his parent's closet and grabbed the expensive bottle of booze stashed there. If they didn't like it, fuck 'em. One gulp, two gulp, red gulp, blue gulp. Drink. Drink away the pain.

The door slammed downstairs. Father called out his name. Jon sluggishly walked out, whiskey on his breath, decked in T-shirt, underpants, and sparkling white socks. Father tossed Jon's cap at his feet. The world immediately became lighter. How had he gotten it?

"Are you done playing the fool?" Father demanded. "Time to stop groveling and bargaining with these creatures and start *commanding* them. That's what the family does. These creatures put up a strong front, but underneath are weak, easily cowed. They have no substance, no identity to call their own. So what kind of a person falls prey to them?

"You are a man, the most powerful being ever forged in the fires of creation. Man is the destroyer. All things eventually crumble to him. There is nothing that he cannot conquer. Where you're going, you will need to stand on your own two feet. I can protect you no longer. The test ahead is for you to pass or fail. In light of what just happened, I'm shipping you out to France tonight."

Jon drunkenly burped in reply.

CHAPTER 14

The Devil's Bellows

WAS THERE EVER a city fouler than Paris? The whole place was putrid. The food stank, the air stank, the water stank, and the people stank worst of all. No wonder it was the French who invented perfume. It was needed to knock out the fetid odors leaking out the hairy crevices of every Parisian. The metropolis was built on a foundation of human waste. Take two steps across any yard and your feet would scuff up some vile fart entombed two millennia ago by Roman soldiers.

Adding to their stinkiness was their foul attitude. People say New Yorkers are rude, but they are nothing compared to the average Parisian. They all speak English but pretend not to. They will shove you aside. They don't break for traffic lights. One whiff of an accent will bring on a barrage of insults spouted right to the person's face—in French, of course. They assume the average tourist doesn't speak their lingua. Even if you make an attempt to speak their language, it makes no difference. Everything costs double when they hear Uncle Sam's twang.

Not that Jon tried to endear himself to the locals.

He wallowed away in his overpriced tourist hotel, bored and angry, forced to eat over-rich and saucy French cuisine. And forget about getting decent French fries in Paris

Jon had been stuck alone in that stink pot for two weeks while waiting on his family to contact him. Father had literally shoved a passport—something Jon did not know had been acquired for him—a plane ticket, and a fat wallet of francs at Jon, then kicked his son onto a plane. After a quick stopover in Toronto, it was off to the land of the croissant.

The only good thing was that he could legally drink here. So, he downed as much as he could. His temper didn't improve after three bottles and that led to many brash altercations with wine merchants, each pretending they couldn't understand Jon's insults.

"Just gimme the fucking bottle, you lazy snail eatin' faggot frog," Jon yelled, throwing a handful of francs at a beard in a beret. "Take your goddamn monopoly money and go fuck yourself."

He stumbled down the corkscrew streets at night, screaming over and over a limerick Michael had composed in saner days, much to the hatred of the locals he awoke.

"There once was a fellow named Glantz
Who, on entering a toilet in France,
Was in such a heat,
To paper the seat,
That he shit right into his pants."

It was Jon's farewell to his oldest friend. One that he'd never be able to complete in person. Apparently once the cuffs were slapped on, Michael went into a delirious state then lapsed into catatonia. There was a debate on whether to stash his body in a regular slob hospital or go right ahead and warehouse him in the loony bin.

Jon did have one task to perform while in Paris. A letter had been waiting for him at the hotel when he arrived after an aggravating taxi ride. In it was a pamphlet about the life of St. Fond, the Catholic Saint, and a note instructing Jon to memorize the contents. The family promised to come for him once he had. Jon had put it off for a while, the lure of alcohol and intense wine hangovers were very distracting, but eventually boredom drove him back to its study.

```
    The Life of St. Fond


    In the third century after the
crucifixion of our lord and savior,
Jesus Christ, Emperor Diocletian
unleashed  the   last   and   most
terrible of the ten persecutions of
the early church. Unto the land of
Gaul was sent Dacian as prefect and
procurator. He  was  stern  of  face
and harder at hand. He was to wipe
out this new scourge of Christians
once and for all. Anyone who would
not  renounce  their  faith  to  the
Lord   was   executed.   Thousands
perished under his direction.
    Fond was  the  name  of  a  little
maiden born in the Auvergne region
of modern day France. Her parents
were wealthy, and she was taught to
```

be courteous and gentle to everyone. Her nature was sweet and pure, and her face was fair with the kind of beauty that shines from within. The town where they dwelled was mostly Christians and they all lived happily together.

Then one day, a great calamity was heard in the center of town. On the horizon, Dacian and his column of Roman soldiers were seen approaching. The reason of his coming was known to all. Upon entering the town, Dacian proclaimed in the marketplace that every Christian who refused to sacrifice to the heathen gods should be tortured and put to death. To make his meaning quite plain, the soldiers spread out all the terrible instruments of torture, so that men might know exactly what lay before them if they refused to deny Christ.

One by one, that night, the Christians in the town slipped away and scuttled to cower in caves in the nearby mountains. Even the bishop of the town was afraid to stand up to Roman might. In the morning, the only one to stand in the marketplace was the maid, Fond. Dacian, angered that so many others had escaped, focused his fury upon the little girl.

Making the sign of the cross on different parts of her body, she uttered this prayer, 'Lord Jesus, who art always ready to assist your servants, fortify me at this hour, and enable me to answer in a manner worthy of you.'

Dacian then asked her, 'What is your name?'

She answered, 'My name is Fond, and I am a servant of the Lord. I am His and you cannot hurt me.'

Dacian asked, 'What is your religion?'

'From a babe, I have served Christ and to Him, I have consecrated my entire soul.'

'Deny Him, and sacrifice to our gods," thundered the prefect. "Else shalt thou endure every kind of torture, until there is no life left in thy young body.'

'You serve the will of devils. How can I sacrifice to them?'

'Dacian, in a rage, said: "You call our gods devils! Well, devils they may be, but you must sacrifice either an animal or your life to them.'

'Without hesitation,' Fond replied, 'My life for my Lord.'

To insult her honor, several townsmen were brought forward to claim that she had prostituted herself to them in order to turn them to the Christian faith. With the lie of her lack of virginity in place, she could be tortured under Roman law. A brazen bed was produced and Fond was tied to it with iron chains. A great fire was kindled under the bed, the heat of which burned her terribly. She was then taken from the bed and salt was pushed into her wounds. Then she was tied to a pillory and scourged with barbed whips.

Just before she perished, a white dove came gently flying down from heaven, and rested on the child's head. Soft dew fell from its wings, which healed the girl's wounds so that her body might rest in perfect state while her soul was transplanted into heaven. Many of the Roman soldiers were touched by the child's death and became Christians. They began to think that such a religion was worth living for if it could teach even a child to die so bravely.

St. Fond's feast day is October 6th and she is represented in art by the gridiron and scourge. She is

the patron of soldiers and falsely
accused women.

The pamphlet then went on to describe various miracles attributed to St. Fond and the resting places of her relics, none of which was interesting.

The next day, Jon received a call in his hotel room. It came in at five in the morning, before he could shake off the inevitable pounding wine hangover. Having gotten only a few hours of sleep, it took fifty rings before he could drag himself to the receiver.

"Wake up, wake up," a heavily accented Frenchman chirped. "It's time to check out. We go."

"Go? Where?"

"To Saint-Fond. Hurry up, I want to miss the early traffic. In Paris, it is the worst."

That was easier said than done. A beach ball inflated inside his skull every other second that was stomped on by a thunderous horse hoof. A brisk shower did nothing to help. He hadn't bothered to unpack, so all he needed to do was toss his toothbrush back in the bag, and then drag it down four floors.

It was Absolom below, sitting in a wire chair, eating an apricot. When Jon stumbled into view, Absolom threw a handful of bills at the desk clerk and offered Jon the pit from his fruit.

"No, thank you."

"I am Absolom," the older man said, throwing the rocky pit away. He didn't need to introduce himself. It would near impossible for Jon to forget the man he saw in a tag-team three-way with his parents. "We are third cousins, once removed. But this has been explained, about the family, oui?"

Oh, yes. Before parting, Father explained a great many things, revealed his grand plan and the insanity of it. By this time, Jon had learned to take it all in stride and let alcohol smooth out the rough edges of life.

I will become number one. The Magus. Father had told him. *And I will shape the world in my own skin.* Here Jon was still the fool, still blindly walking the path towards destruction. Hopefully after this crucible, he would be forged into something else. That was how the unknown test ahead was explained to him.

They zipped away in a red convertible through the dusk-lidded city, at an hour when even the night riding rats had decided to catch a few Zs, and coasted southwards to the commune of Saint-Fond, several hundred kilometers away. Communes, Jon discovered, were left-over bits of villages from ancient times that had been blanketed under a single term in the brief period when the shifting governments of the French Revolution stopped beheading each other long enough to get some paperwork done. The area paid its taxes, were told what national policies to implement, but otherwise Saint-Fond was pretty autonomous. The town, in one form or another, had been there since at least the 5th Century.

"So, you know the story," Absolom said, the wind whipping over his bald head. "And how does our family fits into it."

That seemed a no brainer. "We're all descended from the Saint's family. They probably didn't have a last name, so they took hers."

He laughed and lit up one of those abnormally strong French cigarettes. "No. No. Think of who we are. What little you know of what we do. We are not saints, nor do we pretend to be. It is not the little imbecile we come from, but the one who is strong. We are of the line of Dacian."

"The one who put her to death?"

"Mais oui. After the wholesale and violent conversion of people to the Christian faith, we kept the old ways, but hid them in the new. It's an excellent trick."

"But weren't her bones kept in a church at Saint-Fond village."

"At our private chapel, oui. Well, *bones* were kept there, probably not hers. But the casket was beautiful, done up in gold and velvet. People would come from all over the continent to pray before her and ask for a healing miracle. An excellent source of revenue."

"There are a lot of reports of actual healing from people touching her bones."

"Fake, fake, fake. The original bones were stolen by revolutionaries and the gold melted down to pay for more guillotines. After Napoleon took power, we 'recovered' the bones and built a new casket. Then Hitler stormed in and the Church, with misguided zeal, moved them to a 'safe' spot in Spain and there they have remained ever since. The Church has repeatedly refused to hand them back."

"Couldn't you like sue or something?'

"We considered a lawsuit, but that would involve an international court and a lot of bad publicity. People don't like it when you're seen to be attacking Jesus. So we had no choice but to accept. One of our traditional cash cows gone."

Another trick. Another dodge for money. Was that

all his family did? It couldn't be. He remembered his great-aunt Charlotte and her undying remains. Father proposed a very different route from that which she took to power. Father saw himself as the High Priest of the family's unnamed religion, and the others seemed to regard him this way. Jon had mentioned the old woman and Brian Elder to him and wondered which Father would end up like.

They all attempted to go on beyond to fulfill their power dreams. And to what end? Even if they did succeed, who are they? Their fundamental personality is ripped off and thrown down like a threadbare suit. I want to remain who I am. So instead we will bring one of them here and through that, I will have my power.

How? How? Jon had asked. How will that help you?

By having it conceive the next messiah, a blending of here and beyond. Your sister has been raised to be this creature's womb. A degraded vessel. A defiled conception. She will spawn this new dark messiah, shaped by our wills into our instrument. I will take charge of it and it will elevate me to the cosmic powers.

Father refused to divulge anymore, especially about how exactly this dark messiah would escalate him. More would be revealed later, it was implied. Jon wasn't certain of that. He wasn't certain that this wasn't another massive con.

Saint-Fond was snug up against the Rhone River near the middle of France. It was a pleasant little riverside town. Quaint, quiet, not particularly touristy. The streets were narrow, made of brick and cobblestones. Three-story buildings, alabaster walls, and slate roofs abounded. Traditional small shops were dotted about. The butcher, the baker, the candlestick maker all had a little place on the town's high street. Apart from a few old gents sipping wine at a cafe, not many people were about.

The family manse was a few kilometers away, surrounded by dense woods. Absolom called it a manse, in Jon's eyes it was a fortress. The wall around it was a stone structure straight from the Middle Ages, complete with a gatehouse and battlements. A massive fountain, worn with age and algae, dominated the entrance drive. It was of a weeping young girl, presumably St. Fond, in chains. Water flowed lethargically about her. The main house was more modern, 17th Century, with all the architectural oddities that century provided.

His bag was taken from him by a mute and starry-eyed servant. The car was wheeled away to a converted carriage house holding many high-end vehicles. He was given no time to freshen up. Dusty and unkempt as he was, Jon was whirled into a large ballroom, filled with elegant people picking the finest local cuisine off silver plates.

He was introduced in a whirlwind of greetings to cousins—first, second, third, fourth, fifth, sixth—once removed, twice removed, etcetera. John, Jean, Hans, Ian, Sean, Juan, Eoian, Chon, Jane, Johanna, Sian, Ionna, Janine, Yana, Jana, Gianna, Hannie. Their names blended together. Impossible for him to later attach name to face. The range of races surprised him. The crowd contained the fair skin he was used to, but also olive skin Greeks, Slavic ruddiness, Africans,

Arabs, and even a few Asians, among the mix. Each held the badge name of St. Fond.

Everyone was handed a glass of wine and Absolom lead the toast.

"À la famille!"

They repeated it proudly and drank the wine in one gulp before smashing the glasses against the wall. Absolom pulled Jon into the center of the room. The rest of the St. Fonds stood about, still eating and drinking, but also listening intently to what the pair was saying.

"Now, Jon of Black Rock," Absolom began. "Now, you earn the family name. Even if legally you bear it, you have not earned it, but today you do so. If you pass the test of will that is."

Jon, suddenly alert, simply nodded. The wine hangover had vanished.

"I can only offer you one piece of advice. You have played the game, yes? You have another name, another mind, to use? What is his name?"

"Crixen Runeburner."

"Je m'en fous. This will be his test as well."

"I understand."

"No. You do not," Absolom paused and licked his lips. "We also give you the choice here. If you do not want to be one of us. If you do not feel you *can* be one of us. You may walk away. Be of your own mind and your own name. We will allow this to happen."

Jon looked Absolom in his eyes. Yellow, like Father's. Disturbing. He saw the glint. Heard a rustle beneath his kinsman's shirt. The truth bubbled up rapidly from Jon's subconscious.

"There is no walking away."

"Mais oui," the other smiled. "But we enjoy offering the illusion of choice. Now, we must wait."

"For what?"

"For the hallucinogens you drank to work their magic."

Oh, boy. A minute later he grew weak in the knees and some of his extended family caught him. They dragged him down a long hallway into the basement. The world started folding at the corners. A secret latch behind an ancient cask was flicked and a rock wall creaked open. Jon was tossed into the center of a circular room. Oil lamps were lit. Their flickering light illuminated grotesque images of death, the devil, and torture over every surface. The door was shut and locked. He was alone with the pictures.

A transparent protective coating ripped away from the planet. There, the break sifted through worlds like a broken film reel. One piling on top of the other, until all things cursed at each other in a common tongue. Albatrosses filled the sky and the mud on the ground and clay in the cliffs spoke frankly with men who trod upon it. And his mind was exposed to concepts below the action. All the elements of his life. All the knowledge he had accumulated as a tortured soul. They took shape and clawed at him with demon faces, then melded together into ONE shape that told all.

He ran.
He broke free.
He broke his nose on the wall.
And they came for him.

Jon the boy-man could do nothing
against these fiends from inside and beyond.
He had not the will to fend them off.
To crush them. To conquer them. To command
them.
That would require a mighty hero.
One from a long line of adventures and princes.
One who had destroyed many a fearsome foe.
The name was bellowed
And he came.

On fleet feet he swept in
For half a day
With spell and staff
He crushed the demons of the mind
Threw them back into oblivion of non-space
And of the boy-man there was no sign
He was gone
Sleeping in safety and security
Away from knowledge, harm, and responsibility

Jon emerged from his mental crib only to find his body resting comfortably in a luxurious bed. Thousand thread count sheets swaddled him. The most comfortable pillow ever cradled his head. An IV hung above in the rafters, pumping nourishment into his veins. His broken nose was bandaged up with only the faintest throb of pain. Absolom sat nearby, reading from a book bound in the time of the Renaissance.

"Congratulations, Jon St. Fond."

Jon tried to mouth the question, but no words

came out. The mere act of attempting to ask wore him down. Absolom divined his intent.

"Yes. You and Crixen passed. He was fully formed enough to take on the role. You must have understood that failure meant a permanent vacation in an asylum, your mind fractured to the four winds."

Absolom lifted a glass of port and sipped in short rapid spurts. Jon was surprised to see a softness outline the other's eyes. A . . . concern? Pity?

"The way of the opener has never been an easy one in our famille," Absolom continued. "And while you've stood up to become the type of man we require, the usefulness of your skill will always make one of the others attempt to dominate you into their service. Even now, your father still holds sway, does he not? Is his thumb still not pressed against your spine?"

Jon nodded.

"Of course, he has. It is not easy for the boy to become man when the father is about, non? And this is his greatest triumph. What has he offered?"

With tremendous effort, Jon managed to squeak out, "One million dollars."

Absolom whistled. "That much, huh? Coûter les yeux de la tête. But I will add my guarantee that this debt will be paid. Then you can be your own man, learn the deeper mysteries of the family and secretly pull the strings of the world."

Jon nodded his assent. Absolom went into detail on the ritual, one carefully researched and crafted over the centuries, which culminated in the eighty one day ritual they called The Feast of the Beast. Everyone involved would don their alter egos, their magical names, for the entire time. By their will, by their thoughts, by naming the creature, and mental atmosphere, they would physically pull one of these entities into the Earth's gravity and give it shape. Under the power of their collective will, it would remain long enough to impregnate Jon's sister and then dissipate to the cold lightless reaches beyond the universe.

The key emotional elements of the ritual were lust, degradation, hate, anger, fear . . .

" . . . and betrayal," Absolom finished.

"Betrayal?"

"You will know when the time comes and then you will choose the truly great path. How will you open it? How does the boy become the man?" He stood up and patted Jon on the leg. "But now, I must go. Rest up. Faire la grasse matinée. Gather your resources. I will send in some refreshment."

Jon raised a hand. Absolom stooped down, nearly placing one of his ears on Jon's lips.

"The family," Jon asked in the tiniest whisper, "what are we?"

"We?' Absolom laughed gently. "That's a good sign."

Jon closed his eyes, convinced that there would be no straight answers here. Absolom shook them back open.

"We are the ones who sit unseen in the back rooms making decisions, calling out the names of the damned, and forcing the beyond to do our bidding. We divide the world, pitting one side against another. Wherever there can be conflict—politics, religion, culture—we promote it. For where there is strife, there is a gap, and the family flourishes and profits in that gap.

"All things which push indolence and ignorance are our brainchild. All things which degrade the soul is our design. Wherever there is stupidity to be squeezed for a profit, the family is there. The world is full of pearls for us to pluck. We profit from destruction and then disappear.

"On the outside, we shift like with the wind, changing with every cultural norm, but our bedrock remains solid. We also know our place. We do not dabble with thoughts of beyond. That way has always led to ruin. Until now, we knew how far to extend our hand."

With that last cryptic sentence, Absolom left the room. Jon was too weak to ask anything further. A while later, one of his female cousins brought in cheese and wine. After dropping a few morsels in his mouth, she stripped naked and crawled onto the bed, stroking Jon gently. The girl was very thin and lithe with auburn hair that flowed straight across her shoulder blades. Despite his tiredness, he could not help but be aroused by her tender touches. Without a word, the girl mounted him and rode with a calm rhythm.

It was almost a ritual unto itself. Neither said anything. The girl looked at the ceiling as it progressed. Jon simply stared at the girl's small breasts and thought of how much larger Maria's had been. He eventually reached a joyless, weak orgasm and the girl climbed off. She did a handstand for a minute. Still naked, she walked out of the room, her clothes draped across her back.

CHAPTER 15

SLOUCHING TOWARDS BETHLEHEM

JON CAME BACK to the beginning. For eighty one days, the beast was fed. Crixen Runeburner, in human flesh, ate, drank, fucked, and shit in the mausoleum below Goodleburg Cemetery. All the cousins below, several hundred of the St. Fond family, continued non-stop until they were hollowed-out zombies, merely a shell for their magical egos.

Acolytes scuttled up and down the rows of participants, picking people up where needed, making sure the cauldrons boiling with fat—animal and human—were well-stoked, adding incense to five massive burning braziers, occasionally shitting in them to add extra heat to the aroma, and scooping up animal carcasses littered about the altar. They were just menial ones, clothed only in black. Those in red robes, like Jon, performed the tasks. Endlessly chanting the spells of invocation. Having rough and degrading sex with all genders on soiled mattresses scattered about the chamber. Then taking turns slaughtering a creature on the altar.

Outside of the old tomb, RVs had been set up to help revive and refresh members. Porta-johns and food tables had been installed nearby, enough to fill three trailer parks. They had called in every member that could assemble, spending a hundred thousand on their accommodations, travel expenses, food, and recompense for lost income from their day jobs.

No part of this ritual was done was for the benefit of those beyond. All the pageantry, the blood, the mindless chants, the smells, and sex was to get the heroes into the perfect mesmeric state to open the door within their minds. With Jon as the battering ram, they themselves would crack the seals between worlds to allow the Beast to enter.

Then came the moment, The Great Whore, the Scarlet Woman, the unclean vessel, his sister, was brought in by Father, the High Priest. Jon was pulled before the altar, a gold knife slapped into his hand. The live sacrifice was revealed. Kathy, with whom he had given up his virginity.

"Jon!" she screamed.

That cry, that wail of desperation from the only person left in the world Jon cared about, nearly split the image of Crixen Runeburner in two. He felt his own body again and saw ghoulish hands in the ether trying to grapple his mind. One second, two. He was about to be destroyed from within. The blade was raised.

"Go. Go. My son," Father hissed.

Go on. Go on. The moment had arrived. His vision wobbled. Split between the ultimate adventure Runeburner was on and the reality of Jon's friend screaming her head off on a bloodstained altar. Twin piles of thoughts crowded his head, but there was no time. Heat and pressure mounted around him. He had to act!

A strike. Crixen, no it wasn't Crixen . . . Jon had plunged the dagger into Father's chest. A sigh of orgasmic satisfaction rose up from the crowd. This was the greatest betrayal a boy-become-man could accomplish. They savored its evil. Drank in the dark beauty. Father stumbled back a pace, then forward, stubbornly unaware he was dead. Refusing to admit defeat, despite losing five pints of blood. Nature eventually won out over willpower and Father tumbled forward onto Kathy's screaming body.

A hollow sound boomed, like a rip in reverse. Suddenly a space appeared in front of Jon that had not been there before. From it slithered a yawning, sucking cold. It leeched off his heat, his mind, his soul. Crixen was well gone by now and his true self was naked before the beyond. He felt himself being drained away into a nothingness, wherein dwelled shapeless forces of evil intent. They wanted him. Mind, body, and soul. They would devour him whole and shit out a corrupted parody of Jon.

He jumped away, ripping himself from their grasp, screaming in pain. Damage was done though, he could feel it. Part of him was indelibly gone into that void. He grabbed Kathy, now mute with fear, and roughly dragged her down from the altar by her hair. Father's body flopped over.

In the space, a thing appeared. There was no definite way to describe it for it only had the loosest definition of a form. A moving color which buzzed around a shaky outline of a man. Little pinpricks of light evolved and died around the shape. Grinding noises fell off the thing from no definite orifice.

It leapt across the altar, directed by the mystic

symbols to that spot, and onto Michelle. The form melted around her like a marshmallow before a flame, drawn in by her heat, while the color shook around her frame. The grinding, like rock on rock, increased. Michelle shrieked and twisted in painful spasms. Finally, her body seized up, each one of her muscles arched upwards in an inhuman posture. She fell, eyes rolled up into her skull. The color faded.

All of them, each St. Fond member stared expectantly at her body, not believing that this ordeal was over. The rip to beyond silently sealed up and, little by little, everyone came back into themselves. They emptied out of the foul-smelling room and gazed happily at the overflowing night sky. Cleaners would come in tomorrow and sweep everything under the rug. Michelle was carefully taken away in a private ambulance under the watchful eye of Absolom. A half-hearted applause sprinkled across the crowd. Some alcohol and food was produced, but most were too burnt-out to do anything except sit down and try to remember who they were and what they had been doing before the ritual.

Jon stood apart from them, trying to comfort the shivering Kathy. He didn't feel like celebrating. In fact, he couldn't feel anything at all. He realized he should be hungry, but the sensation was absent from his body. His fingers and toes had gone numb. When Jon stared at his hands, the tips faded into and out of focus, sometimes becoming transparent, other times becoming startlingly detailed, more real than real.

His mother appeared a short distance away. She just looked at him, lip quivering. Old angers and fears danced around her twisted-up face. Her whole body spat curses that she was too afraid to say out loud. Jon, at least for the moment, was a hero to her people and she was just a useless bit of debris.

The next day, after he was dropped off and had a fitful night of sleep, Jon realized he was alone in the house. Where was Kathy? She had curled up next to him on his bed that night. The geas to prevent him speaking had died with Father and he had whispered to her all of the strange doings over these past few weeks, then expanded onto the bizarreness of his life, the murder of her parents, the sketchy history of his family stretching all the way back to the betrayal of a saint.

She had reacted violently when all of the dirty laundry was laid out, but he held onto her tightly, refusing to let go until she settled. Jon had stroked her hair and told her not to worry, that a million dollars was coming his way and that much money would take care of them both for the rest of their lives. They could go anywhere and do anything. Eventually, they fell asleep and now she was gone.

It wasn't just her. Mother had cleaned out her clothes and the safe. A great deal of Catherine's clothes were similarly gone, along with her kiddie pageant trophies. A simple note was left on the kitchen table.

"I'm taking Catherine and leaving. Don't ever contact us."

No fear of that. Their disappearance was a blessing, nothing less. But where had Kathy gone? To the police? That might be awkward. There wasn't any proof of her parents' murder, but there must've been evidence still at the cemetery. No way could all of that be cleaned up so fast.

He pulled a soda can from the fridge and sipped. The soda was flat on his tongue. Strange. Even with these threats against him, Jon couldn't get excited, couldn't have cared less. Everything was placid inside.

Time slipped by. Absolom showed up, wheeling in two large suitcases. The Frenchman was fresh and chipper. The world was doing good by him and all doors were wide open. He laid the cases at Jon's feet.

"Voila," Absolom said, zipping them open and tossing large bills about. "Argent. Un million. All for you."

Jon just sat there, looking at his future laid out in green rectangles. He took another sip, then slowly said, "There might be a problem . . . "

Absolom shrugged and tossed a copy of the afternoon edition of the newspaper on the table. An article was circled in red.

"But before that," Absolom said. "We have all legal matters and so forth to handle, due to your Papa's demise. Naturally we need to cover up his death. Report him missing, so legally he won't be dead for seven years."

Jon nodded. His eyes drifted to the paper. "Local Girl Dead in Old Grain Elevator" it announced.

"I have finagled a power of attorney for your father, so I can handle all of the details," Absolom continued, "but I have to ask, do you want the house?"

Jon was busy skimming the article. Kathy Lauder found dead . . . apparent overdose . . . Agway grain elevator . . . parents missing in Mexico, presumed dead . . . girl fell into bad company . . . local drug dealers being questioned . . . same place ritualistically butchered dogs were found. How long had he been sitting there? It could have been minutes or centuries. Jon had no idea, the concept of time had lost all meaning.

"Hello?"

"What?" Jon said.

"As per our agreement, you are a free agent. Your Mother has left. Do you want to stay and look after the house, or go?"

Jon thought for a moment. What was left here? What did he need? "Just gimme the car, you can have the place."

"Bien," Absolom smiled. "I divined this would be your answer. Young man on the road. Very romantic. Very American."

He produced two documents and a pen, placing them both in front of Jon. "Sign," he ordered. "One we will date later giving me custody of the house. The second transfers the car's title to yourself."

Jon scribbled his signature. Absolom nodded to him and swept up the documents.

"Our business is done," the Frenchman said. "You may return to us when you like. Take the time, take the money, and indulge yourself. We have done great work here."

Absolom left.

Jon sat there for a while, numb in all matters. He thought of Kathy. Of Michael. Even Louis had been affected by this business. Eternal victims. Who would speak for them?

After much slow churning in his mind, Jon decided on a path. He ripped open the bags of money. After taking a moment to gasp at the sheer enormity of a million dollars, he divided a portion of it into another bag and loaded it all into Father's beautiful car.

He drove over to the rundown student apartments that Brian Elder haunted. Jon found the man in a nacho cheese stained shirt and underpants, watching some barely animated cartoon from the 60s. He was eating circus peanuts from a large bag. Jon was regarded with sallow eyes.

"You still in the psychic assassin business?"

Brian Elder cracked his knuckles. "Sure as Hell, if you've got the coin."

Jon dropped a bag at his feet. It held one tenth of his newly gotten wealth. 100,000 in hundred dollar bills. Brian openly drooled over the money.

"A Dark Messiah was conceived in an unclean vessel under the Hill of the Ghouls. That's your target."

Elder laughed. "Consider it done."

That finished, Jon jumped into his luxury car and drove out of the city looking for the next chapter in his life, content in the fact that he was no longer the fool.

ABOUT THE AUTHOR

Born into the blue-collar city of Buffalo, NY, Rex Hurst was traumatized as a small child by the suffocating rabbits scene in the animated adaptation of *Watership Down*. Ever since, his mind twists toward the macabre, until his inevitable blossoming as a horror writer. When not writing, he is an assistant professor of composition, public speaking, and literature.

Rex Hurst is the author of *The Foot Doctor Letters: A Serial Killer Speaks Out* as well as several science fiction books and novellas. He is also co-host of the weekly radio show Write On SC—Yes, radio shows and stations still do exist—on the art of writing. Back episodes can be found on his website at Rexhurst.com.

THE END?

Not if you want to dive into more of Crystal Lake Publishing's Tales from the Darkest Depths!

Website www.crystallakepub.com/
Amazon amazon.com/author/crystalpublishing

Dear reader,

It makes our day to know you reached the end of our book. Thank you so much. This is why we do what we do every single day.

Please take a moment to leave a review on Amazon, Goodreads, or anywhere else readers visit. Reviews go a long way to helping an author, and will help us to continue publishing quality books. You can also share a photo of yourself on social holding this book with the hashtag #IGotMyCLPBook!

Thank you again for taking the time to journey with Crystal Lake Publishing.

Website:
www.crystallakepub.com

Amazon:
amazon.com/author/crystalpublishing

Twitter:
https://twitter.com/crystallakepub

Facebook:
https://www.facebook.com/Crystallakepublishing/

Instagram:
https://www.instagram.com/crystal_lake_publishing/

Patreon:
https://www.patreon.com/CLP

Join the Crystal Lake journey by signing up for our newsletter and receive three eBooks for free: http://eepurl.com/xfuKP

Or check out other Crystal Lake Publishing books for more Tales from the Darkest Depths. You can also subscribe to Crystal Lake Classics, where you'll receive fortnightly info on all our books, starting all the way back at the beginning, with personal notes on every release. Or join our interactive community of authors and readers on Patreon for exclusive content and behind the scenes access, bonus short stories, polls, interviews and, if you're interested, author support.

Since its founding in August 2012, Crystal Lake Publishing has quickly become one of the world's leading publishers of Dark Fiction and Horror books in print, eBook, and audio formats.

While we strive to present only the highest quality fiction and entertainment, we also endeavour to support authors along their writing journey. We offer our time and experience in non-fiction projects, as well as author mentoring and services, at competitive prices.

With several Bram Stoker Award wins and many other wins and nominations, Crystal Lake Publishing puts integrity, honor, and respect at the forefront of our publishing operations.

We strive for each book and outreach program we spearhead to not only entertain and touch or comment on issues that affect our readers, but also to strengthen and support the Dark Fiction field and its authors.

Not only do we find and publish authors we believe are destined for greatness, but we strive to work with men and woman who endeavour to be decent human beings who care more for others than themselves, while still being hard working, driven, and passionate artists and storytellers.

Crystal Lake Publishing is and will always be a beacon of what passion and dedication, combined with overwhelming teamwork and respect, can accomplish. We endeavour to know each and every one of our readers, while building personal relationships with our authors, reviewers, bloggers, podcasters, bookstores, and libraries.

We will be as trustworthy, forthright, and transparent as any business can be, while also keeping most of the headaches away from our authors, since it's our job to solve the problems so they can stay in a creative mind. Which of course also means paying our authors.

We do not just publish books, we present to you worlds within your world, doors within your mind, from talented authors who sacrifice so much for a moment of your time.

There are some amazing small presses out there, and through collaboration and open forums we will continue to support other presses in the goal of helping authors and showing the world what quality small presses are capable of accomplishing. No one wins when a small press goes down, so we will always be there to support hardworking, legitimate presses and their authors. We don't see Crystal Lake as the best press out there, but we will always strive to be the best, strive to be the most interactive and grateful, and even blessed press around. No matter what happens over time, we will also take our mission very seriously while appreciating where we are and enjoying the journey.

What do we offer our authors that they can't do for themselves through self-publishing?

We are big supporters of self-publishing (especially hybrid publishing), if done with care, patience, and planning. However, not every author has the time or inclination to do market research, advertise, and set up book launch strategies. Although a lot of authors are successful in doing it all, strong small presses will always be there for the authors who just want to do what they do best: write.

What we offer is experience, industry knowledge, contacts and trust built up over years. And due to our strong brand and trusting fanbase, every Crystal Lake Publishing book comes with weight of respect. In time our fans begin to trust our judgment and will try a new author purely based on our support of said author.

With each launch we strive to fine-tune our approach, learn from our mistakes, and increase our reach. We continue to assure our authors that we're here for them and that we'll carry the weight of the launch and dealing with third parties while they focus on their strengths—be it writing, interviews, blogs, signings, etc.

We also offer several mentoring packages to authors that include knowledge and skills they can use in both traditional and self-publishing endeavours.

We look forward to launching many new careers.

This is what we believe in. What we stand for. This will be our legacy.

Welcome to Crystal Lake Publishing—Tales from the Darkest Depths